# ENVOY FROM ELIZABETH

The King of Spain, engaged in preparing his ships for war, seeks to ensure the success of his invasion by the death of Elizabeth Tudor. The Queen, aware of the presence in her Court of an assassin, but ignorant of his identity, sends for Nicholas Rokeby, one of her gay, bold sea-dogs. Rokeby and his companions, posing as refugees from the tyranny of the Protestant Monarch, are welcomed in the Court of Spain where they hope to uncover the secret which will save the Queen's life. But as they begin the desperate race against time, they find unexpected complications, and Nicholas loses his heart to Philip's beautiful ward who has her own tragedy to hide. Finally Philip, with cold resolution and undaunted patience, completes his plans and orders his Armada to set sail, but as the dons reach the English Channel, Sir Francis Drake and his captains are waiting for them.

Pamela Bennetts

# Envoy From Elizabeth

NEW YORK
ST. MARTIN'S PRESS, INC.

# ACKNOWLEDGMENTS

I am deeply grateful to the following authors and historians who brought to life for me that brilliant period of our history when Spain challenged England's freedom and the sovereignty of the woman who sat on her throne:

*Philip of Spain*, Sir Charles Petrie
*Master of the Armada*, Jean H. Mariéjol
*The Character of Philip II*, Ed. John C. Rule &
                                        John J. Te Paske
*Queen Elizabeth*, J. C. Neale
*The Life & Times of Elizabeth I*, Paul Hamlyn
*Elizabeth the Great*, Elizabeth Jenkins
*The Lives of the Queens of England*, Agnes Strickland
*Palaces & Progresses of Elizabeth I*, Ian Dunlop
*Elizabeth's Army*, C. G. Cruickshank
*The Defeat of the Spanish Armada*, Garrett Mattingly
*The Spanish Armada*, Michael Lewis

# I

IT WAS January. Deep, white January, with the merry warmth of Christmas now three long weeks away, and spring too distant to thaw the frozen lakes or melt the delicate flowers of snow which hung lightly from the bare branches of the trees in the gardens of the Palace of Whitehall.

The light was fading, for evening was at hand and the sun was a great fire-ball dying on the horizon, but in the dungeons beneath the glitter of the Queen's riverside residence, neither full noon-light nor dusky eventide made any difference to the awesome gloom.

The dungeons were bare and stark, hemmed in by damp stone walls and blackened ceilings, with flags of cold granite beneath the feet. True there were some furnishings, but these only served to heighten the chill, and to freeze the eye which fell upon them. The iron rings set in the walls spoke for themselves, as did the hoist set hard by, and on a rough wooden table lay some of the delicate implements of persuasion used by the inquisitors in their ruthless pursuit for knowledge and truth.

There were pincers of twisted metal, fashioned to tear a reluctant tongue from the mouth; irons for branding white-hot symbols on shrinking skin; pointed prongs for loosening the eye from its socket; the garrotte, borrowed from the sophisti-

7

cated torture-chambers of Spain, and the sharp polished knives which could cut cleanly and finally through flesh and muscle when more gentle methods had failed.

In one corner a huge cauldron bubbled merrily, but the hungry flames which licked beneath it warmed to scalding heat, not water for a cook's pot, but oil, in which to immerse the shaking body of a miscreant. The Queen feigned to ignore the use of torture and would have waxed indignant had she been charged with these means of gaining her ends, and in public, her advisers and counsellors would shake their heads and deny such barbaric practices, stating blandly that they had no knowledge of such things.

But secretly and silently all were aware of the task of those who tended the dungeons; all knew of the molten lead poured into the vicious wounds made with the smouldering pincers, and of the *bassin ardent* white hot and blinding, as it passed to and fro before the eyes of a writhing suspect. None admitted, but all knew, the existence of the scavenger's daughter, whose cold iron grip crushed bones and drove out the breath of life itself; the cat-o'-nine-tails, the Spanish boot, the iron gauntlet and the thumb-screws.

They were not things to talk about, to boast of, but they were necessary when a stubborn tongue had to be unlocked and when vital information had to be prised from a man well paid to keep his silence.

And so, on a cold January day, when flares and torches were being lit in the great chambers and rooms above, and when maids and servants bustled about to begin the preparations for their mistress's toilet, a small group of men stood in the centre of the main dungeon, clustered about the long oak rack.

A man lay beneath the wooden frame, his wrists and ankles strapped lightly to the two rollers one at each end of the structure and as his guardians watched, two soldiers moved the heavy levers which raised the victim's body to the level of the frame. The men moved nearer, bending slightly so that not a word or whisper should be lost to them, their eyes fixed on

8

the prisoner with strange intensity. His face was ghastly in the flickering torch-light. Sweat and blood had mingled to stain his face, for his captors had worked on his trembling agonised body for many hours and he was scarcely conscious of the dull rumble of the rollers as they stretched his limbs taut and still.

The Keeper of the Dungeon, Sir Henry Ruthevan, bent a little nearer. He was a thick-set man with grizzled hair and beard, wearing a crisp white ruff above the steel gorget which encircled his neck.

Atop his doublet of purple velvet he wore a heavy fur-lined gown to ward off the seeping cold, and pulled over his yellow netherstocks were tall boots of Spanish leather, made to withstand the rigours of the icy floor.

He scanned the prisoner's face without compassion, and when he spoke, his voice was harsh and without feeling.

"Come, sire," he said shortly. "I pray you to use your wits. Your silence we will not accept; this stubborn will of yours will be broken, never fear." His lips thinned. "Have we not made our intent plain this day, *señor*? Dost doubt that we are fully determined to wrest from you the names of those who aid you in this plot?"

The man's lips moved in a faint grimace of pain, but he did not open his eyes and Sir Henry bared his teeth.

"So be it," he said coldly. "If we must tighten your sinews to loosen your tongue, we are well equipped for the task, but you would do well to answer freely now, for naught can save you. Marry, man! We know that there is a plot afoot, for we have as many spies as his Catholic Majesty of Spain. We know also that 'tis some mischief which will affect our lady Queen, and thus we will stop at nothing to draw from you the secrets which you cling to with such obstinacy. Now, sire! You were sent hence, to this Court, to plan some evil, yet you were not sent alone; this we also know. Who is· it who aids you? Who stands by to help you in this infamy?"

The man gave a slight moan, but still he kept his eyes tightly closed against Sir Henry's burning gaze, and with a quick oath, Ruthevan straightened and snapped his fingers at the guards.

"Turn the wheel again, Captain Rayne, for it seems your caress is still too mild to prod this obdurate fool to a confession. Turn it again, and mayhap this will make him see the folly of his silence."

Bertram Rayne, a burly man of steel and leather, with little imagination and even less pity, obediently turned the rollers with slow, callous deliberation, and the prisoner bit his lip as he had bitten it so often since he had first come to this abominable place. After a moment, however, as the levers drove the rollers relentlessly on, his legs and arms were slowly stretched until the bones began to start from their sockets, and then the man began to gasp in agony.

His eyes opened, blank with horror, as he felt his body breaking beneath the vicious pull of the cords and wheels. First he cried aloud, the Spanish words strange and unintelligible to his torturers, and then he swore and cursed, but still the wheels ground inexorably onwards, and when he gave a sudden sharp scream, Sir Henry held up his hand to stop the guards at their work.

"Wait." He bent again to his victim, his face thrust close to the dying man's. "Well, sire? What have you to say now? Who are these men who aid you? What are their names? Tell me, or by the Blood of God, I will tear your living body apart!"

The man's eyelids flickered and his swollen lips moved with difficulty.

"Here . . . here . . . at Court," he managed finally. "Here . . . at Court . . ."

"Yes, yes! Who!" Ruthevan's eyes glittered eerily under the flares. "Who at Court?"

The man mumbled something and seemed to drift into unconsciousness, but after a moment, he managed to open his eyes and began to speak again.

"There . . . there . . . are others . . . others . . . three others . . ."

"Others? Who? Their names?" Ruthevan was sharp for he could see the man's life was nearing its end, and he dared not fail in his task. Too much was at stake. He gripped the torn shoulder of his prisoner, and the man groaned in pain. "Their names!"

Again the man's lips moved, and in pain-thickened tones whispered the names Henry Ruthevan so badly needed to know and for which he had worked so hard and so long during all that dull, winter day.

Ruthevan gave a quick sigh of relief. "Good, good. You shew sense at last. And the man at Court? Who is he?"

The prisoner's face was grey now. The sweat on his brow stood out starkly on the bloodless skin, and his voice became more slurred.

"He . . . he . . . has been here . . . here at your Court for two years. Two years . . ." The pale lips twisted into something like a smile. "A favourite of your virgin Queen, *señor* . . . a great favourite." The eyes closed for a moment, then opened once more to meet Sir Henry's hot blue ones. "She . . . she does not know . . . your . . . your Queen . . . that she has with her one who will destroy her."

The group round the rack moved nearer still, pressing close to the man who mocked them from his wooden bed of death. Ruthevan's brows met fiercely, and the veins on his forehead stood out thickly as he clenched his hands.

"Tell me," he said in a low, venomous voice. "Tell me, you miserable jackal, who it is who seeks the life of our sovereign lady. Who?"

He struck the prisoner across the face, cutting the ashen cheek with the heavy rings on his right hand, but the man seemed unaware of this final assault upon his person, for his eyes were slowly closing for the last time.

"Answer me! Speak! Speak!" Ruthevan was shouting now, his voice ringing round the silent dungeon like a peal of violent bells, but it was too late. Even as his heavy hands grasped desperately at the mutilated shoulders of his victim to shake the truth from him, the man gave a faint sigh and his head fell sideways into merciful oblivion.

"Curse of heaven!" Ruthevan let go of the man and looked

11

at his companions. "He is dead, and we are no whit wiser now than when we started."

"We know the name of some of those concerned, my lord," said the Captain of the Guards quickly. "These men we can take, and perhaps they will not be able to withstand our questions as readily as did this man."

"If we can find them," said Sir Henry bitterly. "The names are not known to me, and mayhap they have already left the country, bound for Spain, if their part in this plot is done."

"Yet if we could search them out, sire, then could we discover who it is who is close to her Majesty."

Ruthevan turned to look at Rayne, and his mouth was grim.

"And if we cannot, we shall have small chance of learning who is so favoured by the Queen. Which man this is who stands by her side and receives her smiles; who kisses her hand and plies her with golden trinkets whilst in his black heart, he plans her destruction."

The others paled slightly and turned to look at one another in consternation.

"Wh . . . what can we do, my lord?" asked the sergeant-at-arms finally. "How can we discover who this may be?"

Ruthevan shook his bearded head and raised his hands in despair.

"By the devil, I know not," he said, and his voice was oddly quiet. "Yet we know 'tis one who has been at Court but two years. This will narrow down the number who must be considered. Further, since this varlet is a Spaniard." He paused to look down at the dead man. "'Tis likely that he who is close to the Queen is also of his blood."

"But, my lord." The sergeant-at-arms tipped back his steel helmet and rubbed his worried brow. "There are no Spaniards at Court. All England knows that the time for false friendship with Spain is past, and that his Catholic Majesty now prepares his ships to sail against us. If there had been a man at Court who had come hence from that accursed land, he would have been sent packing long since."

Ruthevan was fingering his beard thoughtfully. " If 'twas known he were Spanish; ay, that is true. But not all Spaniards are dark of hair and swarthy of skin, and many speak our native tongue as well as thee, good Bondman. No, 'tis possible there could be one here at Court, at this very moment, whose flaxen hair and pinkish cheeks do fool us all, and whose gallant English compliments mask a devilish and devious plot of death."

" But, sire, if 'tis not a Spaniard . . ."

Henry Ruthevan turned to look at his secretary who had dared to whisper his inner fears aloud. A small, sad man with dark unhappy eyes and wispy hair falling to the collar of the neat black gown he wore. A man whose shaking fingers were stained with ink, and whose timid mind could scarce absorb the horrors he had been forced to witness that day.

" Ay." Henry Ruthevan nodded and pursed his lips. " Ay, Blackwell, ay. If 'tis not a Spaniard whom we seek, then 'tis a traitor. A son of England, who would turn his hand against his Queen, and stain his honour with a deed more foul than any of Satan's devising."

Peter Blackwell trembled anew, partly from the intense cold which wrapped itself around him with chilling fingers and partly because of the subdued menace he read in his master.

" My lord, what reason could a man have for seeking to harm the Queen? Why should he . . ."

Ruthevan laughed shortly, breaking into his secretary's tremulous words.

" God's mercy, Peter! Reasons there are a plenty. First there is the lust for gold, which turns honest men into rogues and worse. The promise of a chest full of good Spanish escudos could well seduce a faithful servant and make him the willing tool of Spain's illustrious monarch. Then there is the more subtle persuader of faith, good Blackwell. Our gracious Queen is pleased to give her subjects much freedom in their worship, though, bless her, she is a stalwart Protestant, like her sire. Yet for all this, she doth not persecute the Catholics as Bloody Mary harassed and slew the Protestants whilst she sat upon the

13

throne. But, Peter, there are those who would be done with this tolerance; those who seek to establish once more Papal rule in this fair land of ours. Philip of Spain is one such man, for his purpose in gathering his Armada to sail against us is not a single one.

" 'Tis true that he cannot hope for peace in the Netherlands whilst England aids her valiant people to resist the Spanish tyrants, and it is also true that whilst Sir Francis Drake and our other gallant seamen scour the seas and scuttle the Spanish treasure ships, the King of Spain's coffers will never be full enough, but there is another reason."

Ruthevan's voice softened. "Philip of Spain is a fanatic. A man with a single-minded devotion to an ideal, which has warped and twisted his mind and rotted his immortal soul. He will have England Catholic again if he has to torture and burn every last man, woman and child in this island, and he is not alone in this dream of his. There are men; Englishmen, who share his vision. Such a man could be the one we seek."

For a moment there was silence. Under the glow of the torches, the faces of those about Sir Henry were scarcely less pale than that of the corpse below them, for they understood him well, and a shiver of dread ran through Blackwell's thin frame. Then Ruthevan struck his thigh with a clenched fist.

"Come, sires, we can do no more here. I must away and make known to my lord Burghley what has come to pass for he, being wiser than us, will know what to do, and what steps must be taken to protect our lady Queen. Come."

He turned on his heel, his boots striking determined notes over the flagstones as he led his party up the winding stairs to the main part of the palace. As the flares disappeared from view, the darkness fell quietly over the corpse, laying the shadows and silence like a merciful shroud over the tortured flesh and broken bones of King Philip's harbinger of death.

The Palace of Whitehall, set close to the banks of the Thames, was not to be judged by the grimness of its dungeons, for when these were left behind, the aspect was fair indeed. Once the seat of the Archbishops of York, the somewhat jumbled and scattered buildings had been enlarged and enriched when it had become a possession of Cardinal Wolsey, but scarce had that worthy prelate finished the work of building the great hall and the lavish improvements to the private apartments, than King Henry, casting a predatory and approving eye on this riverside haven, took it for his own, and continued the expansion in his own inimitable way.

Thus, since so many hands had dabbled in its building, Whitehall had something of a lack of unity in its overall design, but the gardens were large and pleasant, the orchards well-stocked, the paved and tree-lined walks gracious and welcoming, and for all that the palace sprawled rather untidily round three sides of the gardens, it needed little more, either in the state rooms and galleries, or in its chapels, tiltyard or servants' quarters.

The Queen, constantly on the move from one palace to another, chose a modest enough apartment when she came to Whitehall. An unpretentious set of rooms lying between the grey-blue river and the Sermon Court, a sweep of green turf, laced with paved walks, boasting an open-air pulpit in its centre.

Her bedchamber was not lofty, but its ceiling was richly gilded and though its diamond paned windows were small, its walls were hung with rich tapestries and its furnishings were dazzling to behold. The great four-poster bed was carved of oak, with a heavy matching tester above, and from the wooden scrolls and leaves, fell hangings of damask shot with gold and silver thread which glinted marvellously in the light of the log fire and the blaze of a score of candles.

On one side of the room a long polished table was strewn with the trappings of beauty. Silver bowls of powder, phials of belladonna to make lack-lustre eyes glow like stars, rouge to colour ashen cheeks and pallid mouths, kohl to darken lashes, flasks and bottles of lotions for the hands and neck, soliman to whisk away freckles and sun-spots, red peach blossom and pomegranate peel to whiten the teeth, and perfumes from the great Italian masters. Here too was a profusion of wigs and ornaments for the hair, the tiny brazier for the iron setting-sticks which crimped and coaxed the great cartwheel ruffs into rigid shape, the jewel-boxes and the sweet coffers, those tiny boxes of gold, alabaster and enamel in which the rare and precious scents were housed. Yet this was but a fraction of the items needed to keep her Majesty's illusion of youth and beauty alive.

A whole chamber had been set aside for the Queen's gowns, another for her wigs, and yet another for her shoes, fans and jewels, and in the servants' wing was the great distilling room where her maids produced the rose-water, violet-dew and other sweet-smelling fragrances which were sprinkled so liberally over the chambers to be used by the Queen.

The army of sewing women, when they were not engaged upon yet another fabulous gown of silk and satin, stitched industriously at the miniature cushions filled with rose leaves and violets, which were tucked between the linen and lawn sheets and in the chests where the royal undergarments were kept.

Elizabeth had a sensitive nose, and care was taken to see that this was not offended by such smells as arose from the river or from the domestic quarters of the palace.

Near to the table, and within range of the warmth of the fire, stood the Queen. A slight, rather frail figure, her rigid, upright posture aided by the tightly laced underbodice, moulded and stiffened with busks, which encased and flattened her bosom and pinched her waist to fashionable slimness.

Beneath the low point of the bodice, a huge wheel farthingale was fastened, the forward tilting circle of hard wire and whalebone thrusting out a foot or more from the waist, its shot-silk fullness held out by hoops of increasing width from waist to floor.

She watched silently as her maids and ladies-in-waiting moved quietly and efficiently about their allotted tasks, her head held proudly in the glow of the coals. Her hair, originally fiery red, was now streaked with grey and thinning about the temples, and the skin which had once been of luminous pallor was faintly yellow and wrinkled about the mouth and eyes, but as the lotions and powder were gently applied to cheek and brow, something of the lost youth seemed to return, and in the kindly light of the mellow candles, it was easy enough to imagine that the delicate flush on the cheek and the redness of the lips were natural. The brows, high and arched, were left undarkened, and no artificial aids were needed to brighten the sparkling brown eyes under the heavy lids.

At fifty-five, Elizabeth's body was wasting, and the fresh loveliness of youth had died many long summers before, but her spirit burned as strongly and as fiercely as ever. In the quick, intelligent eyes was all the uncanny magic which had enthralled her subjects from the very day she had ascended the throne of England, for this was as indestructible as time itself.

A strange, unaccountable, inexplicable enigma, this woman born of a sensuous Tudor king and his light-of-love, whom he had made his Queen, only to destroy her so few years after their marriage. Gloriana, their daughter, who had once had an elusive, tantalising beauty which had seemed almost unearthly, and who still retained something of that elfin quality as time robbed her of all else. Proud, arrogant and fastidious, she decked herself in gowns of such magnificence that the crowds which watched her pass by gasped in awe, but she could ride her stallions like a trooper, with such speed and recklessness that her Master of Horse, the faithful, adoring Leicester, clutched his head in anguish and begged his wayward mistress to have more care.

She could stitch the finest of seams, and draw sweet music from a lute, but she could also swear like the roughest of her soldiers and often reduced the boldest of her ministers to quivering silence by the quality of her passion.

She spoke several languages with fluency, and wrote in a hand near to perfection, yet her highly tutored and scholarly

17

mind could relish a bawdy joke with the ready gusto of a farm-hand, and she could switch her attention from the design of her latest robe, to the intricate and dangerous affairs of State without the slightest flicker of concern or hesitation.

She understood statecraft; thoroughly and completely. She had studied history diligently in her childhood and knew well what a monarch's duties were, and if at times she indulged too freely in the light-hearted fickleness of womanhood, she could cast this shallow mask aside at a second's notice when the need arose, and could apply her sharp, astringent wit to any problem which put her throne in jeopardy.

And her hold on men was absolute. For all the physical charms of her girlhood, she had never relied upon her body to keep faithful the courtiers who surrounded her, and the bold English sea-dogs who roamed the high seas seeking wealth and fame. She caught their imaginations and their minds and held them fast.

She understood their dreams and their ambitions and she listened with ready ear to their plans and aspirations, setting them afire with her own enthusiasm.

She did not always agree with them, but she always responded to them. She spoke sharp words to them when they displeased her, but when they succeeded in their missions, she made them feel like gods. She was always their sovereign; autocratic, and demanding, but had enough of womanly uncertainty in her to make them feel protective.

She infuriated them, dazzled them, bewitched them and exploited them, and she kept them eternally faithful to her cause.

For her, they would have gladly risked death a thousand times, and for her, they scoured the globe for gold and gems to lay at her feet. Because of Elizabeth, they grew in stature and daring, straining away from the old, outworn shackles of indifference and apathy, eager to seek a new vibrant exciting world to make their own.

If Elizabeth had favourites, and these she most certainly had, none held the place deepest in her heart, for this was reserved for England alone. That she had warm affection and perhaps a little more for Leicester, and flirted with the Earl of Oxford and Christopher Hatton, her handsome Vice-Chamberlain; that she smiled winningly upon each new and comely gallant who came to Court, was of no lasting consequence, for in the final analysis, nothing could turn her away from her first love.

Wise enough to see that a monarch could only rule successfully with the love of the people, she had made plain from the first that none could turn her from the needs of those over whom she reigned. To England she had promised her hand, and to England she had given her heart. All that she did was for her realm, and for the common people, whose welfare and safety was her first charge, and her most sacred duty.

She stirred slightly as the rustling maids finished their work and stood aside to allow the ladies-in-waiting to come forward. First came Jane Mordaunt, sweet and twenty, with sunshine hair and saucy eyes. The Queen looked severely at the low cut of Jane's gown, and the mischievous gleam in her eyes, for she was strict and stern with these high-born maidens of hers, but she said nothing as the girl carefully fitted the jewelled bodice into position, her slender white hands deft as she fastened the golden hooks and eyes together.

Then came Mary Kildare, dark-haired and lovely, with azure eyes and a winsome mouth, who helped her friend, Agnes Trewlace, to fix the sweeping underskirt of embroidered and jewelled damask to the farthingale. Finally came the skirt itself, lemon-satin, sprinkled with topaz and diamonds and trimmed with golden aiglets from waist to hem.

It needed all the girls' skill to settle the great skirt into position, but finally it was done, and then the huge bishop's sleeves with their wings of golden cord and gems were tied to the bodice.

Lastly the snowy cartwheel ruff was fastened round the Queen's neck, its delicate, sharp folds a welcome cover for the ageing muscles of the neck, and Penelope Fitzallen stepped back to admire the effect.

" Stop gawking, girl," said the Queen, finally breaking the silence in the chamber. " Would you have me stand here all night whilst you simper and smirk? Get me my wig."

Penelope, barely seventeen, and newly-come to Court, flushed, but turned quickly to take the elaborately curled wig of bright red from the near-by maid, and with the aid of her companions, slipped it carefully over the Queen's own fading locks.

When each last jewel had been fixed to the wig, so that it glittered like some monstrous bauble, and the fragile, wired headrail, sprinkled with gems, had been fastened into place, the ivory fan with plumes of faintest cream was handed to the Queen, and Elizabeth of England was ready to face her audience chamber and to partake of supper with her courtiers and favourites.

The servants were left behind to clear the silk-strewn chamber, but the maids-of-honour and ladies-in-waiting clustered behind the Queen, and as the great doors were opened, a dozen magnificently clad men turned as one to bow low to their sovereign.

The Queen's eyes sparkled. Despite her devotion to England, and to her duties, she was woman enough to love the attention these handsome young men laid so devotedly at her feet, and her nightly task of deciding which of them should be favoured with the royal hand, was one she greatly enjoyed.

Finally she selected a tall young man of some two and twenty summers, clad wondrously in a doublet of pure white pinked velvet on which pearls and diamonds fought for supremacy. His scarlet cloak, waist length, was slung with studied carelessness over one shoulder, and his paned breeches of white and scarlet silk were distended with bombast to absurdly fashionable width.

Elizabeth cast a quick admiring eye over his strong, shapely legs concealed by the white hose, and then returned to regard with favour the young, earnest face above the full stiffened ruff.

" Zounds, Sir Charles!" she said gaily. " You wear fine

20

feathers this night. I am persuaded you mean to put me in the shade, so dazzling is your raiment."

She held out her hand; a long, slender member with carefully tended nails and soft skin which needed no artificial aids to beauty.

Charles Trenton took the proffered hand as if it were made of the most delicate glass, and with another profound bow, touched it lightly with his lips.

" Ma'am, how may this be? This charge I can deny with heart and conscience as clear as a mountain stream, for could I hope to match perfection such as yours? Your Majesty rebukes me for my poor attempt to fit myself for your company, yet we both know, madam, that I have failed, and most miserably."

The Queen laughed happily and allowed him to kiss her hand again. " You are a rogue, Charles, and you have a ready and plausible tongue, but I will not punish you too severely for your extravagance on this occasion. Come, I will take your arm."

She smiled warmly at the other young men, who were now frowning and starting to protest at this favouritism, for it was an understood thing that such indignation should be shewn to the one fortunate enough to win the Queen's hand.

" Alack, sires," she laughed, entering into the spirit of the game which she loved so well. " Do not frown so, for it ill-becomes you, and who knows with whom I shall sit at supper this night, or who shall play primero with me when our meal is done? Enough of your scowls, sires. Let us join my lord Burghley and the others, for we have kept them waiting long enough."

The procession glided in stately fashion along the corridor and down the sweeping staircase, the Queen's fingers resting lightly on the slashed sleeve of her chosen courtier, the others falling behind to flirt noiselessly with the delectable and nubile ladies-in-waiting, now that their nightly ritual with the Queen was over.

In the great audience chamber, William Cecil, Lord

Burghley, awaited his royal mistress. He had served her for long years, giving unstintingly of his wisdom, experience and guile, and offering this slender, delicate woman his love and devotion in a way she did not mistake.

One of Elizabeth's greatest charms was her loyalty and affection for those who served her well. She did not take them for granted, nor expect their lives to be hers simply because she was their Queen. She took care to earn their respect and love, and when she had it, she guarded it and treasured it more covetously than she cared for the most valuable of her jewels.

Burghley's appointment as Chief Secretary of State had been a shrewd one, for he had guided the Queen since she first assumed the Crown, and now, in an age when adventure was on the wing, and young men were reckless in their search for fame and fortune, and when England was aflame with a new determination and drive, Burghley's old head was wise and stable, and his counsel and advice to the Queen was sound and reliable. She called him her spirit, and valued him for his true worth, and as he bowed low before her, she took her hand from Trenton's arm and extended it to Cecil.

He kissed it gently, his faded blue eyes affectionate as they met the Queen's, and for a moment, the gay artificial quality of the Queen's smile changed.

There was no need for coquetry with Burghley; they were old friends and knew one another too well for flirtations. Elizabeth's dark eyes softened as the old man straightened up.

"Well, William," she said softly. "How is your gout this night? It doth not trouble you too much I hope."

William Cecil, a martyr to the ailment, shrugged ruefully, acknowledging the Queen's concern with a quick grateful smile, but then the smile faded and his worry returned.

"I thank your Majesty, but I fear there are other things that trouble me this night."

"Oh?" The sharp eyes flashed, for Elizabeth heard the note of real apprehension in Cecil's voice. "What is this, my lord, which causes you unease?"

Cecil hesitated and glanced quickly at the group behind the Queen, now still, and waiting for his answer. Then he gave a half-glance at the remainder of the assembled Court and sighed faintly.

"Madam, 'twould be as well if I spoke with you alone, for this is a matter of some urgency."

Elizabeth frowned, but she did not argue, for Burghley did not panic easily, and if he sought her private ear, there would be good cause for it. She nodded.

"Very well, good Cecil, if we must put aside our supper for a while, it will not do us much harm." She smiled round at those standing near. "We shall not be long. I pray you forgive us." And with that she laid her hand on Burghley's arm and walked slowly to the door, matching her pace with Cecil's painful steps.

In the small ante-room, Burghley settled the Queen on a long stool by the fire, and stood doubtfully by her side, but she made an impatient gesture.

"God's body, my lord, sit you down. There is no need for ceremony between us now; we are alone. Sit down, Will, and tell me what it is that makes you look like this."

Burghley bowed stiffly and took a seat opposite the Queen, and his lined face was grave.

"Madam, there is only one thing which could make me fear as I do this night."

The Queen was very still, only the blaze of jewels in the firelight seeming to live. Then the heavy lids dropped a little to conceal the shrewd dark eyes.

"Go on, Will. What may that be?"

"Your life, madam," he said briefly. "Your life and safety."

Elizabeth nodded slowly but without trace of fear, for plots against her life were nothing new, and she realised only too well how vulnerable she was despite her soldiers and guards and how the throng of courtiers and servants hedged about her.

She, like other rulers, recognised with grim resignation that unheralded death was one of the hazards of the monarchy.

All the watchful guards of William of Orange, the brave defender of the Netherlands, had not been able to save his life from an assassin's bullet after five abortive attempts, and Elizabeth, hearing of his end, had smiled bitterly, knowing that her own situation was hardly less insecure and dangerous.

"A new plot, Will?" she asked finally. "Another attempt on my life? And what is it this time?"

Burghley shook his head and found it hard to meet her eyes.

"Alas, madam, we are not sure. We know little of it, and this is why my mind is thus troubled."

"But you know something of it," said Elizabeth sharply. "Tell me what you know."

Hesitantly, Burghley outlined what had taken place in the dungeons earlier that day, and as she listened, Elizabeth's mouth grew thin.

"I do not like the use of torture, my lord. I have told you this before."

"Yes, madam." He was patient. "We would not have used these ends had there been any other way. The man was stubborn and would not unlock his secrets."

"And courageous too, if what you say is true," returned the Queen acidly. "I do not like to think of . . ." She broke off and gave a deep sigh. "Yet you are right, Will. You had to know what was afoot. And you say you have names?"

Cecil nodded, the anxiety in his eyes deepening. "Three names, madam, only three. These men, if they are still in England, we will find, but the fourth man . . . the other man . . ."

He stopped abruptly, and the Queen's mouth curved into a grim smile.

"Ah yes; the fourth man. The man who stands by my side, eh, Will? And who is he I wonder."

Burghley, looking at her with troubled gaze, wondered if it was but his imagination which made her face seem paler, but before he could offer her any words of comfort or reassurance, Elizabeth said softly:

24

"Only three men close to the throne have come to Court within the last two years, Will. Stephen de Vere, John Dyke and Robert Blandford."

Burghley was startled at the speed with which Elizabeth had assessed the situation, and when she saw his expression, she laughed caustically.

"Oh yes, my lord," she said shortly. "I can see danger as readily as the next, but which of my handsome gallants is it who seeks my life?"

Burghley shrugged helplessly. "Madam, I know not. They are all of old and honoured families. On their loyalty, I would have staked my life. I cannot believe that one of them would . . ."

"But what if one of them is not whom he seems." The Queen's voice was softer still. "Until they came to Court, we did not know them. All we knew of them was their heritage and the quality of the names they bore. What if one is an imposter?"

Burghley sat upright, his gnarled hand tight on the arm of his chair.

"An imposter! I had not thought of that, ma'am. But how can we decide if this is so? How can we tell which of them is privy to this plot?"

"I know a way," said Elizabeth, and now her tension had left her and her mouth was smiling in a different way. "I know. Send you a messenger to Devon, good Will. Tell him to go to Blandon Point; to the house set hard by the cliff."

"Monks' Walk?" Burghley's eyes met the Queen's. "You will send for Nicholas Rokeby?"

"Ay, Will. We will send for young Sir Nicholas. 'Tis time he came to Court again in any event, for he has sadly neglected me of late. Send for him, my lord, and I will charge him with the task of finding which of these men is a murderer or worse."

Cecil pursed his lips and gave a slight shake of his head.

"But why Rokeby, ma'am? There are others nearer at hand who could equally well undertake such an enterprise. Men with brave hearts, and a shrewd eye for a conspiracy."

"But not with a tongue which speaks Spanish like a native," said Elizabeth with a faint smile, and her eyes were brighter now. "He has many unusual gifts, this young man of mine."

"You think he will be able to do this, madam?" Burghley was still doubtful, but the Queen gave a quiet laugh.

"Oh yes, he will be able to do it, Will; never doubt it. He is made of steel and fire, my lord, and has a mind more devious and cunning than your own. He is bold, resolute and has the courage of a lion, and of his loyalty there is no shred of doubt. Yes, send for Sir Nicholas, but say nothing to any other yet, for clearly we know not who our enemies are, and the slightest word might mean Rokeby's arrival would be too late."

Burghley whitened, but he nodded. "I will do as you say, ma'am," he said slowly, "and I pray to God that Nicholas Rokeby will comprehend the measure of his task."

The Queen gave a slight, crooked smile. "Fear not, my lord," she said gently. "He will understand, for he was born to live with danger, and hath a sixth sense for death."

She rose, straightening the shimmering farthingale with a thoughtful hand. "Yes, my lord, you need have no concern; he will understand." She smiled at the old man and held out her hand.

"Come, Will, let us take supper together, and put these distressful thoughts from our minds. We can be of greater watchfulness until Sir Nicholas arrives, and when he does . . ." Her smile grew warmer. "When he does, my lord, all will be well, as you will see."

And with that she took Burghley's arm and returned to the great hall and as she ate sparingly of the extravagant fare spread before her, and sipped the carefully tested wine in the gold and enamel goblet, none would have guesssed what had passed between her and the Secretary of State, for Elizabeth knew how to keep a secret, and her courage was as high as that of the man to whom a messenger had already been sent.

Burghley, watching her, felt his apprehension lessen as his admiration for his mistress grew. Tartar she might have been;

a coward she certainly was not. Slowly he raised his own goblet to her in a silent toast, thanking God, not for the first time, that Elizabeth Tudor was a brave woman.

# 2

IT WAS two days later that Burghley's messenger spurred his hard-pressed steed over the rolling downs to Blandon Point. Despite the warmth of his uniform, and the heavy cloak he wore about his shoulders, he shivered as he raced onwards, for the tentative snowflakes he had encountered at Blackley Moor were now a swirling mist of whiteness which made him jerk his horse to a halt every now and then when he could no longer see the path ahead.

He cursed heartily, but did not check his speed, and before long was racing up the steeply rising ground to Monks' Walk. The house lay back from the face of a rocky incline which fell almost without break to the fretful, icy waters below, and now, in the coldness of winter, the winds howled angrily about its walls, feverishly seeking a chink or crack through which to whisper its chill venom.

But Monks' Walk had been too well built for such intrusions. It was a legacy of an earlier age, and the foundations had been laid long years before when Edward II was England's feeble king. Later, when his vigorous son ascended the throne, the building had been finished, the masons and craftsmen putting loving touches to the gracious house with precise care, the carpenters and joiners securing the last span of the great hammer-beam roof with justifiable pride and satisfaction.

The history of the house was obscure. At first it had been occupied by the noble family under whose direction the building had started, but it seemed that they did not stay long in the mansion they had created, for the next record shewed that the building had become the home of a small and austere Order of monks. The fate of the monks was as difficult to discover as the whereabouts of the family which had deserted its Devonshire paradise, but it was rumoured that the Brothers had left suddenly, almost overnight, and were never heard of again, and that in the deep cellars beneath the house, red stains had been found upon the floor which could not be explained.

Later when Jonathan Rokeby, Nicholas's grandfather, had brought his young bride to Monks' Walk, some of the darkest whispers had dissolved under the happiness and laughter which filled the house, but it was John Rokeby, Nicholas's father, who had wrought the greatest changes.

A strong, vigorous and wealthy man, with a great love for beauty, he had preserved faithfully the exterior of the house whilst completely replanning and refashioning its interior. Built round a square, central courtyard, Monks' Walk rose to three storeys, linked by a fine polished oak staircase with richly carved newel posts and satin-smooth handrail, and by the smaller, narrower staircase at the rear reserved for the servants.

On the ground floor was the long panelled hall with its impressive carved stone fireplace and the simple, beautiful andirons preserved from the Middle Ages. Here too, was the great parlour, and the smaller winter parlour, the buttery and the kitchens with their spits and shining pots of copper and bronze, the chafing dishes, the rows of gridirons and boilers and the white scrubbed tables cluttered with mortars and pestles, cleavers and axes, kneading troughs and platters. Near at hand was the mealhouse and the spicery; the pastry, where the baking was done, and the bolting house, where the sacks of grain and flour were stored, and at the rear was the squillerie, or coal house, which supplied the vast open fireplaces throughout the house, and warmed the cooks' furnaces and ovens.

On the floor above was the Great Chamber, a lofty and gracious room with sparkling windows and fine furnishings, and at this level were to be found a number of well-appointed bedrooms, each boasting a four-poster bed with sumptuous hangings of velvet and silk, with rare Turkish carpets upon the polished floors.

It was here too, that the loveliest room in the house was to be found; the gallery.

Stretching the whole width of the house, it looked out over the restless water, its tall windows opening up a wide spectacular vista to the sea. On the opposite wall hung portraits of earlier Rokebys, cheek by jowl with the glow and splendour of the canvases of Italy's undisputed masters. Each window had a cushioned seat beneath it, where one could sit and gaze in lost wonderment at the scene below, and beneath the paintings a number of marble-topped tables were placed with wondrously wrought curios in ivory and jade, porcelain and gold upon their smooth surfaces. There were niches for the alabaster statues of Greek gods, and smaller resting places for the clocks with exquisitely engraved cases and jewelled dials and hands.

The gallery was lit by candles, some in heavy silver holders and some fixed to wrought-iron rings suspended from the high beamed ceiling like a series of misty aureoles. There was little other furniture, save for a carved chest or two of cedar wood and cypress, for the gallery was reserved for dancing and for strolls when the elements outside were too rough, but it needed nothing more, for it was perfect to the last inch of polished floor and in the final curls of ironwork on the two vast fireplaces.

John Rokeby had not ignored his gardens either. Modest in area, the grounds were trimly designed, with a fountain which played soothingly in summer, set in a square of neat hedges and white-flagged paths running between the flower beds. There was a narrow little orchard packed with trees and fruit bushes, and a rose-arbour with rustic benches and rain-washed marble figures to guard it well. At the end of the garden was the yew walk. A long, rather dusty path, running between the tall straight trees on either side, which kept the sunlight away with jealous waving arms.

The servants, and those coming from the near-by village, avoided the yew walk if they could, and none would venture near it once night had fallen, for tales were told of it which froze the blood and made the fingers unsteady with fear.

Some said it was this path which had given the house its name; that down this narrow strip had trod the mysterious monks who had once lived in the house beyond, and who had started down this leafy avenue only to vanish into thin air as they passed by the last tree into open meadow land.

And they had been seen. On nights when the moon was full, and even the thick yew branches could not keep out all the silver light, shadows had loomed oddly between the trees; blurred outlines which could not be explained and once, many years before, a maidservant, looking from the attic window of the servants' floor, had seen a cowled figure hurrying down towards the walk, and had fainted on the spot.

Since that time, the villagers and servants had kept well away, and averted their fearful eyes from this strange, haunted place.

Whilst Burghley's messenger thrust his determined way through the icy, snow-laden wind, Nicholas Rokeby was entertaining his aunt, the Lady Caroline Fitzmorton. They were partaking of supper in the winter parlour, a cosier, warmer place than the great parlour where Nicholas normally entertained his guests, and in the glow of the fire and the light of the candles, it was a delicious haven from which to listen to the blizzard outside the heavy velvet curtains.

The meal had been a simple one; a saddle of mutton, a few capons, a joint of tender veal, served with spiced sauce from the shallow dishes of silver and glass in the centre of the round table, a platter of lampreys and a chine of salmon. In addition to the dishes of colewort and artichokes, the kidney-beans sprinkled with chervil and the cornsalad, there was the new wonder, the potato, white and floury and marvellous on the palate. For Lady Caroline, who had a sweet tooth, the cooks had conjured up a miracle of jellies of all flavours, small rich cakes iced with almond paste and marchpane, and had filled crystal dishes with suckets, those delicious fragments of rose-leaves, violets, rosemary and walnuts, dipped in boiling syrup, cooled and dipped again and again in the heavy liquid until thickly coated with crisp hard sugar.

In the slender crystal goblets there was vernage, a cool Italian wine, and a steward hovered near with muscadel and malvesey, should more potent refreshment be required.

Caroline Fitzmorton nibbled a candied cherry and regarded her nephew thoughtfully.

He lay back in the great, carved chair, one hand clasped round his goblet, the other resting idly on the table. Tall, lithe and graceful, he moved with all the powerful, delicate precision of a panther, but when he was at ease, he had a strange quality of utter stillness which was almost superhuman in its control.

His crisp dark hair was brushed back from a face of carefully designed bones and a skin lightly tanned by a benevolent sun and quick restless winds. Under black, mocking brows, his eyes were clear and sapphire bright, their gentle derision matching the slightly sardonic lines of his mouth. The short pickdevant beard gave him a faintly satanic air, and there was that in him which made the eye pause to consider with more care the handsome, striking face which at first glance had seemed so innocent.

This night his doublet was of deep blue velvet, elaborately pinked to shew the silver cloth ruffling beneath it, the huge bishops' sleeves tapering to immaculate wrist frills falling over strong, slender hands, tanned brown by a sun England had not seen for many months. The cartwheel ruff boasted no less than four rows of snowy, stiffened lawn, and over one broad shoulder, a blue and crimson waist-length cloak fell in negligent folds, half-concealing the deadly rapier strapped to a jewelled belt around the slim waist.

32

He wore paned trunk-hose of silver cloth and blue satin, fashionably puffed, and cutting in sharply to strong, muscular legs clad in white netherstocks, terminating in shoes of pliable Spanish leather.

He looked the perfect courtier; poised, elegant and self-possessed, each last detail of his toilet a work of art, but that second and more careful survey aroused a feeling of faint doubt, for under the lavish finery his body was hard and supple, and every now and then the brilliant eyes had a gleam of something unexpected in their depths.

To his fellow nobles he was a puzzle; an enigma whose depths they could not plumb, and there were many who questioned the odd disappearances of Sir Nicholas, when he was to be found neither at the Queen's side nor at his retreat in the soft Devonshire countryside. He was popular enough, for he was gently civil and had a ready sense of humour, and to the ladies of the Court he was excitingly gallant, but no one knew him really well. It was difficult to get beyond the first layer of the elegant creature that was Nicholas Rokeby; impossible to discover what lay beneath the lazy smile and light, casual courtesies.

Only a few knew the secret, and they were as close-mouthed as Nicholas himself. Elizabeth was one; Burghley another. Christopher Hatton and a thin, dour secretary, who spoke little, but observed much, also knew. So did Francis Drake, the vibrant, dynamic seaman who had already aroused England's admiration by his daring exploits at sea, and with his victories on the other side of the world. Drake, and his companions; Hawkins and Frobisher, Seymour and Raleigh, and the gentle, aristocratic Lord High Admiral of England, Charles, Lord Howard of Effingham. They knew well enough what lay beneath the silks and satins and the soft tongue, for they had good cause to be grateful to this man who now sat staring into the fire.

England's quarrel with Spain was an old one. For years the truce between the fervent Catholic monarch of Spain and the determinedly Protestant Queen of England had been a shallow mockery, designed only to prevent the final rupture which would end in bloodshed and disaster.

Both rulers were cautious by nature; both reluctant to dip their hands into the royal coffers to find the money needed to equip armies and ships for conflict, for neither treasury could really afford the reckless luxury of war.

And so, whilst Elizabeth had given succour to Philip's rebellious subjects in the Netherlands, in a manner which was secret in name only, Philip had not hesitated to seize English seamen, foolish and careless enough to come within his waters, and to consign them to the unrelenting care of the Holy Office, looking broodingly towards the coast of the heretical island of which he had once been titular king, as he signed the death warrants of his doomed prisoners.

He had looked also, with even blacker disapproval, at the New World, which had once been Spain's undisputed domain, but which now was prey to the outrageous English pirates who sailed boldly into the alien waters to claim a share of this *paraiso* for themselves. And this was not all. Not content with encroaching on the territories which Philip claimed as his alone, these privateers of the English Queen had been steadily draining his income away by seizing and plundering his treasure ships as they sailed gracefully home, laden with gold, silver, ivory and jewels of every fabulous shape and colour and size.

Hitherto, Elizabeth had denied vigorously the charge that her navy was engaged in acts of aggression against the King of Spain, and she had spoken truthfully, for men like Francis Drake sailed under an independent flag, on a purely commercial basis, and would have been the first to admit that the Crown had had no hand in their ventures.

Yet it was as well known in Madrid as it was in London, that when Drake and his fellow adventurers set sail, they lacked nothing in financial support, for the Queen and the English nobles were glad enough to invest their money in such enterprises, knowing full well the return would be rich and rewarding.

When Philip, sending a bitter protest to Elizabeth concerning one of Drake's more insufferable atrocities, had read her conciliatory reply, his lips had tightened forbiddingly, for news had already reached him from his spies in England that Elizabeth had dubbed Drake, knight, almost before the ink was dry on her plausible note of apology.

And so, the war, which was never called openly by that name in its early stages, had continued, and Drake, a stocky man of medium stature, with a fresh, lightly tanned complexion and quick, intelligent eyes, had pursued his ravages upon the Spaniards with untroubled calm.

He was the epitome of the spirit of his day, this son of Devon. Daring, resourceful, always ready to grasp an unexpected opportunity when it offered itself and to turn it to spectacular advantage, he had a cunning and inborn wisdom which protected his seemingly headlong exploits from the dangers of rashness and want of caution. He was a child of his time. A man who understood, and felt instinctively, the sudden upsurge of new life in England, and rode on the crest of its wave with a bold confidence that did not recognise the possibility of defeat.

He did not stop to measure the might of Spain; he was solely concerned with England's potential strength and the place he considered she should hold amongst the nations, and because he was, above all else, a brilliant and experienced seaman, the target he set for himself was no misty vision of a dreamer, but a cold, realistic probability.

Yet there was also a personal animosity underlying his actions. He had never forgiven the Spaniards for their treachery at San Juan de Ulua where, years before, he and Hawkins had been engaged upon the repair of their small fleet of ships in the harbour. The Spanish Plate Fleet, hovering outside the harbour, had given its solemn promise to leave the English ships unmolested if its own were allowed to dock. Drake, younger then, and more trusting, had agreed, and the Spanish ships flocked into San Juan de Ulua in quiet good order.

Once there, they had rounded upon the smaller and weaker

fleet and scattered it, and although Hawkins and Drake had managed to escape, many ships were taken, and the unfortunate crews relegated to the rôle of galley slaves, or burnt at the stake as incurable heretics.

Drake hated the Spaniards with cold, concentrated venom, and they knew it. For all their fierce Castilian pride, they were afraid of him, for he seemed to them to have powers which were unnatural and inhuman. It was whispered that he had a magic mirror into which he could gaze, thus seeing all that his enemies were about and could frustrate their every move since they could have no secrets from him. They called him *El Draque*, and crossed themselves hastily when his name was mentioned, their own hatred growing apace as they did their best to keep out of his way.

Finally the war of nerves and diplomacy took on a different shape. Tempers rose, and resolves hardened, and the Marquis of Santa Cruz put his specifications for a great invasion fleet before Philip. The King had read it with habitual calm and with the painstaking thoroughness which attended all his undertakings, then with a gentle sigh, had laid the papers aside, remarking only that the enterprise was too costly.

But time did not stand still, nor did events. The wheel of history rolled relentlessly onwards. In 1585, following an attempt by Philip to seize English cornships in a manner which called into question his honour, Drake sailed to Vigo Bay, helping himself generously to food and water at Philip's expense, then sailing blithely on to Santiago, which he left in flames. This done, he moved to San Domingo, the proudest jewel in Philip's crown of golden islands, which he sacked and left in ruins. From there, he went to Carthegena and to St. Augustine, Philip's new settlement in Florida; both were left smouldering and crushed under the heel of Drake's contempt.

Hearing of the Sea Dragon's latest infamy, Philip's face had grown thoughtful, and he had pulled from under a large pile of documents on his desk, Santa Cruz's blueprint for the invasion of England.

If he had needed any further spur to quicken his determination he got it when the ill-fated Mary Stuart met her end on the block. The Queen of Scots, claiming to the end that the throne of England was rightfully hers, named Philip as her lawful successor, and Philip began to think in earnest of his Enterprise, which would quell England's impudent sea-vandals, and bring that country back to the true faith at one and the same time.

He studied Santa Cruz's figures, slashing them ruthlessly to more manageable proportions, and started to supervise personally the re-conditioning of his fleet. Recognising Philip's change of mood, and learning of Spain's plans from Francis Walsingham, who had his finger on the pulse of every intrigue in the Western world, Elizabeth also commenced her preparations, but like Philip she was aghast at the sums demanded by the Lord High Admiral, and by Drake, now Vice-Admiral of her fleet.

In the spring of 1587, England was far from ready to withstand an attack by Spain, and Elizabeth gave tacit agreement to Drake's plan for staving off the onslaught of Spain a little longer. At the last moment, her courage seemed to fail her, as if she feared that this final, defiant and irrevocable step would dissolve for ever any hopes of peace, but her instructions to Drake to turn back were too late.

Whether Drake ever saw the peremptory demand of his mistress, no one ever knew, but whatever was the truth of that strangely misplaced missive, Drake sailed into Cadiz Harbour and routed Philip's fleet of royal galleys, scattering them, and rendering them useless.

Again the rumour of his magic mirror waxed loud, but *El Draque* had, in fact, no such device to aid him. Instead, he had a small band of men who sailed the wide seas, quietly and without fuss, gathering facts and news about the movements of the Spaniards; an intelligence system which worked with smooth efficiency and which furnished the English Vice-Admiral with all he needed to know of his enemy's doings.

One of his aides thus engaged was Nicholas Rokeby, who had made a fortune by relieving Spanish treasure ships of their precious cargoes, and who now, in addition to this lucrative occupation, kept a watchful eye on the growth of the new fleet which Philip was once more gathering together with undaunted and patient care.

Rokeby, whose presence was feared almost as much as that of Drake himself, sailed his ship, the *Bullen Lass*, under a flag of crimson with a single white star upon it, sweeping boldly across the oceans, plundering ships, and harrying coastal towns and villages, taking prisoners when he felt they might provide useful information, and sinking such shipping as he caught at anchor in the harbours which he visited in his whirlwind fashion.

The Spaniards had a superstitious fear of him, for he seemed to arrive suddenly and without warning, and to vanish again with equal rapidity. Their terror was fanned by the fact that his victims never saw his face, for he always wore a mask, and, whilst engaged upon his work of destruction, never spoke a word.

His appearances seemed to the Spanish seamen to have an uncanny touch of the supernatural, and they named him *El Espectro*, or the Phantom, and for all their undoubted courage, shivered when they saw the crimson and white flag come fluttering arrogantly along their starboard side.

There was little to connect the courtier who bowed low over a lady's hand and whispered quick, delicious compliments in her ready ear, with the man who drew his sword with swift purposefulness as he leapt aboard a ship to which his grappling irons were fastened. Nothing to shew that the man who considered with grave concern the relative merits of a doublet of slashed green velvet, and one of paned aquamarine silk, was the same as he who wore a steel breastplate and high leather boots as he swung a long leg over the side of his adversary's crippled galley.

When Rokeby encountered his Vice-Admiral at Court, his greeting was formal and brief, but in less public places, in darkened rooms where only a few candles burnt fitfully to lighten the gloom, Drake listened with an intent ear to his lieutenant's report on the strength of Philip's growing Armada.

Blissfully unaware of Rokeby's double existence, the Lady Caroline finished her sweetmeat and wiped her hands carefully with a silk-tasselled handkerchief.

Of some fifty years, she was a formidable woman. Rich, autocratic and peppery, her one weakness was her fondness for Nicholas; a fondness she took good care to hide from him, for she would acknowledge no such chink in her armour.

She effected an elaborate toilette, crushing her ample form into the agonising tightness of a firmly-boned bodice, and rejoicing in the concealing fullness of the great French farthingales and stiffly starched ruffs. She wore a wig of carefully dressed curls, in which diamonds glittered brightly under the light of the candles, and her fingers, white and plump, were laden with costly gems, whilst long ropes of perfectly matched pearls hung to waist length with a large and unusual string of pomander beads.

Her nose was strong and curved, her mouth firm and uncompromising, and the spark in her dark eyes gave warning of her unbending determination.

She tucked the kerchief into the pocket of her slashed and ruffled sleeve, and gave Nicholas another severe look.

" Nicholas," she said finally. " It is time you were wed."

Rokeby, comfortably warmed by the fire and by the excellence of his wine, stirred slightly and shot his aunt a quizzical look.

" God, madam! What brings this to your mind? Is my table so poorly served that you feel I need a woman to supervise my establishment?"

Lady Fitzmorton clicked her tongue impatiently.

" Don't be absurd, Nicholas. 'Tis naught to do with that, and well you know it. It is time you married and settled down, for you are far too restless. God a mercy, boy, you have not been at Monks' Walk for months."

Nicholas smiled. " I have been at Court. When the Queen sends for me . . ."

" Nonsense! " Caroline took a quick sip of wine. " You

have not been at Court. Do you think I do not know who is at Court and who is not? Mayhap I do not spend my time within earshot of her Majesty, yet do I know who serves her and when. Moreover, the winds are as chill at Nonsuch and White-hall as they are here." She gave Nicholas a piercing glance. "You did not get that warmness of skin in England. Now, where have you been?"

Nicholas shrugged slightly, but his eyes were more wary.

"In truth, good Aunt, I did make a short journey, but it was nothing."

"You make many journeys," returned Lady Fitzmorton significantly, "and they are not always short. Beshrew you, boy; do not treat me as if I were senile! Oh well, if you will keep silent about your comings and goings, and will tell me naught, that is your business, but still I say you should be wed. Would you have the name of Rokeby die with you?"

"There is time," said Nicholas with a quick smile. "Ample time, for I am not senile either."

"You are twenty-six," snapped Caroline, her eyes kindling again with renewed disapproval. "The years go by quickly, Nicholas, and if ought should happen to you . . ."

The anger was suddenly gone, and her eyes were fearful. Nicholas saw her look of anxiety and gave a low, comforting laugh.

"Nothing will happen to me, sweet; I have nine lives, and, marry, I take good care of myself, of this you need have no fear."

"But . . . but . . . anything could befall you, Nick, when you sail forth in that great ship of yours."

"My ship?" Rokeby was suddenly very still, the affectionate amusement dying out of his eyes. "What ship is this, Aunt?"

The Lady Caroline saw the change in him, and for once was a little uncertain as she spoke.

"*The Bullen Lass*, of course." She pulled herself together, and the hesitation was gone. "Don't talk like a fool, Nick. Did you think to keep secret the existence of such a vessel? What you do, I cannot think, but I am not one to pry." Her lips compressed in frustration. "But you must see that it is your duty to take a wife, so that the line does not become extinct."

Nicholas relaxed and drank more wine, the smile returning to his eyes.

"Perhaps I will one day, madam; perhaps I will."

"Not one day, Nick; soon." Caroline leaned forward, a militant glimmer in her eyes. "I know the perfect wife for you. A girl who will add lustre to our family, and who will give you the sons you need."

"Faith, Aunt! Who is this paragon you have selected for me? Do I know the wench?" Nicholas pulled a slight face, seeing the determination in his aunt, and she nodded, opening the small ivory fan and whisking it back and forth impatiently.

"Yes, 'tis the Lady Anne Courtney. Her family is an old one, and she is wholesome and healthy with good broad hips to bear your children."

"God's body, madam, you make me sound like a stud bull," said Nicholas shortly. "And if the Lady Anne is well favoured in her hips, God has not been so gracious in the fashioning of her visage, for she has the look of a brood mare. No, Aunt, no! You will not get me to the altar with her, that I promise you."

"Stuff and nonsense," said Lady Fitzmorton sharply. "She has a fair enough face, and even if there are others more favoured in this respect, she is of strong sound stock, and this is what matters."

Nicholas roused himself and poured more wine. "I am not of a mind to wed yet, dear Aunt," he said firmly, "and when I do, the wench will be of my choosing."

"Yes." Caroline was short. "And you have had much experience, have you not?" She looked at her nephew with disfavour. "I am not unaware of the reputation you have earned for yourself with women, Nick, and it is time this folly stopped."

"I congratulate you," said Nicholas smoothly, "for you are as well informed about my affairs as Sir Francis Walsingham is about King Philip's plans, but I pray you, do not disturb yourself. I do none any harm, and when the time is ripe, I shall marry; but not yet. There are things I have to do."

"Things? What things?" Caroline was curt, but Nicholas merely smiled.

"Mere trifles, dearest," said Nicholas with studied casualness. "Nothing for you to concern yourself with. Now, tell me; when do you leave for London again?"

The question was a pointed one, but Caroline was not in the least put out.

"In a day or two," she said with a tight smile. "Have no fear, Nick, you will not be saddled with me for much longer."

"You are always welcome, my dear," said Nicholas, and meant it, for he had a fondness for Caroline, and was not misled by her sour tongue, knowing well the affection she had for him. "I am glad to know that I am not to lose you yet."

Lady Fitzmorton favoured her nephew with another frown, and would have spoken again, but at that moment the door opened and a page approached the table, bowing low, first to Lady Caroline and then to Rokeby.

"Sire." He gave Nicholas a wide smile, for he doted on his master. "There is a man here who asks for you."

Nicholas raised a brow at the child, but his gaze was kindly. "And who is this man, Thomas, who comes through a night such as this to see me? A villager?"

The child's eyes were round with wonder now and he shook his head vigorously. "No, sire, he has come from London; from the Court of her Majesty." He took a step nearer to his master. "He has ridden for two whole days without rest, my lord, and he is sorely tried."

Nicholas rose to his feet, and Caroline, watching him, saw the sudden hardening of his mouth and something in the clear blue gaze which half-frightened her.

"Where is this man, Thomas?" he asked quietly, and the

page bowed again, sensing as Lady Fitzmorton had done, some indefinable change in Rokeby's manner.

" In the kitchen, sire, for he was in dire need of food."

Rokeby nodded. " I will go to him. Thomas, tend the Lady Caroline's wants. Madam." He turned to his aunt. " You will forgive me?"

" But Nicholas." She raised a hand in protest. " Why do you go to the kitchens? Let the man be brought here."

Nicholas shook his head. " No, I will go to him. Drink your wine, sweet, and Thomas here will keep you company whilst I am gone."

He kissed her hand and strode to the door before she could put forward any further arguments, moving in his graceful, easy way to the bright warm kitchens at the rear of the house.

There he found giggling maids and eager servants plying his unexpected visitor with hot spiced wine and with thick slices of meat and rye bread, but he waved them impatiently out of the room and turned to the man, now bowing low before him.

" Well?" Nicholas did not waste words. " You have come from Court?"

The man nodded, drawing from his leather jerkin a sealed parchment which Rokeby quickly opened.

When he had read it, he glanced back at the man.

" Finish your meal and rest here tonight. I shall leave at once, but there is no need of such haste for you."

" Sire!" The man was perturbed. " You cannot travel alone."

Nicholas smiled faintly. " You did, and so could I, if I had to, but in fact I shall not be alone. Now drink that good strong wine before you, and do not trouble your head about me."

And with that he left the man staring after him, and made his way back to the winter parlour.

When the Lady Caroline heard that he intended to leave Monks' Walk that night, she threw up her hands in horror and was voluble in her objections.

" God's pestilence, boy; are you mad? There is a blizzard

blowing, and 'tis cold as death outside. Wait until the morrow, for then you will at least have daylight."

"There is no time to dally till the morrow, love." Nicholas took her hands in his. "The Queen has need of me, and I must go this night. Now, I pray you, do not concern yourself for me. No ill will come to me, I pledge my word on this."

He kissed his aunt's flushed cheek, and listened to no more of her arguments. Instead, he went to his own chamber, calling for his body servant, Jacob Blount, and ordering his steward to send word to the grooms that his horse be made ready.

Jacob Blount came with unhurried calm. He was a stolid man, with a thatch of brown ruffled hair and small sharp eyes of light blue. His nose was thick and broad, but his mouth was kindly and smiled readily. He wore his fustian doublet with some reluctance, for he preferred the rough garb he wore at sea, but since he fully understood the need for secrecy, he accepted philosophically enough the burden of donning the fancy, foppish clothes for which he had so much scorn.

"We are to go to Whitehall, Jacob," said Rokeby, unfastening his ruff with a quick, impatient hand. "I have a message from my lord Burghley."

"Ah." Jacob smiled thoughtfully. "I thought 'twas time we had a summons, for 'tis many months since you have been at Court, sire." He gave Nicholas a quick, friendly wink. "Her Majesty is a jealous mistress, my lord, and mayhap she has heard rumours of the Lady Mary."

"No, no." Nicholas finally succeeded in freeing himself of the great cartwheel of starched lawn and threw it on to the bed. "No, it is not that, Jacob, though doubtless I should have some convincing explanations to make were a whisper of that affair to reach the Queen. No, 'tis something else."

Jacob watched him frown, and moved placidly forward to unfasten the ties of his doublet.

"Something which is amiss, my lord?"

His deft, experienced hands removed the costly doublet with care, turning with the same phlegmatic air to pick up a fresh linen shirt.

"Perhaps." Nicholas bit his lip. "I know not. It is something in the way Burghley's message is phrased which fills me with unease. His pen is wont to be as calm as the words he speaks, but this time . . ." He hesitated. "This time, I read something of fear in his despatch."

"Fear, sire?" Jacob, as imperturbable as Philip of Spain, shewed no surprise or alarm, but continued to vest his master in the plain black velvet doublet and modestly bombasted trunk hose of black silk. "'Tis not like my lord Burghley to shew fear. Doth he say, sire, what troubles him?"

"No. No word as to the reason for requiring my presence at Court, save to say that no minute must be lost." Nicholas fastened a narrow jewelled belt about his waist. "Give me my sword, Jacob, for in truth this seems the one thing I must not leave behind."

He threw a cloak of scarlet velvet lined with vair about his shoulders and sat on the stool at the foot of the bed to allow Jacob to pull on the high boots of soft, sweet-smelling leather. "These are perilous times, Jacob. Although war is not yet honestly declared, King Philip doth make ready for the encounter with all speed, and whilst he waits until each last keg of water is on board his galleons, and each sack of gunpowder truly stacked, he doth watch with his dangerous, unwavering patience for the opportunity to strike a blow at us. And where better to strike that blow than at Court, Jacob; at Elizabeth herself?"

Jacob got to his feet, his labours with the boots at an end, and eyed Rokeby thoughtfully.

"You think, sire, there is a plan afoot to end her life?"

"Why not?" Nicholas was bitter. "It has been tried before."

"And failed, sire."

"We do not know that it will fail this time," returned Rokeby almost curtly, and Jacob smiled comfortingly.

"We do not know that the plot even exists, my lord. Maybe there is some other reason why Lord Burghley has called you

45

to Court. We do not know for certain that her Majesty is in peril."

Nicholas stared at Blount for a moment, then the tension left him and he laughed slightly.

"God a mercy, Jacob, you are right! I must not make mountains where there are none. Mayhap 'tis something else which needs my presence at Court, though if 'tis to explain to the Queen the affair of the Lady Mary, I am in worse toils than would her Majesty be if a Spanish plot were being hatched about her ears. Ah well! We shall see soon enough. Now, Jacob, I must have clothes fit to be seen at Court. The new crimson doublet; the green and silver one with the diamond buttons; the blue and gold and the lemon-silk. That will do. No; wait! The black and silver is a becoming garment, and should your worst fears be realised, and I am called to task for unfaithfulness, Jacob, I shall need the finest plumes in my wardrobe. And Jacob." He smiled a little. "In my closet there is a casket; made of silver and gold, with a crown of diamonds and rubies atop its lid. Fetch me this, for if I am disgraced, the contents of this box should wipe away the fiercest frown from the royal brow, and do me good service in my hour of need."

Quickly Blount assembled the splendid apparel, adding some more modest garments for himself, holding carefully the exquisite box he had taken from the cedarwood closet, and when this was done, the two men made their way to the stables where the grooms had saddled the fine white stallion Nicholas normally rode, and a handsome black mare, solid enough to bear Jacob's ample weight.

Nicholas mounted quickly, and pulled the cloak tighter about him as they left the warmth of the stable for the cruelty of the storm.

"Let us be gone, Jacob," he called, raising his voice above the shrill cry of the wind. "First to Devil's Pond, there to collect Sir Peregrine, and thence on to Tollemarche, where Lord Greville lies this night, and thus to Whitehall. And ride you hard, Jacob, for despite the comfort you would offer me, I fear there is something wrong, and shall have no rest until I know what is afoot."

And without another word, he drove his spurs hard into his horse's flanks and was gone.

# 3

DEVIL'S POND lay three miles east of Blandon Point, and despite the adverse elements, it did not take Rokeby and Blount long to reach the low, timber-framed house where Sir Peregrine Grey's family had dwelt for a hundred years.

Unlike Monks' Walk, which stood boldly on the cliff's edge challenging the sea, Devil's Pond lay quietly relaxed in a gentle hollow of land, with tall poplar trees swaying above the tiled roof, its natural oak studs and sill-pieces mellowed to a darkish-grey.

There was a splendid barn near-by, full thirty foot in length, which was shared by the proud thoroughbred horses which were Peregrine's joy and delight, the end bay boarded off to accommodate the hay and meal which the horses needed for their well-being, and not far away a windmill's stiff wooden arms rotated slowly against the skyline.

At a respectful distance were the cottages and the timber and wattle houses of the villagers, and south of the small Norman church of St. Goderic, ran the crofts of the farmers, neatly divided by trim hedges and bordered by a fast moving stream on one side and by a narrow beaten path on the other.

Here, in the village of Marlbeck, of which Devil's Pond was the much-loved manor house, the men farmed the land and tended the sheep on the gentle hills, keeping stolid, well-fed cows to give milk, and plump chickens scratching in the dirt outside the cottage doors to provide fresh eggs. They fished in the stream and in the pond by Blaise Wood, whose thick trees and bushy shrubs provided fuel for the smoky fires in the villagers' dwellings, and they hunted boar and hare through the tangled undergrowth to furnish meat for the cooking pots.

It was a happy, close-knit community, and few strayed far from it, for there was no cause to look further than the village for their needs. There was a blacksmith, a fiery, black-browed man, with sinews of steel, to hammer out new shoes for the horses and to help with the repair of a barn roof or a broken window frame; there was a physician, old and short-sighted, but faithful to his calling, who aided the sick and helped new lives into the world with infinite patience and undiminished wonder, and there was the priest, who dwelt in calm austerity in the small stone house behind the church. The women of the village were proficient at their weaving and dyeing, the baking of bread and churning of the rich milk to produce butter and cream, and for those who could not read or write, there was a small, erudite man who lived in the copy-holder's house by the village green, who could write in fine, graceful script any letters which were needed, and who taught the sons and daughters of the farmers how to form their letters, and helped them to study their catechisms.

Thus, there was little cause for any to journey far away, for all that was needed for life's fulfilment was to be found in this quiet patch of England, and only the master of the great house beyond the bridle path, saw any reason to turn his eyes to other things outside the village green.

Peregrine Grey, the only son of the bluff old squire who had died gallantly in the service of the Queen, spent little time in his timbered paradise, with the retinue of servants bequeathed to him by his father. It would have been simple enough for Peregrine to have slipped into the easy, undemanding ways of the village, and to devote his time to hunting and hawking and to the other pleasures available to the young and wealthy, and, indeed, he might well have succumbed to these delectable temptations had he not met Nicholas Rokeby.

Theirs had been a chance encounter. Peregrine, riding his sleek, raven mare across the fields towards Blandon Point to keep an assignation with a fair damsel who dwelt in giggling modesty with her indulgent parents, took a briar hedge too quickly, and was thrown heavily to the ground. The mare, shaking herself to her feet, trotted off in high indignation, leaving her stunned master to fend for himself, and since he had suffered a sharp blow on the temple, he might have lain for several hours in discomfort, had not Nicholas Rokeby chanced to ride by some fifteen minutes later.

Within the hour, Peregrine's life was changed. Once his injuries had been tended, and he had been given strong, reviving wine to soothe his ruffled spirits, he had found himself engaged in conversation with his host, a conversation which suddenly, yet quite naturally, changed from polite small talk to something entirely different. He had seen nothing strange in the manner of their discussion; there was an inevitability about his meeting with Nicholas which he did not attempt to resist, for it was as if he had been waiting for it all his life.

When he finally returned to Devil's Pond, something in him had changed, and the servants shook their heads and wagged their tongues at this remarkable metamorphosis, exclaiming in bewilderment when he ordered a few of his clothes to be packed, and set out on a journey to some mysterious destination of which he would not speak.

Gradually his household grew used to his sudden disappearances and his equally sudden return, and no longer gaped in amazement as Peregrine, somehow stronger, and harder of body and spirit, came bursting through the door to pick up the threads of his life at Devil's Pond as if he had merely ridden across the meadows from the neighbouring hamlet.

Whilst Rokeby and Blount spurred on their reluctant horses through the white-splattered night, Peregrine was comfortably ensconced by the fireside, engaged in the pleasant pursuit of seducing a plump, delicious maiden, who had slipped away from her father's farmhouse, uncaring of the cold and snow, in order most willingly to fulfil her rôle as Peregrine's latest quarry.

The servants had provided a well-planned and ample meal, and then, with their customary tact and diplomacy, had vanished to the kitchens and to their own quarters, leaving Peregrine to chuckle a little as he pulled the girl into his arms.

" Faith, Martha-Ann," he said softly, " you are a satisfying armful for a man on such a night, and I do swear that you are more fair than when last we had an encounter."

Martha-Ann's full red lips parted in a contented smile, and she made no protest as Peregrine's hand pulled open the bodice of her gown and stroked her shoulder and breast with a seductive hand.

" You are a baggage," said Peregrine after a moment, and his hand became more demanding. " Marry, girl, were I your father, I would flog you for your wanton ways."

Martha-Ann giggled with pleasure and pressed her soft white body closer to him, and with a slight exclamation, Peregrine caught her hard against him and covered her inviting lips with his.

With Martha-Ann's capitulation so near, and with her quickened breath sounding urgently in his ear, Peregrine was not best pleased to be interrupted, and gave a sharp curse as he heard the peremptory knock upon the front door, reluctantly releasing the girl as he straightened his doublet.

Martha-Ann, as eager as he for the climax of their love-making, pouted and her eyes were bright with vexation, but she made no attempt to cover her nakedness which she still flaunted in bold temptation before his frustrated eyes.

When he heard voices as his steward admitted his visitors, he shrugged philosophically, and pulled the girl's frock into place, patting her cheek and whispering a soft endearment.

" Sweet Martha-Ann," he said regretfully. " This night is not to be ours, and lest this be your father come to run me through, and to lay about you with his whip, I pray you leave me now, through this door, for there will be other days and other nights for us."

He gave the disappointed girl a quick kiss, pulling her to her feet and wrapping her discarded cloak about her shoulders as he urged her to a small door set in the panelling near the fire place. It opened silently as he turned a carved rosette by the mantel, yawning wide to reveal a dark passage stretching into infinity, and Martha-Ann drew back in alarm.

"My lord," she cried in protest. "'Tis so dark! What if there be ghosts? I cannot go through there; I cannot."

He laughed and took a candle from the mantelpiece.

"There are no ghosts, love, and the passage is not long. See, here is a light for you, and if you hurry, you will be free of the house in but a few minutes. Run you back to your home, Martha-Ann, for I can hear steps near the door. Quick! Away with you, but never fear; we will meet again."

He pushed her through the opening and let the panel slide back into place and before he had reached his chair again, his steward was ushering into his presence Nicholas Rokeby, his heavy cloak white with snowflakes.

"God's blood, Nick!" said Peregrine as he went forward to greet him. "You have chosen an ill night to come hence. Is ought wrong?"

Nicholas surveyed his friend in silence. Peregrine was tall and agile, with the light spring of youth in his step and the strength of his forebears in his broad shoulders and long, sinewy legs. His hair was mid-brown and curled with careless charm about his face, which, though not classically handsome, was well-formed and pleasant, with eyes of hazel hue under straight brows. In the fashion of the day, he wore a short, neatly trimmed beard and his skin had the same warmth as Rokeby's.

"What is it, Nicholas?" he repeated, and the smile had left his eyes. "There is something amiss?"

Rokeby nodded and flung off his cloak, coming to the blazing fire to warm his chilled hands.

" 'Tis possible," he said slowly. " We are called to Court by Burghley."

" Tonight?" Peregrine's brows shot up. " Lord save us, Nick, not tonight?"

" There is no time to lose." Nicholas looked unusually sombre. " I do not know the manner of the problem, yet I know that there is something which troubles Cecil, for it is apparent in his words. Come, Peregrine; call your servant and bid him pack some clothes for you, for we have still to get to Tollemarche."

Peregrine did not stop to argue any more, for it was always this way. If Rokeby ordered, he and Greville West obeyed, whether it was a command to saddle a horse to ride a mile to a game of dice, or an order to board a ship to sail to the sunlit islands of the tropics to raid an enemy port. They accepted his leadership with unquestioning obedience, revelling in the life of danger and excitement he had opened up to them.

With him, they had made their fortunes, and with him, they had become men. They had learned courage and fortitude; the ability to lead men in times of peril, and under his guidance, had seized Fate by the throat and forced it to bend to their stubborn, implacable wills.

They followed Rokeby gladly and with delight, both to the ante-chambers of the Queen's palace and to the strongholds of Philip of Spain, not once questioning his judgement or doubting his decisions.

As Peregrine made for the door, shouting for his servants, Nicholas poured himself some wine, smiling faintly as he noted the two half-empty goblets on the table, and the small cambric kerchief which lay beside the velvet armchair, but since he was apprised of Peregrine's bolt-hole, he did not ponder on the manner of the girl's disappearance, but merely shrugged in slight regret that he had been the cause of her headlong flight.

When Peregrine returned, warmly clad, with brightened and expectant eye, they made their way from the shelter of the house and took the winding road to Tollemarche, where, in the grey stone manor house, they found Lord Greville West playing a single-handed game of chess with bishops of fine ivory and queens of pearl and silver.

West did not stop to protest either, abandoning his solitary game with alacrity, and taking the polished stairs three at a time as he prepared to make ready for the journey.

Greville West, at twenty-four, was thin and studious-looking, and loved nothing better than to spend his leisure hours amongst the leather-bound books in his large, panelled library. He read quickly and avidly and in several languages. He absorbed the works of the ancients with as much relish as the bawdier writings of his contemporaries, constantly acquiring new books to stock his already overflowing shelves.

His hair was blond and carefully dressed, but unlike his companions he did not sport a beard, and although his raiment was expensive and well-cut, he wore it more as a matter of necessity than of pleasure. His grey eyes looked sleepy and his mouth gentle. He was entirely at home amongst the treasures and works of art which surrounded him on all sides, and it was hard to imagine him as a friend and follower of the dashing Nicholas Rokeby.

His meeting with Rokeby had been little short of fantastic. Sent by his father, the Earl of Tollemarche, to escort a treasure ship home from the East, Greville, having satisfied himself that all was quiet aboard, had settled down in his well-appointed cabin to read an ancient Persian manuscript which he had acquired from a glib and hard-bargaining trader in Cathay. Poring over the strange, faded lettering, West had been blissfully unaware of trouble until he had heard shouts and yells from the deck, and had become conscious that the ship had swung about to a standstill.

Flinging aside his newly-acquired treasure, he drew his sword and raced up to the deck in time to find himself confronted by a masked man, naked blade in hand, whose followers held his own men transfixed at the point of their rapiers.

If West had been true to his mild and inoffensive appearance, he would have dropped his sword and stood meekly aside in capitulation, but the dreamy scholar had another side to his nature.

Charged by his sire to bring the treasure ship safely home, his fingers tightened round the hilt of his sword and his mouth hardened.

The masked man, seeing his challenge, raised his own blade, and the respective crews fell silent as their leaders met in combat.

The struggle was grim and silent, neither man speaking as their swords said for them all that needed to be said. West, loving peace, had been well taught by his father in the arts of war, and he gave his enemy no quarter as they fought bitterly under the blazing noon sun.

Finally, the invader, thrusting Greville away, gave a faint laugh and said in faultless Spanish.

"*Madre del Dios!* You are a stubborn man, *señor*. Can you not see that you cannot win this encounter? Must I run you through, or will you shew wisdom and surrender your sword?"

Greville gritted his teeth and swore in good plain English.

"Be damned to your soul, you infernal Spanish pickpocket! I will not surrender so much as one gold coin to you, to feather the nest of your black-hearted monarch. If you want my ship, then, by God, you will have to kill me first!"

Expecting a quick and lethal response to this defiance, Greville was stunned when his opponent stopped dead in his tracks, lowering the point of his rapier, and slowly raising his hand to tear the mask from his face.

For a long minute Nicholas Rokeby and Greville West stared at each other; then Rokeby said softly:

"You are English, my lord?"

Greville nodded, his eyes widening a fraction as he studied Rokeby's face.

"Then in God's name, sire, why do you fly the Spanish flag?"

Greville started, his reverie done, and glanced quickly up to the mast where the colours of Spain fluttered arrogantly in the gentle summer breeze.

"Heaven above!" said West in a shaken voice. "I knew not that we did. When we left harbour, I commanded the Master of the Ship to fly the colours I had set aside in my cabin, but 'tis true that there was a Spanish flag taken from a merchantman we captured on our voyage, as well as the Queen's ensign.

He rubbed a rueful hand over his forehead and gave a warm chuckle.

"Now I recall it, sire, he did seem a thought reluctant to obey my command, but I paid little attention at the time. Doubtless he assumed I had adopted the flag of Philip's empire to ensure a safe passage through his waters."

He sheathed his sword and smiled again. "And you, my lord? Since 'tis clear you are no Spaniard for all your ready use of that tongue, what task are you about, which brings you to my ship?"

Since Nicholas had by now seen the quality of his host, he made little bones about his explanation, and Greville, roaring with laughter at the whim of Fortune which had brought him so near to death at *El Espectro's* hands, soon found that the pleasures of his library and the joys of scholarship were not enough.

They made a good partnership; using their skill and talents to frustrate the Queen's enemies and to fill her coffers with gold, whilst ensuring at the same time that their own financial needs were not neglected. They revelled in the life they led; in the wide, spacious freedom of the sea; the blood-tingling excitement which came when a Spanish galleon bore down upon them, and the exquisite fulfilment of a well-fought victory.

They were true companions and fast friends, West and Grey giving to Rokeby the kind of devotion that a leader has to earn and can never buy with gold.

They knelt humbly at the Queen's feet, but it was to Rokeby that Grey and West dedicated their hearts, and for him, they would willingly have laid down their lives, without a second thought.

Now, when he called them to his side, they did not hesitate, and when Grey had completed his preparations, Nicholas led them to the horses once more, and though the night was dark and without mercy in its penetrating chill, they mounted up and turned their steeds towards the road to London, there to offer to the Queen all that three brave and gallant men could give.

Elizabeth was in a temper. She had awoken with a slight headache and an even stronger realisation than usual of the passing years as she felt her bones ache in the coldness of the morning.

This day, none could please her, for she was fractious, unreasonable and demanding, and all attempts to placate and soothe her ruffled spirits had failed.

Her ladies-in-waiting were wary, but their caution gained them nothing. Agnes Trewlace got a sharp box upon the ears for pinching the Queen's arm as she fastened the huge embroidered sleeve into position; Mary Kildare was tartly reprimanded for day-dreaming, and Jane Mordaunt was sent to change her gown for something more seemly, and promised a sound beating should she venture into the Queen's presence again with her bosom thus exposed.

The servants and maids were snapped at, scolded and berated, and even Lord Burghley found his morning session with her Grace a trying and exacting penance.

Finally, after a cup of wine and some sweet biscuits, the Queen consented to lie upon her downy bed. The great hooped skirt was removed, then the quilted bodice and the sleeves, and finally the underskirt, and the small, rather pathetic body was wrapped lovingly in a silk bedgown and covered by a fur-lined wrap. With a sigh of relief, the royal household went about its various tasks, moving carefully on tip-toe, and speaking in hushed whispers lest a single sound should rouse its royal mistress.

Near to the hour of six, the Queen awoke, greatly refreshed and in a considerably better temper, and it was with an almost light-hearted frivolous air that her ladies prepared to dress her for the evening.

Now Elizabeth smiled upon Mary Kildare as her blue eyes began to dream again, and she hardly winced as once more Agnes Trewlace nipped her arm when fixing the gauze-covered trunk sleeves into place, nor did she comment on Jane Mordaunt's gown, which was of softest blue, dipping enticingly over her swelling young breasts.

When word came that Sir Nicholas Rokeby had arrived, the Queen's eyes brightened further still, and her mouth smiled her genuine pleasure.

"Alack, the boy must have wings," she said, and there was a note of soft affection in her voice. "He hath lost no time in coming when I called him." She turned to Jane. "Hurry, girl, hurry; the wig! The new one, freshly sent from France; be quick!"

The women's fingers flew, settling the wig into position, nestling diamonds and rubies midst the bright red locks, and gently pinning the great ruff about the Queen's thin neck. The rebato was fastened to the neck of the gown, which was fully as low as Jane's, and ropes of matchless pearls were wound about the throat and left to hang to where the Spanish farthingale burst into its full glory above the jewelled and spangled forepart of the gown.

Finally their work was done; the last speck of powder was pressed to the fading cheek, the last smear of scarlet salve applied with care to the lips, and the ruby and diamond rings slipped on to the slim, lovely fingers, the only reminder of Elizabeth's lost beauty. Stilling the chattering of her women, the Queen made her way slowly and with dignity to her audience chamber, her pleasure and excitement at the news of Rokeby's arrival not bending one inch the regal calm she displayed to the world when she was on her best behaviour.

With a gracious smile, she allowed Christopher Hatton to settle her on the throne, and exchanged a kindly word with Burghley, as if their unfortunate exchanges of that morning had never taken place. When this was done, the Queen gave a faint sigh.

"Now do you leave me, sires," she commanded, and her eyes were brilliant, yet curiously warm. "Send Sir Nicholas to me, for I have a task for him."

Hatton and Burghley looked doubtful, and Burghley even went so far as to utter a mild protest that he should be excluded from so important a discussion, but the Queen waved aside his objections with an airy hand.

"Perdition, Will! Think you I cannot tell Master Nick what I would have him do? I need no help, my lord. Be about your tasks, for you have many which press for your attention. Leave the tutoring of Nicholas Rokeby to me, I pray you for this is something I am well fitted to undertake."

Her two ministers, recognising defeat when they saw it, shrugged resignedly, but not too openly, and bowed their way from the presence chamber, leaving Elizabeth to smoothe an imaginary crease from her farthingale.

When the doors opened to admit Nicholas, the Queen watched in silence as he walked towards her, wondering what it was about this man which set him apart from the other gallants clustered about her throne. There were many as fair of face and as strong of body; others with the same dash and gallantry, and the same sweetness of tongue, but they were not Nicholas Rokeby.

It was a hard thing to analyse; the indefinable difference between this man and her other courtiers which had made her thoughts fly instantly to him when she knew her life to be in danger. When it was a matter of a game of one-and-thirty, or a question of treading a lively galliard, there were plenty of comely young blades, such as Charles Trenton, on whom to call, but when it was life itself which was at stake, then the Trentons of the Court would not do. Then, Elizabeth, the Queen, who was also a woman, needed the certainty of a man's strength to protect her; the quality of steely, indestructible determination which she saw clearly in the man who now went down on one knee before her.

Her eyes softened yet again. He was a handsome one, this rogue of hers. Handsome and charming, and had he wished, he could have grown much closer to the Queen, seeking favours she would have been delighted to grant. But he had made no such overtures, and now Elizabeth had accepted regretfully that he never would. He would serve her, honour her, and love her, but he would always remain a trifle remote from her, and perhaps it was this very thing which made him so exciting and desirable.

" Well, Nick?" The Queen's voice was quiet, and when Nicholas raised his head to look at her, he saw the true affection in her eyes, and smiled in that special way of his.

" Well, ma'am. I am here."

She nodded and gestured him to rise.

" At last, Nick; at last. 'Tis many months since you have been at Court. Must I always needs send for you?"

Nicholas laughed gently, and bowed again. " Ma'am, I have been about the Queen's business, and I venture to say with some success."

Elizabeth shared his smile for a moment, then it faded and she said slowly:

" Ay, Nick, ay. You have done well, for my coffers are richly swelled by your last endeavours, but gold is not everything. There are other things . . ."

Her voice trailed off, and Rokeby saw something of uncertainty in her.

" It matters not what it is, ma'am," he said softly. " Save that it is your pleasure. I am yours to command, whether it be to relieve his Catholic Majesty of his gold, or to uncover some plot which works to your Majesty's ill."

" What! " Elizabeth's uncertainty was gone and she sat upright, her voice sharp. " Plot? Why do you speak of a plot? What have you heard? Tell me this instant, Sir Nicholas; what has come to your ears?"

Rokeby's eyes narrowed faintly. So that was it. His first guess had been a right one, for there was no mistaking that sudden flash of surprise which the Queen had quelled as quickly as it had appeared. He gave a quick shrug, and his voice was soothing.

" I have heard naught, ma'am. 'Twas a mere hazard."

She gave him a straight and penetrating look, but the cool blue eyes did not waver, and it was hers which fell first. He saw her fingers tighten about her fan and his brows came slowly together. Elizabeth was not a nervous woman, and there had been plots a plenty in the past. He wondered what it was about this latest mischief which caused her such disquiet, but he said nothing, waiting in still patience for her to speak again.

" A shrewd hazard, sire," she said finally, and her mouth moved in a wry grimace. " Very shrewd, but then you are a devious one, Nick, as I told my lord Burghley. That is why I sent for you. Because your mind works in a subtle and complex way; cunning and cleverly. Because of that and because . . ." She broke off again and closed the fan with a slight snap. " The rest is not important."

She rose from the throne and stepped from the dais, her hand on Nicholas's strong arm.

" Come over to the fire, Nick," she said, and her voice sounded tired. " Sit with me here, and I will tell you what is to do."

Rokeby led her to a padded coffer-seat, and when she leaned back and closed her eyes, he sat on a low stool opposite the hearth and watched her.

Presently she stirred and opened her eyes again and gave him a brief smile.

" There is a man here, Nick, in my Court, who would have my life."

" What! " Rokeby was almost curt. " Ma'am; you are sure of this?"

" I am sure." The Queen's voice was now completely under control. " I will tell you of the circumstances, my lord, and you shall judge for yourself whether 'tis a feeble womanish fear that besets me, or whether 'tis a matter of consequence which will affect the Crown itself."

Nicholas listened in silence as the Queen outlined the story, and when she had finished, she opened her fan again, moving it slowly to and fro to cool the ardour of the roaring blaze at her side.

"Well, my lord? What say you now?"

Nicholas nodded, and his mouth was a hard line. "I fear there is no doubt, ma'am. The man was dying; he had no reason to lie."

"No." The Queen's agreement was unemotional. "I do not think he lied, for God knows there have been enough attempts on my life to lend credence to his tale."

"And his fellow conspiritors? Have they been found?" Nicholas leaned forward. "Has my lord Burghley traced them yet?"

Elizabeth made a negative gesture and Nicholas's mouth moved in an unpleasant smile.

"So, 'tis the nobleman at Court we have to find. Well, marry, madam, that should not be difficult. De Vere, Blandford and Dyke can be questioned, and if this does not suffice to tell us who is guilty, then enquiries can be made of their families and friends, for this would shew which was the imposter."

"If he is an imposter." The Queen did not meet Rokeby's eye. "It may not be a matter of an imposter."

Rokeby saw the pain of her mouth and cursed under his breath.

"Nevertheless, ma'am, these men must be questioned and ..."

"No!" Then the Queen did look up and Nicholas saw all the Tudor stubbornness in her gaze. "No, I will not have this."

"But, ma'am ..."

"No! God's body, Nick, two of these men are faithful and honourable servants of the Crown. I will not insult them with probing questions and degrading enquiries, nor will I have their families put under suspicion."

"Your life is at stake," said Nicholas sharply. "Do you not understand this?"

The Queen smiled, ignoring Nicholas's tone which was not of a kind normally used to address a reigning monarch, for she understood his concern, and loved him for it.

"I understand, Nick; I understand. Yet I will not take this path to uncover the secret. Do you think, my lord, that because I am a Queen, and a woman, I am insensible to what honour means? Do you think I should behave like an ungrateful shrew because Philip of Spain seeks my life? Shall I drag the names of the two innocents into the mire because I am not wise enough to tell which of these men is my enemy? No, Sir Nicholas, I will not do this. I know that I am a difficult mistress to serve; as I grow older, I know my tongue becomes sharper and my temper more uncertain, yet my love for my loyal subjects grows deeper with the passing of the years. A sovereign cannot rule without the affection of the people, Nick. The crown and sceptre are empty symbols if there is no love from the nation to support them. And love I have had from my subjects; love and loyalty. My people give me what they can. Some give great wealth with their ardour, but some have only their hearts to give, but this does not matter. They give me what they can. Thus, I will not throw back into the faces of the two men who are innocent of guilt, that which they have laid so unstintingly at my feet."

"No matter if it costs your life?" Rokeby's voice was barely audible, but the Queen's sharp ears heard his words.

"No matter that it costs my life. I would not preserve it by such means." She drew a deep breath. "You think I am a fool, my lord, because I will not follow your advice?"

Nicholas rose and moved slowly towards the Queen, bending as he raised her hand to his lips.

"I think you are a great lady, and a most worthy monarch," he said quietly, "and if you will not take these ends, then I will accept your decision without further question."

"God alack, Nick!" she said, for once half-embarrassed. "I do no more than any man would do. Now, sit you down again, boy, for I have a plan which may uncover me this villain, and I would have you aid me."

Rokeby sat down again, smiling warmly at Elizabeth. "Then tell me, ma'am, what plot you hatch yourself, and how I may be privileged to serve you."

Elizabeth hesitated for a moment, then she said slowly:

"'Twill not be easy, Nick. There will be great risks."

"You would condemn me to a life of comfortable boredom, ma'am?" He raised his brows in mock indignation. "Would you have me dream my life away in Devon with never a hint of danger, which is the essence and very spice of existence?"

The Queen did not return his smile.

"This is no ordinary risk," she said sombrely. "I want you to go to Spain."

Nicholas fingered the tip of his beard thoughtfully. "I see. Secretly, ma'am?"

"No." Elizabeth held his eyes with hers. "Not secretly, Nick. I want you to go openly to the Court of Philip of Spain."

Still Rokeby shewed no trace of surprise or perturbation, and she chuckled.

"You do not even raise a brow, Nick. God's teeth, boy, you are a cool one, and you will need to be." She sobered again. "Yes. I want you to go to Philip's Court, claiming asylum from the tyranny of a Protestant monarch, seeking the protection of the upholder of the true faith. There have been others; many others. English Catholics who have fled to Spain, so this part will not be difficult. But then, Nick; after that, the danger will grow, for once there, your mission is to find out whom Philip has sent to England, to my Court, to take my life."

Nicholas nodded, still unmoved by the thought of the perils Elizabeth had laid open to him, and the Queen laughed again.

"It is a risk, my lord, for all your calmness and courage. Once there, you will have to gain the ear of his Majesty, his ministers and those at Court who have his confidence. One false step, Nick; one mistake and there is only one end for you."

Rokeby shrugged. "Then I must walk with care, ma'am. But what if there are those in Philip's Court at this time who know me? If there should be English traitors fawning on his most Catholic Majesty, I shall have scant chance of gaining my ends."

"There are none; this we know." Elizabeth's mouth thinned slightly at the thought of her treacherous subjects. "Master Walsingham keeps me well informed, and I would not send you to your death so lightly, Nick."

"Then before I go, ma'am," said Rokeby. "I would crave a day or two at Court. I would get to know more of these three men, one of whom is known in Spain. I would speak with them and question them, but with care, of course. Then, when I am at Philip's Court, perchance some remark that is made will cause me to remember that which I learned from the knave whose life I would take with my own hand, should God grant me this opportunity."

Elizabeth nodded. "Very well, my lord; this is a fair boon that you ask, and I will not deny it, yet tarry you not too long, Nick, for each morning that I wake, I wonder if . . ."

She stopped and drew herself up slightly. "Well, that is arranged. You have other questions?"

"Who else knows of my mission, ma'am? Are there others privy to this secret?"

"Burghley and Walsingham; Walsingham's secretary who is beyond reproach, and Francis Drake."

"Drake?" Nicholas cocked an eyebrow and gave a rueful smile. "Marry, ma'am, I warrant he will not let me sail for Spain lest I undertake some task for him as well."

The Queen inclined her head. "It seems likely, sire, that you will be so constrained, for he frets impatiently for news of Philip's Armada, but I have told him not to pester you, for you will need all your wits about you to come out of Spain alive. Elizabeth bit her lip. "I do not like to send my men to what seems certain death, yet . . ."

"Ma'am, this is foolish talk," said Nicholas, and his eyes were calm as they met hers. "Death and I know one another well, for we have crossed swords many times before. Do not fear for me, for I shall come to no harm. I have your faith and trust as my shield; your affection as my amulet. What more could any man ask than this?"

He got to his feet again and turned to a small side table on which he had laid his feathered court bonnet and the precious casket which Blount had held against his breast during their long ride to London. The Queen watched him silently as he turned back to her, and held out the box.

"What is this, sire?" she asked, taking it between her slender white hands. "A gift for me?"

"A trifling bauble, ma'am; nothing more. A small remembrance until we meet again."

Elizabeth smiled and opened the casket, drawing from its velvet depths a long rope of black pearls, each larger than a fat pea, each perfect in its sheen and quality. For a moment she stared at the necklace in silence, running one hand down the priceless beads.

"Lord save us, Nick," she said finally. "Whence came these? In all my treasure chests I have nothing like this."

"It came from a land far away, ma'am," said Rokeby, enjoying her pleasure. "When I saw it, I knew of only one woman fair enough to wear it. Thus did I acquire it to lay at your feet."

"Acquired it?" The Queen shot him a quizzical glance. "How so, Nick?"

He laughed but shook his head. "On my honour, poor thing though it be, ma'am; this trinket I did not take at the point of my sword, but did purchase it most righteously for your sake."

"'Tis a rare thing, my lord, and for all my days I will cherish it, not least because it came from you, but mark this well. I would relinquish this, and all the others gems in my possession, rather than lose your life in this engagement."

He bowed low, taking her hand in his once more, touching the fingers with his lips.

"Until this day, my life has been of little account, ma'am, but if 'tis of such concern to you, then I pledge my word that I will bring it back to you unscathed, for I would not rob you of that which is yours by right. Be you content; I will not fail you, nor take from you the services of the meanest of your courtiers."

The Queen watched him bow from her presence, wondering why, as always, this man affected her so, and praying with all her stout Protestant heart that he would come back to her unharmed.

# 4

Two DAYS later, Jane Mordaunt sat in her chamber wrapped in a robe of deep rose velvet, stitching a headrail of point devise. Her golden hair, freed from the jewelled pins and combs, fell down her back in a glowing cascade, and by the light of the fire, her blue eyes were dark with excitement.

Jane found Court life a trifle dull, for though there were many handsome gallants to be found there, few dared to shew more than a passing interest in the Queen's ladies lest the sovereign's wrath should fall upon them. There had been those, of course, who had dared all for love, but they had found themselves in the Tower or banished from Court, whilst the woman who had coaxed their attention from the Queen had suffered equally dire punishment.

Thus, the day's passed too quietly for one of Jane's buoyant nature, for she had a thirst and hunger for life which the sedate walks with the Queen, incessant games of chess and gleek, and the pleasures of the chase could not assuage. Only in one pastime did Jane share the Queen's enthusiasm, and that was in dancing, for then she could throw off something of the restrictions of Court etiquette and lose herself in the satisfying beauty of motion and music.

Even then she needed to have a care for the Queen watched her constantly, convinced that she needed a firm hand, and when Jane's lovely body moved too seductively, the Queen brought her sharply to her side and sent her about some dull and harmless task where her sparkling beauty could do no harm.

But now Nicholas had returned to Court. Nicholas, who was tall and strong and demanding, and who had been prepared to risk the anger of the Queen for the sake of holding Jane against his heart and stroking her soft flesh with his cool, firm hand.

Jane trembled anew as she remembered their last meeting, and wondered if he had forgotten the ecstasy they had shared. She did not know why he had returned to Court, for the buzz and hum of rumour which kept the Court in constant turmoil had nothing to suggest, yet it was hinted that his stay would not be a long one, and thus there was little time to lose.

She laid aside her work, crossing to the table where a silver mirror reflected the gentle flush on her cheeks, and the rosy mouth curved in a smile of eager anticipation.

Would he remember? And would he still want to hold her as he had held her before? She touched her slender white throat with perfume from the tiny enamelled sweet-box and let the gown fall open at the neck to reveal a hint of the delicate swell of her bosom. There was only one way to find out. It was a risk, of course, but a risk worth taking, for to lie in Nicholas's arms again would compensate for any retribution which might fall upon her in the future.

Silently she opened the door of her chamber, taking a single candle, and moving noiselessly along the corridor to Rokeby's room. She had friends amongst the maids, for she was a warmhearted and good-natured girl, and it had not been difficult to discover that Rokeby was accommodated in the wing which adjoined that occupied by the Queen's ladies. There were no guards on duty in this stretch of passage, for such precautions were not considered necessary, although two stalwart troopers kept a nightly vigil at the entrance to the wing itself.

However, they were too far away to impede her progress, and with heart in mouth she managed to reach Rokeby's door, turning the handle cautiously and slipping into the room without a sound.

When she moved to the bed, her heart jumped again, for he was just as she had remembered him. The same strong, unforgettable face, the blue eyes now closed in sleep; the same broad shoulders and sun-tanned hands, which could arouse a thousand shivers when he touched her.

She smiled down at him lovingly, and moved aside to place the candle on a near-by table, but before she could turn again she felt a hand go over her mouth and a strong arm pin her own trembling arms to her body. She tried to struggle, but the grip was steely and unbreakable and her heart thudded violently as she was swung sharply round to face her captor.

"Jane!" Rokeby's biting hold on her wrist slackened and his eyes widened. "God, girl, what do you here? Art mad? Did any see you?"

Jane could hardly speak, so great was her relief, but she managed to shake her head and gave a little whimper as he caught her arms again.

"What are you doing here?" he repeated, and his voice was neither welcoming nor loving. "You little fool; do you not realise the folly of coming here?"

By now she had recovered some of her self-possession, and as the fear drained out of her eyes, he saw them light up with something else which made him frown harder still.

"Nicholas." Her voice was soft and inviting, and in the faint light from the candle he saw her eyes repeat the invitation a thousandfold. "Dearest Nicholas. Oh, 'tis so good to see you again. It has been so long, and I thought I would not see you again, but you have come back."

He released her arms and tightened his fur-trimmed robe about his waist.

"You are bereft of your senses, Jane," he said shortly. "God's blood, girl, you are within a stone's throw of the Queen's chamber. What are you thinking about? Is your palate for life so jaded that you would throw it away by being found here?"

She swayed towards him, uncaring that her wrap had fallen further from her throat, and laid a soft hand upon his arm.

"I care not, Nick. For an hour with you, I would willingly spend a lifetime in the Tower, for I should have remembrance of our precious time together to strengthen me in my solitude."

He took a deep breath, but even as he answered her, his reluctant eye wandered from her fresh young face to linger thoughtfully on the sweet white roundness of her breasts.

"You talk like a fool," he said, but his voice was quieter, and there was less anger in its depths. "You have no conception of what would await you in the Tower, nor are you sure that this is all the Queen would mete out to you for your folly."

She drew closer still, and he felt her warmth, and smelt the perfume in her silky hair as it fell lovingly over one cheek.

"I would not care," she whispered. "Let her beat me, imprison me, or do with me what she will. It would be worth it, love, to spend this night with you."

Rokeby swore silently, but somehow his arm was round her waist, and her body was pressing closer to his.

"And what of me?" he asked, half to himself. "What of my life? Would you see that taken by the Queen for seducing one of her maidens?"

She gave a low laugh and laid her head on his shoulder for a moment. When she looked up again, her eyes were alight with mischief.

"You do yourself much injustice, my lord, when you call me maiden. You risked it before, sire; are you now less bold, or do I no longer please you?"

"Fate was on our side before, Jane," he said slowly. "Mayhap it will not be so on this occasion, and I would not have harm come to you because of me."

He felt her hand on his cheek; a light, gentle caress, and as he looked down at her, he saw again the desire in her eyes.

"I care not, Nick; I care not. Is safety all you value now, love? Am I not worth a little hazard?"

He bent his head to kiss her lips, and suddenly she was locked in his arms, her body hard against his, her hand gripping his arm in frenzy as their passion mounted. She gave a little moan of pleasure as he stripped the robe from her and pulled her to the bed, stopping only to blow out the candle before pressing down upon her in quick and urgent demand.

Fortune smiled once more upon the lovers, for the next morning, Jane, contented and lovelier than ever, went about her tasks with demure propriety, leaving Nicholas to continue his study of the three men he had to get to know in so short a time.

The first, Stephen de Vere, was his prime concern, for it took little time to learn that this elegant young gallant was in love with Eleanor Strickland, a girl whom Nicholas had known since the cradle. Thus it was easy to renew his acquaintanceship with Eleanor, and to coax her to walk with him in the long picture gallery to talk of old times.

She was a small girl, with russet-brown hair and pansy-hued eyes. Not a beauty, but a pretty, gentle woman, with a soft laugh and dimples by her wide, generous mouth. At first they talked of Devon and of the days of their childhood, but gradually Nicholas managed to turn the talk to de Vere, and when he saw Eleanor's eyes glow, he knew she cared as greatly for her beau, as he did for her. It was not a pleasant task he had to accomplish, made less palatable by his affection for Eleanor, but he was ruthless in his determination, and coldly efficient in his approach.

Eleanor was happy enough to talk of her love, painting him in terms which made Rokeby's mouth grim, but when he asked idly how long she had known him, and learned that they had not met until de Vere had come to Court, the hardness deepened.

"And his family, Eleanor? What of them? Have you yet met them?"

Eleanor shook her head and smiled happily. "Not yet, Nicholas, but soon I shall; very soon, for Stephen has promised that ere long he will seek the Queen's consent to our marriage, and when this is done, he will take me to Norfolk so that I may meet his father."

"Does he speak of what he did before he came to Court?" Nicholas's question was still light and casual, but he saw the sudden wariness in her eyes, and his attention sharpened.

"N . . . no." She hesitated, and would have turned to other subjects, but gently he pressed his question again.

"Have you not asked him, sweet, what manner of things he did before you met?"

She did not answer at first, one hand fluttering uncertainly on her cheek, but finally she looked at Nicholas with unhappy eyes.

"Yes, I have asked, Nick, but he will not answer. He laughs and says his life did not begin until he met me. I have tried to find out more, but he turns my curiosity aside, kissing me to silence. Oh, Nicholas, I know that whatever he did, it was an honourable life that he led, but I wish he trusted me enough to talk of what he did and those whom he knew, for I would share everything with him if I could."

Nicholas remained calm and his voice shewed nothing of concern as he smiled down at her.

"Of course, love, and it is right that you should. Ask him again, Eleanor, but gently and without heat, for I would assure myself that he is a fitting husband for you. Your parents are dead, and though you are the Queen's charge, yet do I feel some responsibility, and great affection, for you. We grew up together, and I would not have you wedded to one who was not fitted for the task of caring for you."

Eleanor's face softened and she took his arm as they walked on down the gallery.

"Dear Nicholas, I thank you for your concern, but there is no need for you to fear. Stephen is all that I want, and if he does not choose to tell me what he did until we met, then I will not pry. I am assured that he is the man for me; the one with whom I would spend my life in sweet contentment."

"Yet ask him, love, so that ere I leave Court, which must be very soon, I may go with a quiet mind. Do this for me, Eleanor."

He caught her shoulders and looked down at her. "Ask again, my dear."

She nodded, warmed by his concern. "If you will, dear Nick. I will try, but he may not want to answer, and I will not plague him with my questions."

With that, Nicholas had to be content, and turned instead to Robert Blandford.

Blandford was a very different proposition from Stephen de Vere, who was young, engaging and seemingly innocent at heart.

Blandford was in his early thirties. A dark, saturnine man with hooded eyes and a thin mouth. He dressed in magnificent style and was watchfully attentive in the presence of the Queen, but when Nicholas found an opportunity to engage him in conversation, he had the uncomfortable feeling that Blandford was laughing at him. It was as if Blandford knew that Rokeby's casual enquiries had something of urgency behind them, but he made no attempt to conceal anything, answering Nicholas's questions with a faintly mocking smile and a sardonic lift of one eyebrow.

"You seem interested in my circumstances, my lord," he said finally, and lay back in his chair to regard Nicholas benevolently.

The two men were playing a game of chess in one corner of the Great Hall, amidst the gentle hum of voices and the swishing of the ladies' skirts over a floor strewn with sweet herbs and rosemary.

Nicholas moved his queen, and gave Blandford a quick smile.

"Forgive me, sire, if I have appeared too inquisitive, but I seldom get to Court these days, and when I do, then I like to learn the latest gossip and to meet new faces."

"Mine is not so new, Sir Nicholas." Blandford paused to consider the board reflectively. "I have been here two years, no less."

"I have been away much of that time," said Rokeby. "I fear I have not noticed you before."

"Nor I you, sire, but I have heard speak of your name, for there are those who say . . ." Blandford broke off and his hand hovered over his bishop.

"Those who say?" prompted Nicholas gently, his eyes still on the board.

Blandford shrugged. "Rumour, my lord; rumour, nothing more."

"Of what, sire?" Then Nicholas did look up, and found Blandford smiling in the same mocking fashion.

"It will not please you," he replied coolly, "and I would not have you run me through for repeating another man's word."

Suddenly the game of wits on the chessboard was no longer important; the contest was now of a different kind, and Rokeby smiled slightly.

"I do not use my sword so lightly, Lord Robert. Now come, you have whetted my curiosity. What is it men say of me?"

Blandford stroked a finger along his black marquisetto beard and chuckled.

"They say, sire, that perhaps you serve two monarchs, since you spend so much time away from England, but then you are, I am sure, well versed in the quality of spite which is used to make the fabric of rumour."

Nicholas controlled himself with an effort and his expression did not change as he inclined his head.

Damn the man. Lord Robert was deliberately baiting him, twisting the words into sharp little barbs to rouse him to anger. Rokeby relaxed, for Blandford was skilful at his work, and emotion had no part to play in this duel of words.

"Indeed, my lord, and I am surprised no worse things are said of me than that, for this is a charge so foolish that none with sense could believe it."

His eyes held Blandford's and the latter's mouth curved in frank amusement, as if he read Rokeby's discomfiture beneath the impassive façade.

"Of course, sire; none with wits could entertain such a

75

notion for a moment, but, alack, there are others whose senses do betray them, and whose wagging, foolish tongues . . ." His smile broadened. " Ah, but there! " He leaned forward to study the board again. " Let us waste no more time on such blockheads, my lord. If there is no truth in the gossip, then 'tis of no consequence."

Swallowing the ' if ' like a bitter pill, Nicholas ground his teeth and gave his attention to the game once more, but after it was over, and Blandford, smilingly victorious, had bowed from his presence, Nicholas watched him go with tightened lips.

Blandford was a much more likely suspect than the boyish de Vere. Blandford, who was both experienced and quick of wit, with a smooth, caustic tongue and very expert in turning suspicion from himself by a sly counter-attack. Yes, a much more likely suspect; perhaps too likely. Would Philip's counsellors have sent someone quite so obvious?

Rokeby mulled over his thoughts until that evening when Elizabeth appeared, clad as usual in breathtaking splendour, and with a gracious smile accepted Blandford's hand.

Nicholas, who had been watching the Queen, suddenly glanced at Blandford, and became very still. Blandford's face had lost its satirical hardness, and something of his sophisticated poise seemed to have dropped from him as he raised his head from his deep bow, and for one startled moment Nicholas saw the way he looked at Elizabeth.

As he watched Lord Robert lead the Queen to the banqueting hall, Nicholas stroked his beard in perplexity. If Blandford was Philip's spy, then he was the most consummate trickster he had ever met, for the look of devotion in Lord Robert's eyes as they met the Queen's was something which left Nicholas shaken and uncertain as he followed the throng of chattering courtiers and ladies to the table.

His opportunity to consider John Dyke was made the easier because of a ready friendship which had been struck up between his third suspect and Greville West. Their love of books and literature was a common bond, and Dyke had shewn

Greville his collection of rare manuscripts with barely concealed pride.

So far, Nicholas had not told West or Grey of the mission they were to undertake, for he proposed to delay the telling of this tale until they set sail for Spain, but he was quick to take advantage of West's acquaintanceship with Dyke, for it made his quest for knowledge a simpler thing.

Dyke was a well-built young man of medium height, with dark hair and eyes and a graceful carriage. He had none of Blandford's polished assurance, yet his manner was easy, if a trifle shy. From West, Rokeby learned of Dyke's family and of his home in Cumberland, and on the face of it there seemed nothing to raise any suspicions, and watching Dyke laughing with Grey and West, Nicholas had to remind himself sharply that though the home in Cumberland probably existed, peopled by the charming family Dyke had described, they might well be unconnected with the man who now turned to bow to a group of the Queen's ladies who had come to seek the company of her gay young courtiers.

The days passed by and Nicholas continued to watch and listen, but on the sixth day he found he was no nearer to the truth than on the day the Queen had first laid bare the secret, and with no small irritation in his soul, he sought an audience with her Majesty.

She saw him in her own chamber, shooing the maids and ladies-in-waiting away with an impatient hand, and beckoning Nicholas forward with an imperious finger.

" Well now, Sir Nicholas? Have you news for me? Have you yet uncovered the identity of this man who would have my life?"

Rokeby bowed low, straightening up to shake his head ruefully, and Elizabeth gave a sour smile.

" Nor did I think you would, Nick, for if 'twere as easy as that, my lord Burghley or Kit Hatton would have unmasked the rogue by now."

" True, ma'am, yet I now know more about these three men.

I have talked with them and learned something of their character by listening to their words. Tomorrow I shall leave London and shall take with me some small knowledge which may be of use to me in Spain."

"You have told Lord Greville and Sir Peregrine?" The Queen studied an emerald ring on her forefinger with care. "You have made known my plan to them?"

Nicholas shook his head. "No, madam, not yet. There is time for this later."

"And you trust them?" She was sharp. "You have no doubts?"

Again Nicholas shook his head. "No doubts, madam. I would trust them with my life, and more. I would trust them with yours. No, there is no doubt of their loyalties, but my ship is a safer place to talk of this matter."

The Queen gave a slight sigh. "Ay, Nick, that is so. Then we make our farewell this night." She rose and gave him her hand. "Go with God, Nicholas," she said quietly. "And keep you safe, for I would have you come back to me. I have sacrificed enough brave men to feed the fires which Philip lights in the name of his Holy Church. See to it that you do not become kindling for his senseless, fanatical priests." Her lips moved in derision. "Of all the sins that men commit, none, surely, are so base as those designed to fulfil the Will of God. It is fortunate for mankind, Nick, that the Almighty is more merciful than we are, for He will accept our prayers and our hearts no matter the manner of their offering."

When Rokeby left the Queen, he made his way to a small ante-room, poorly lit, as if seeking to deny its existence by its secrecy. Behind a scarred oak table sat a man, not unduly tall, but with a strong, deep chest and sturdy shoulders under a velvet doublet of dark crimson. The triple ruff of starched linen framed a round head of brownish curls, now receding slightly from the broad brow, the short neat beard and trimly curled moustache giving the wearer a debonair and jaunty air. His complexion was fresh, his eyes small and brightly intelligent, and when he greeted Rokeby, his voice still held traces of the soft Devonshire drawl of his forebears.

At forty-eight, Francis Drake was at the prime of life, exuding an air of health, strength and determination which struck like a blow. It was impossible to be indifferent to him, for this he would not allow. One could love and admire him for his zest, his courage, his loyalty to the Crown, and to his Queen, or one could hate him for his conceit, his savage reprisals, and his calm disregard for law and order, but one could not overlook him.

And Nicholas did not try to do so. He had a warm affection for the cheerful little Vice-Admiral, whose merry smile and ready laughter gave little warning of the ruthlessness which lurked beneath the surface. He had served Drake for several years, furnishing him with the vital threads of information his leader required, and following him more than once on expeditions which were both rewarding and exhilarating.

Drake, who was studying a report by the indifferent light of a few candles, laid the parchment down and raised a hand in welcome as Nicholas made his bow. " Nick! 'Tis good to see you, boy. Sit you down, for we have much to talk about."

Rokeby smiled broadly, moving rolls of charts and maps from a near-by bench and sitting quietly by Drake's table whilst Sir Francis reached for an exquisite flagon of gold encrusted with precious stones.

" A pretty trifle eh, Nick?" Drake held it aloft, where it glittered like some fairy treasure in the soft light. " A dainty beaker, worth a handsome sum." He eyed it pensively. " Ah, but then, there are many more whence this has come, and one day, who knows, we may have them all."

He winked at Rokeby and poured wine into the matching goblets, handing one to Nicholas with a chuckle.

" Spanish wine too, Nick. Rich and red and full-blooded. I like not the temper of the Spaniards, nor their climate nor yet the food they eat, but by the Holy Saints, I have a weakness for their wine."

He sat down again, sipping his stolen nectar with appreciative lips.

" Ay, 'tis a warming thing, this wine of theirs. Now, sire."
He turned to look at Rokeby, and his gaze was sharper. " You
leave for Spain ere long?"

Rokeby nodded. " A day or two, sire, not more, for there is
little time left to us."

Drake twirled the goblet stem between his strong, blunt
fingers.

" No, that is so. Which ship do you use?"

" *The Raven*." Nicholas laid his goblet upon the table. " She
is small, 'tis true, but she moves swiftly, and is not known in
Spanish waters."

Drake nodded approvingly. " A good choice. And the
port?"

" Plymouth, my lord, and thence to Cape Lorcana."

Again the Vice-Admiral nodded. " Wise, Nicholas, wise.
You take a cautious route and avoid the major ports. And once
at Lorcana? What then?"

" There is a man there, sire. A man who will provide us with
horses and mules for the baggage."

" To be trusted?" The bright eyes were watchful. " No
time for errors now."

" To be trusted, my lord," said Nicholas calmly. " He is
one of my own men. I left him in Spain lest the need should
arise for us to visit King Philip, and whilst he waits, he keeps
his ear alert for news of interest."

Drake gave a quiet laugh. " Efficient as always, Nick. And
how does this man of yours get his news to you?"

Rokeby raised his goblet again, and for a moment was
silent, then his white teeth shewed faintly in an apologetic
smile.

" 'Tis a complicated system, my lord. Tangled and complex.
I would not weary you with details."

Drake roared with laughter, for he was too big a man to
resent the gentle reminder that his lieutenant's affairs were his
own.

" Capital, capital! " he said finally. " If I cannot find out
what you are about, Nick, there is scant chance of Philip

having greater success." He sobered. "And then? When you have horses and mules; what then?"

"To Valladolid, sire, where the King holds Court at this time."

"The journey will not be easy. There are the mountains between you and the goal you seek."

"There are passes, sire, and these I know. Also we shall have a guide."

Drake nodded. "Very well, but have a care. I know you have much courage and great spirit, but you will not have a good English ship under your feet this time. You will be on alien soil, and every man will be your enemy."

"I trust not, my lord," said Rokeby easily, unmoved by his Vice-Admiral's caution. "I seek asylum under the wing of King Philip. No longer can I stand the rigours of a Protestant sovereign, and would seek the sanctuary of the Spanish Court that I may once again live in spiritual freedom."

Drake grunted. "Let us hope they believe this." He did did not sound particularly optimistic and Rokeby smiled.

"They have believed others, my lord. Why not me? I have a plausible tongue, and my indignation at my plight in England will be righteous."

Sir Francis gave a deep sigh, but then he put aside his doubts and his cheerfulness returned.

"Yes, Nick, maybe you are right, and perhaps on this occasion I am too wary, but take care, boy, for it will not be that simple. However." He grinned. "Since you are commanded by the Queen to go to Spain it would seem a pity to miss this opportunity of seeing how the King's invasion plans mature."

He sat upright, pulling a map towards him, and tracing a line on it with his forefinger.

"See you," he said, and his voice grew lower. "The time is coming when we shall have to face this fleet of his. Like you, sire, I have ways and means of learning what is afoot and I tell you, we have little time left for our own preparations. This will be no small company which sails to meet the forces of the Duke of Parma from the Netherlands; it will be a formidable Armada.

He bared his teeth in exasperation. " I gave England a few months' grace when I scattered the royal galleys at Cadiz, but I also taught the dons a lesson which they have marked well. The King has done with galleys; now he has taken unto himself the stalwart Portuguese galleons, and those of the Indian Fleet. He has taken merchantmen and converted them to ships that will fight us on our own terms, and he has strengthened his greatships, and commandeered galleasses from Naples and Portugal. I am told he has no less than eight and sixty ships of fighting quality."

Rokeby watched Drake carefully. The Vice-Admiral's voice was thoughtful but completely without fear or concern.

" And his leaders, my lord? What of them?"

Drake gave him a sidelong glance. " As good as ours, sire; as good as ours. He has Juan Martinez de Recalde as his second in command. He has Miguel de Oquendo and Pedro de Valdez, both men of fire and spirit; he has Hugo de Moncada and the comely young Alonso de Leyva, who, for all his charm and fair looks, is a fine seaman. And he has Martin de Bertendona."

He paused and his eyes began to twinkle. " Only in one respect are we fortunate Nick. Fortunate that death claimed Don Alvaro de Bazan, the Marqués de Santa Cruz, before he could lead this Armada against us." Drake's voice was warmly appreciative. " There was a man, Nick; a true seaman, and I would have deemed myself honoured to have sailed my ship against his, but Fortune would not have it so."

Nicholas nodded. " No, sire, and perhaps this is as well, for, as you say, he was a formidable man. Now we have another adversary, perhaps less able to withstand the rude conflict which faces us."

Drake laughed a trifle scornfully. " Indeed, my lord, you speak in truth, for Spain's commander does not measure up to her greed or to her ambition. He has a proud name, and a long one; Don Alonso Perez de Guzmán el Bueno, Marqués de

Sanlucar de Barramada, Conde de Niebla and Duque de Medina Sidonia. Faith, Nick, with such a name he should be fitted to lead the hosts of heaven, but he is not, nor is he able, I would judge, to lead the smallest of flotillas against the weakest of his King's enemies.

" He is one of Andalusia's greatest nobles and one of Spain's worst leaders, with little or no knowledge of the ways of the sea. I have learned much of him whilst I have waited for his onslaught. I am told he is a quiet man and an affable one. He adheres to the tenets of his faith with great devotion, and is generous and kindly to those who serve him. Further, he has little of that arrogant pride of the Castilians, being almost meek and diffident in his manner, and it is said that when the King called him to take command of the fleet, Medina Sidonia protested most vigorously that he was not the man to have this honour and was not equipped by Nature to undertake so grave a task. Indeed he listed his many shortcomings with rare honesty in an attempt to convince the King, but Philip would not heed him." Drake tugged his beard reflectively. " He is an odd choice sire; an odd choice indeed, for Philip does much of our work for us when he gives his own fleet such a man to follow. The only useful service Medina Sidonia is likely to render his sovereign is that he has put a fortune at Philip's disposal for his Invincible Enterprise."

Rokeby sighed gently. " He is a nobleman, my lord. An aristocrat of a proud people. Can we be so sure that he is a weakling? May not the sight of battle rouse in him something of the valour of his heritage?"

Drake laughed shortly. " We can be sure, Nick. He is the noblest of Philip's proud grandees, that I grant you, but he is neither a leader nor a seaman. To lead a fleet, one needs a sailor; a man who is part of the sea, understanding its moods and tantrums, knowing how to coax his ship against the torrents; well-versed in the reading of the wind and its capriciousness."

Nicholas smiled. " Yet my Lord Howard of Effingham was not born to the sea. His appointment bears much resemblance

to that of the Duque de Medina Sidonia. He too, is a nobleman, distantly related to the Queen herself, and for all his good
qualities, of which I am most sensible, he is no seaman. Thus,
my lord, there seems little to choose between the two Admirals
who will one day face each other across the English Channel."

Drake drank down the remains of his wine, and his eyes
were mocking as they met Rokeby's.

"There is a difference, Nick, and an important one. All
that you say may be true; this I will not deny, but Charles
Howard has me as his Vice-Admiral, and the Duque de
Medina Sidonia does not." He fingered his beard again and
his eyes were thoughtful. "That is the difference, sire, and this
is what will count when the time comes."

Rokeby smiled faintly. Francis Drake was not one to hide
his light under a bushel, nor did he feign a modesty he did
not possess. He knew his worth to England, for he had tried
and tested his value to the realm many times before. He had
accepted willingly and without question the appointment of
Lord Howard of Effingham as England's Lord High Admiral,
for Drake greatly admired him both for his qualities as a man,
and for the quiet wisdom and simple dignity which was his. He
welcomed his own appointment as Howard's second in command, knowing his leader to be possessed of a rare broadness
of mind, scrupulous fairness, and a ready understanding of
the abilities of his subordinates.

Under Howard, Drake could achieve his ends, for Howard
would not hamper him with petty jealousies and endless, pointless demands for adherence to protocol. Howard would hold
in his wise old hands the reins of command, and Drake would
be free to serve England in the way he knew best, with all the
daring and courage that was peculiarly his.

It was not blind conceit which had moved Drake to make
his observation, but cold realistic truth, and Rokeby, for all his
affection for the courteous, charming High Admiral, admitted
without reserve that Sir Francis's prediction was undoubtedly a
true one.

"And so, young Nick," said Drake, laying aside the broader

canvas for the fine etchings of detail, "since you have been ordered to Spain by the Queen, you can serve me at one and the same time."

"My lord?" Rokeby was resigned, knowing from the first moment the plan had been uncovered to him by the Queen, that Drake would not waste this opportunity. "And what may I do for you?"

"I want more information about the day on which the Armada will sail." Drake leaned forward, his eyes bright and eager. "I want to know the week, the day, the hour, if possible. I want to know from which port it will sail, the number of the ships, the weight of guns and men. My spies have done well, sire, and furnished me with much detail, but you will do better, for you will have the King's ear."

"Perhaps, my lord."

"You will either have the King's ear, Nick, or you will be dead," said Drake bluntly, for he was not one to mince words. "Either that charm of yours will get you into His Majesty's confidence or into one of his prisons, awaiting the arrival of the familiars of the Holy Office. If the latter, my lord, I will offer my prayers for you, for by God you will need them, but if you succeed, then listen well to what is said, and send me word when you can."

Nicholas laughed and rose to his feet. "That I will, my lord. I will do what I can, for the Queen, and for you."

"Then we shall both be well served, my lord," said Drake quietly. "Now leave me, for I have much work to do, and doubtless there are others to whom you must make your farewells." The diamond-bright eyes were mocking again. "And watch your step, Nick. You could find the bedchambers of Whitehall more dangerous than the Court of Spain."

And with a brief wave of his hand, he turned his attention to his charts again, leaving Rokeby to make his way silently to Jane Mordaunt's chamber.

She was waiting for him, sitting by the fireside, the flames lighting up the golden hair and throwing a pink and magical flush on to her flawless cheek. For a second Rokeby watched

85

her as he closed the door noiselessly behind him, but as he moved towards her, she turned her head and her face lit up in welcome.

"Nicholas." She rose, holding out her arms to him, her red lips parting in a joyous smile. "Dearest Nick."

He caught her to him, holding her tightly and kissing her hard.

When he finally released her, he drew her back to the fireside, pulling her on to his lap as he found refuge in a generously proportioned armchair.

"Sweet Jane," he said softly. "Sweet and lovely Jane. Of all things that I regret leaving, you will be the one I shall miss most."

"You are going, Nick?" The blue eyes were suddenly clouded with sorrow and anxiety. "Nicholas! When?"

His arm tightened round her. "I leave Whitehall tomorrow, love, for I must be on my way."

"No! Oh, Nicholas, no!"

"Alas, yes. There is no help for it, but you know that I shall come back. Do I not always return, and to your arms?"

Jane's mouth drooped and a faint frown touched her pencilled brows.

"To mine, and to others, my lord," she said tartly. "For do not think my love for you makes me deaf to rumours, Nick, nor blind to the looks you cast at other women."

"Oh come, Jane." He laughed and would have kissed her again, but she pulled away from him, still sulky at the thought of his going.

"You cannot deny it," she said, and would not look at him. "You are unfaithful and cruel, Nick, and now you are leaving again after so short a stay."

Rokeby studied the perfection of her cheek and jaw and let his appreciative eye stray down to the curve of her breast. Then he said quietly:

"I do not leave because I grow tired of you, Jane. I go because there is a task for me to do. If I were a man who could be turned aside from duty by the petulance of a woman, I should not be a man at all, and you would cease to care whether I went or stayed. Now enough of this, Jane, for the time we have together is short. Must I spend these last few hours with you coaxing you from a fit of pique? Must I remember you with a frown upon your brow and ill-temper in those wide blue eyes of yours?"

She turned her head to meet his gaze, and her peevishness was gone.

"Forgive me, Nick," she whispered and her mouth touched his cheek in soft apology. "I am a shrew. Why do you not beat me for my childishness?"

"By God I will, if you favour me with such tantrums again. But now, since you have come to your senses, I will not waste time with such stern discipline, for the hours go by on swift wings, and I will not squander a moment of them."

He bent his head and covered her mouth with his, drawing her closer to him, feeling the urgent desire in her as his hold tightened.

"Will you remember me, Nick?" she asked after a moment, and her voice was barely above a whisper. "When you are gone from here; will you think of me?"

Nicholas smiled, but he did not answer as he stroked the satiny tresses with a gentle hand.

"Will you, Nick; will you?"

He gave a quiet laugh, and slowly drew the wrap from her shoulders, pausing to admire the white flesh now shadowed by the warmth of orange flames.

"I will remember you," he promised finally, and let the gown slip from her body. "When I am alone, sweet Jane, and there are things to vex me sorely, I will remember you. I will think of your eyes, which tell me what is in your heart; your mouth, which is fashioned in desire, and your body, created to satisfy the every whim of man. Yes, dear love; I will indeed remember you."

As he caught her fiercely in his arms and carried her to the bed, there were tears on her cheeks, and even the satisfying

87

excitement of their love-making did not entirely salve the grief in her heart.

She was a gay wanton, who gave her body readily and without reserve, but until now she had never loved deeply.

To her, love had meant delicious, secret meetings with such of the handsome gallants of the Court who were bold enough to risk the Queen's wrath. The nights when the world was shut out from her chamber, as she lay contentedly in the arms of her latest conquest, satisfying both his demands and her own desires with their physical union. She had not looked for more, nor had she wanted anything else, but with Nicholas it had been different from the start.

He had taken not only her body, but her mind and soul too, and she was afraid. Afraid, because her longing for him grew apace, and although she felt his hands firm and decisive upon her body, she knew instinctively and unquestioningly that he would never be hers.

He would take her with affection and pleasure, raising her to heights of ecstasy she had not believed possible, but even as she reached out to grasp the inner spirit which was his, she found that her hands were empty as he slipped away from her, and her heart was blank with pain.

She lay relaxed against his strong shoulder, feeling the wonderful hardness of his body under hers, knowing with surety that she had already lost him, and in the quiet silence which followed their passion, she wept silently and hopelessly for a love that she could never possess.

# 5

In a quiet chamber in the centre of the bustling and splendid Court at Valladolid, a man sat at a desk littered with papers and documents, carefully annotating a report on the condition of the water supply to the nearby village of Santa Teresa.

He was of medium stature and slight of build, with light brown hair and beard, and large eyes of undistinguished blue. His skin was pale, as if he spent little time outside in the sun and wind, and there was about him a curiously reserved air which made him appear unapproachable and remote.

It was typical of Philip of Spain that he should select the quietest corner of the palace to make his own, and characteristic too that he should hate to leave his beloved Escorial, where he could find the true peace he loved so well, but his duties required him to move from time to time to his capital at Madrid, or to Toledo or Valladolid, and these duties he did not shirk.

Nevertheless, the time he spent in his fabulous palaces was limited, and even then, he lost no opportunity of slipping away to his own apartments, there to pursue his self-imposed task of reading the avalanche of despatches and reports which flooded into the Court day by day.

His enemies, and of these there was no lack, claimed that in him, absolute power had corrupted absolutely. He was the ruler of the most powerful empire the world had ever known, and as such, had unquestioning and unquestioned authority over his people.

He was their supreme master. He could grant life, or take it away with equal ease. He could raise to a position of power any whom he favoured, and could swiftly cast down those who had incurred his cool, controlled displeasure.

The epithets bestowed upon him varied from the approbation of Philip, *El Prudente*, through the mild criticism of Spider King, to the bitter indictment of Master of the Black Legend, which condemned, with no shred of tolerance, the barbarous inflexibility of his tyranny.

Possessed of all the haughty arrogance of a Castilian nobleman, he could be touchingly patient with, and readily accessible to, his humblest subjects; he could exercise an occasional shrewd and penetrating judgement whilst spinning his life away in a useless web of detailed paperwork, a task more fitted to his clerks and secretaries than to the man who ruled half the world.

In his youth, he had combined the fervour of strict, unbending religious orthodoxy with the unbridled pleasures of frank sensuality, his regular attendance at daily Mass in no way conflicting with the delights of the visits he paid to his plump and comely mistress. His appreciation of paintings of Biblical subjects and personalities had not for a moment quenched his zest for Titian's pink-tinted, fleshy beauties, which Philip called poesies, and which, at his request, were sent so regularly to his galleries.

As the years wore on, sated perhaps by four successive wives and a number of mistresses, he turned aside from physical diversions, contenting himself with memories of love and passion, and plunging wholeheartedly into a pattern of life which threatened to bring affairs of State to a grinding halt.

He had a precise and tidy mind; a mind which lacked the discipline or vision to stay on course and to confine itself to essentials. He strayed with blind persistence into a maze of petty irrelevances which grew in magnitude by the hour.

King of a great nation, Nature had granted him all the grave dignity and majesty necessary to fill this office, but had failed to endow him with that one vital and essential requirement of leadership, the art of wise delegation to others that for which a ruler had no time.

His ministers and counsellors chafed in impatience, longing to prise from their master's grasp the problems and posers with which they could more easily have dealt, and which, in the hands of the King, sank lower and lower in the pile of unread documents which cluttered his desk.

And whilst time was thus halted on the wing, Philip plodded steadily on, reading every missive and despatch which came to hand, dwelling on their content and implication, with unhurried deliberation, finally writing in his strange, sprawling hand a few illegible notes in the margin, mostly confined to the correction of a mis-spelt word, or a gentle and courteous reference to a minor grammatical error.

There was much of the monk in Philip, for all his earlier passions. He had the iron control and inflexible endurance which the discipline of a strict Order demanded, and he had the true and fervent love for his faith which made penalising sacrifices a joyous gift to God. He genuinely welcomed solitude, and for this reason preferred the silence and isolation of the Escorial, where the passages and ante-rooms had been designed to preclude the press of courtiers and nobles which normally thronged about him in his larger palaces.

At the Escorial, no one troubled him. He could sit for hours at his desk, writing letters and instructions which few could read, the silence broken only by the monotonous scratching of his quill and the chiming of the clock on the mantelpiece. From this small, cell-like room of his, he could move, soft-footed and unseen, to the chapel, where he could hear the sacred words which gave refreshment to his complex soul, and where, with great humility, he would kiss the celebrant's hand at the close of the Office, padding quietly back to his book-lined retreat, there to embark upon yet another pile of papers.

But now he was at Valladolid, and the peace of his chamber

was a shallow, mocking thing, for outside in the great hall were the assembled *aristocrata*, who waited for him to finish his work and take his place amongst them.

*La grandeza*, the highest ranking of Philip's nobles, were an arrogant, unbending class who, whilst generously acknowledging the Almighty as supreme, gave almost equal due to their own honour and dignity. Their families were ancient, their blood unimpeachable, and their names of a quality to arouse awe and reverence amongst their lesser brethren.

Once possessed of great power, they now had little left but their rank and wealth, for many years before, King Ferdinand and Queen Isabella, recognising the danger of a ruling class of this kind, had slowly but remorselessly robbed them of their significance, a policy which Philip's father, the Emperor Charles, had pursued with equal vigour. Charles V had tutored his son well in this respect, pointing out clearly the risks of allowing the grandees to reclaim their former positions, and Philip, shrewd enough to see the force of his father's teaching, had given his aristocrats little chance to regain their former glory.

He honoured them and spoke softly to them, but he sent them abroad on pointless diplomatic missions, or established them in comfortable and far-flung embassies where they had little chance to gather armies of loyal peasants and soldiers about them. He conferred high military rank upon them, encouraging them in their exploits outside Spain, but never allowing them to remain long at Court, keeping them isolated from the affairs of State, where they might cause mischief or wreck the absolute power which belonged to the monarchy.

In addition to the grandees, there were the hidalgos, equally conscious of their dignity and pride, but of less danger and therefore of less concern to Philip, whilst to serve the King and his nobles, there was a veritable army of equerries, major domos, grooms, valets, cup-bearers, physicians, grooms, aides, musicians, cooks, barbers, tailors, and all the other well-trained servants which were required to make life smoothly pleasant for the rich and high-born sons of Spain.

Philip laid down his pen and glanced at the clock. It was a pretty time-piece, made of marble and gold filigree, with a different jewel for each hour of the day, but now it told him in its relentless fashion that the time had come for him to leave his haven and to make his way to the audience chamber to greet those who clamoured for his presence.

He sighed, wishing he could avoid this interruption of his work, but finding no excuse for shirking his duty, he rose and walked a little stiffly to the door, for he suffered much agony from the gout which afflicted him. As he put out a hand to turn the ornamental handle, his eye fell upon the small painting hanging on the wall to one side of the door, and, as always, he felt a small, dull pain in his heart.

His hand dropped to his side, the door and the waiting Court forgotten, as he studied the face of the young man in the portrait.

The face was thin, the lips full and sensual, the eyes strangely adult, as if the boy had learned a life-time's decadence in the brief span of years allotted to him. He had been a weak and sickly child, the *Infante*, Don Carlos, his slight immature body deformed by one shoulder hunched higher than the other, and by thin, unsteady legs. It had not taken Philip long to realise the enormity of the blow which fate had dealt him. Even before the fall down a flight of stairs which had accelerated his son's violence and wildness, the lad had been oddly backward in some things, and uncannily precocious in others. He had reached the age of five before he could speak, and when he did begin to talk, his voice had been thin and high-pitched, rising to shrillness when the passionate, infantile tempers shook his narrow frame with their fury. Yet at a remarkably early age, he had learned the exciting gratification of ordering the young daughters of his father's servants to be brought before him for painful and wholly unmerited punishment.

Philip had watched Don Carlos grow, and his unease had increased as the years went by, for he had had no illusions. All his power and wealth had not been able to stave off this disaster, for there had been no doctor in the land able to give

93

this precious son of his a healthy body and a balanced mind. The stock was tainted, and the insanity which had manifested itself in Queen Isabella's mother, and again in her daughter, Joan the Mad, had come once more to the surface in this off-spring of Philip and the Doña Maria Manuela of Portugal.

Philip's face was expressionless as he gazed upon the portrait of Don Carlos. He shewed nothing of his feeling as he looked upon the painted canvas; no more emotion than he had revealed when he had learnt that the birth of the child had cost its mother her life. He had accepted it as the Will of God, and had not fought against the tribulation which the Almighty had sent to him, but inside, where it was not visible, the pain was still there.

He had wanted a son. An heir to the mighty kingdom over which he ruled, and it had taken all that icy self-control of his to stop the anguish of his heart shewing, when he finally had to accept that Don Carlos was a twisted, perverted travesty of a man, with a penchant for destruction, and a lust for blood.

But he had accepted it. With the same impassive calm which attended all that he did, he had accepted it. And when, on that cold day in January 1568, the King had accompanied a handful of carefully chosen nobles and a dozen or so guards to his son's chamber, he could have been calling to bid the boy good-morrow, rather than condemning him to perpetual confinement. After a few days, the chamber had been exchanged for the more permanent prison of a cold room in the tower, a short distance from the apartments which Don Carlos had occupied so unbecomingly, and as the door shut with metallic finality behind him, Don Carlos had been cut off from the world as if he had died. In fact, it took several months of captivity to extinguish the spark of life, and it was not until July of that year that he lay dying, calling to his father to pay him one last visit.

Philip had turned a deaf ear, and would not see him. The decision had been made long months before, and there could be no going back. The King had had to choose between his son and his empire, for if Don Carlos had lived to reign, the future of Spain was clearly doomed, and Philip was first a King and then, and only then, a father.

The malicious whispers of his enemies made much capital of Philip's decisive action, and there were even tales spread abroad that when Don Carlos's coffin had been opened, the small, shrivelled body was no longer joined to the head, but these dark rumours had never been proved, and were soon lost in the passing of time and in belated caution, for Philip still lived, and remained an all-powerful emperor, capable of making short work of those who would impugn his name.

Later, by another of his wives, he had had a second son, the heir he sought so eagerly, but sometimes, when he was least expecting it, the memory of Don Carlos returned to him, and he would bow his head in silent sorrow.

The King, taking one last, careful look at the painting, in which the artist, with delicate discretion, had managed to conceal the heartbreaking truth, turned once more to the door, and made his way down the stairs to the audience chamber to give his cool, unhurried greeting to the ambassadors and the other impatient peers who awaited him there.

Whilst the King paused to give a quiet moment's remembrance to his ill-fated son, Catalina de la Vega, with the assistance of her maid, Luisa, was putting the finishing touches to her toilet.

The Court of Spain was an awe-inspiring and formal assembly. It had none of the gay freedom of Elizabeth's royal circle, nor the wanton extravagances of the Court of Valois, where the French monarchy permitted licence and excesses which would have caused the Spanish grandees to blanch in horror.

And since Philip was a man who cared little for pomp and ceremony for the greater part of his life, it was natural that when the Court did gather together, it made the most of its opportunities, and dressed itself most splendidly, donning its most particular and exacting manners for the occasion. Although it was the normal custom for the ladies of the Court to remain apart, for once, this somewhat dampening restriction had been lifted, and when Catalina received the royal summons to Valladolid, she found to her surprise and pleasure that she was not expected to remain closeted in her own apartments, sharing only the company of the other women, but was encouraged to mingle with the *grandeza* and Court officials, and, not least, with her betrothed.

She was a lovely creature. Not yet nineteen, she had somehow achieved a serenity and poise normally lacking in one of her years, and the King had expressed his approval with something approaching warmth when announcing the news of her engagement to one of his favourite Knights of Castile.

Catalina moved her head slightly to one side to consider the effect of the jewels Luisa was fastening into the shining black hair, and nodded faint approval. She was slim, but most sweetly curved at breast and hip, with small hands of delicate whiteness, used gracefully to emphasise her words. The dark hair was drawn back from a smooth brow, and her skin was of palest olive, flawless and translucent, with the merest hint of warmth on the cheekbones. Her nose was small and narrow, her lips warm, red and strangely sensual in their fullness, but it was hard to dwell long on these charms, or on the slender, shapely neck and small, firm chin, for the gaze was captured almost immediately by the magnificence of the eyes under thin, pencilled brows. They were wide and dark, fringed with sooty lashes which curled back extravagantly or fell entrancingly on the cheeks when Catalina had a secret to hide.

When Luisa was finally satisfied with the arrangement of the diamond and jade billiment, Catalina rose, shaking free the heavy folds of deep-rose satin over the stiffened farthingale, and touching with light finger tips the dainty rustle of the crisp, lawn ruff. She let her eye wander critically over the gown, splendidly jewelled and embroidered in the bodice and fitting with exciting exactness the contours of her body. She wondered if it would please her betrothed; that aloof and overbearing nobleman who had successfully sued for her hand, and for a moment her mouth was sad.

Left an orphan when her father, Don Fernando de la Vega had been killed at sea, she had been forced to shoulder the responsibility of a large fortune, and of a small sister (whose birth had robbed Catalina of her mother, and whose brown, solemn eyes were totally without sight) for her brother, Don Manuel, had been brought up in the Court of Spain, and since he had reached manhood, had spent most of his time abroad in the King's service. Catalina had accepted her burden with courage and resolution, for her upbringing had been strict and efficient, and she had been well trained for the part she had to play amongst Spain's *élite* society. She found little difficulty with Margarita, her sister, who for all her disabilities was a merry, happy child with a true zest for life, and there had been many advisers to aid Catalina with the management of her father's estate whilst her brother was away.

But Catalina and Margarita were also wards of the King, and Philip took such duties seriously. During their earlier years at their father's palace outside Madrid, the King's lieutenants and guards had formed part of their household, and when Catalina had reached the age of eighteen, Philip had written in his own hand to tell her of the plans he had made for her future.

She had not been surprised to receive the King's missive, for, understanding with gratitude the interest he took in her welfare, she had anticipated that in the fullness of time he would arrange her marriage, just as her father would have done had he lived, and when she learned the name of the man chosen by the King for her future husband, she had been pleased and flattered by his choice.

He was the scion of one of Spain's oldest families, this Don Cristóbal Luis Lanuza, the Marqués de Avila y Manrique, and he was greatly beloved by the King, who saw in him, perhaps, something of what he had lost in Don Carlos. Catalina, reading the King's letter, had felt her heart flutter at his words, and with nervous fingers had unwrapped the small packet which accompanied the note, which contained a miniature of the man she was to marry.

97

When Catalina had freed the portrait from its wrappings she had stared at it with eager eyes, but as the seconds ticked past, her fingers tightened slightly on the gem-encrusted frame, and she had felt a sudden and curious dread fill her mind.

It was a thin, clever face, with eyes as yellow as a cat's under supercilious brows and heavy lids. The nose was aquiline and proud, the lips narrow and hard above a well-trimmed beard, the brow lofty and calm. Catalina had shuddered suddenly, and had not known why.

The face was not unpleasing; almost handsome, and certainly distinguished, yet she had found herself trembling a little as she laid the portrait down.

She had chided herself for her folly, reminding herself sharply that the King did her great honour that he had bestirred himself from his labours to select a husband for her, and she was fully conscious of the compliment he paid her by choosing so great a man for her spouse.

But as she had looked back again at the painted face, her heart had fluttered once more, not now with pleasurable anticipation, but with a strange, sick dread which she could not comprehend, and when she had finally come to Valladolid to meet her betrothed, she realised that her apprehension had not been mere girlish fancy. Her first instinctive reaction had served her well.

When Philip had led her forward to greet Don Cristóbal, the Marqués had bowed with the exact degree of courtesy required by the precise code of manners set down by the Court, and when he had taken her hand and raised it to his lips, it was with a graceful, easy charm, but even as he paid lip service to convention, the curious yellow eyes had stripped her naked, and the thin mouth had moved in a smile which made a shiver touch her spine.

In that one moment, with her small, cold hand in his, Catalina had read and understood this man with whom the King had decreed she should spend her life. She had seen in those clear, odd eyes, all the cruelty and viciousness that was in him, and his soft words of greeting had done nothing to ease the panic in her heart.

Now, as she stared at herself in the mirror, she felt her heart beating faster. One day, and a day which could not be put off much longer, she would belong to Don Cristóbal. She would be his possession and chattel, to do with as he wished. She felt icy cold, despite the warmth of the fire, and tried to close her mind to what would happen on that night when the sacred nuptial Mass was over, and the rejoicing of the wedding feast was done.

But try as she would, she could not stop her frightening thoughts, and the fingers which paused to adjust the long rope of pearls were unsteady.

There was so little time left, for the King would not stay long at Valladolid. His heart was already winging back to the Escorial, where he could find the solitude and peace which was so dear to him, and before he left, he would arrange the marriage ceremony, thus completing his task as guardian, and would hand his charge over to her new master.

Suddenly she thought of Antonia Ruiz, the shy, frightened girl whom the King had sent to her as lady-in-waiting on her first day at Court. Antonia had honey-gold hair, thick and smoothly coiled about a small, proud head, with grey eyes and a tip-tilted nose. She was gentle and sweet, and Catalina had felt an instant warmth towards her, but from the first moment of their meeting, she had been aware of the fear in Antonia. It shewed in the large, watchful eyes, and in the sudden uncertainty of the lovely rose-red mouth, and Catalina puzzled silently about this, until the third day of her stay at Court, when she was making her way to her chamber.

She was crossing the wide gallery towards the corridor which led to her apartment, when she heard voices from one of the recesses in the gallery. She would have hurried on, unmindful of the speakers, had she not heard a sudden cry of pain which made her turn quickly.

Even then, Catalina might have ignored the sound, for it was not in her nature to pry, but the cry was repeated; a low sound of pain, followed by a whimper which trailed off into silence. Soundlessly, Catalina had moved towards the alcove, and since the main gallery was lit only by a few candles, the semi-darkness provided her with secrecy as she grew nearer to the lighted recess.

Then she had heard Antonia's voice, low and full of pain, and her brows met in a sharp frown.

"Don Cristóbal, I beg you; I beg you . . ." Antonia's words were cut off sharply as the Marqués struck her hard across the face, the sound stark and shocking in the stillness.

"Do not beg." His voice was cold and venomous. "You are not a peasant. I have given you an order, and you will obey it."

"But, my lord . . ." Antonia's voice was trembling now as she choked back tears. "I cannot . . . I . . . cannot come this night. Oh, sire, do you not see . . . ah!"

Her protest was bitten off in a further gasp of pain as Lanuza caught her wrist and twisted it spitefully behind her.

"Enough of this!" The Marqués was savage now. "I am tired of your whining and snivelling. You will come to my chamber this night, and I will teach you then what risks you take when you defy me in this manner. Now get back to your room before you are seen, and dry those tears. It would be unfortunate for you, my dear, if my precious *novia* should see you thus, and question you, for if she should discover our meetings, *querida*." His voice was very quiet and terrifying. "It would be the worse for you. Now be gone."

Catalina had watched in frozen silence as Antonia had fled from the gallery, and had stood flattened against the wall until Don Cristóbal had sauntered in his casual, effortless way down the wide staircase, before she turned and rushed back to the shelter of her own room.

There, she had dropped to her knees at the prie-dieu, raising stricken eyes to the statue of the Virgin, carved to a mystical perfection from a single piece of ivory, and had prayed most earnestly for a miracle which would deliver her from the hands of Don Cristóbal.

But her prayers had not been answered. On the following day when Antonia came to her chamber, Catalina saw the misery in the girl, and saw also the shadow of a bruise on the delicate cheek, and her heart had ached for her. Antonia moved about her tasks stiffly and almost awkwardly, and when one of the maids stumbled and fell against her, she gave a smothered cry of pain which she quickly checked with a shaking hand.

It was then that Catalina began to hate Don Cristóbal, and when she had met him later that day, it took all her self-control to return a small cold smile as she curtsied to him. She longed to throw convention to the winds and to shout her accusations into his disdainful, unfeeling face. She longed to strike him hard across the cheek, as he had struck Antonia, She wanted to seize the riding whip he held lightly in his gloved hand and belabour him with it, as he had belaboured Antonia. She wanted to spit her fury and disgust at him, and to cover him with her scorn and contempt.

But she had been powerless to do anything but acknowledge his greeting, and to accept his hand as he led her to the King's presence, but with each moment that she spent in his company, her loathing for him grew deeper.

Catalina's hand dropped from the rope of pearls and with tightened lips she accepted the jade and pearl fan from Luisa. There was no escape from it. The time had come when she had to join the King and those assembled below; when she had to endure once again the sardonic courtesies and glib compliments from the Marqués with such control and calmness as she could muster.

When she reached the audience chamber, she found the King had already arrived and was talking to a tall, elegant man with vivid blue eyes and a smile which made Catalina's heart jump unexpectedly. As she made her obeisance to Philip, he smiled a little, and taking her hand in his thin, dry one, led her to the stranger who was staring at her with a queer intenseness.

Nicholas and his companions had found it surprisingly easy to gain the King's ear. Their whole journey, from the moment they had left Plymouth in *The Raven*, until they reached Valladolid on the horses provided by Rokeby's agent, had been uneventful and without mishap.

When Peregrine and Greville had learned the reason for the journey, their reactions had been mixed. Eager enough to do service for the Queen, Greville, particularly, had been strangely quiet on learning that one of the men suspected of treachery was John Dyke, for he had grown attached to him, but neither had questioned Rokeby's orders, nor hesitated for a moment to pursue the task set for them.

Philip had been gracious when they were first led to his presence. Gracious and sympathetic, for he had a genuine compassion for those who would sacrifice everything to follow the true faith, and was glad enough to give them shelter in his Court, for when he possessed himself of this rebellious island, men such as these would serve him well.

And so Nicholas and his friends had been welcomed by Philip and by his Court, with all the stilted graciousness of the Spanish nobility, and although only a week had passed since their arrival, they had already adapted themselves to the formal pattern of life laid down at Valladolid, and were beginning to make cautious overtures of friendship to a number of the *grandeza*.

But until this moment, Nicholas had not seen the girl whom the King now led forward, and he felt a sharp emotion he did not recognise as she curtsied before him. He bowed low in homage, and raised her small white hand to his lips, and for a moment there was a silence between them.

Then Nicholas controlled the extraordinary feeling which had beset him, and his voice was light and casual when he spoke:

" Lady Catalina," he said softly. " I crave your pardon, for I am guilty of the most monstrous discourtesy that I stare so, but, faith, madam, can I really be blamed for my bewilderment?"

Catalina, held by the same spell which had momentarily transfixed Nicholas, was acutely aware of the King's watchfulness, and aware also of the speed with which her heart was beating. In that small fraction of time when Nicholas had held her hand in his, she had felt all her fears and dread fall away from her, as if he had lifted from her a burden too great for her to bear. And when she had stared into the cool sapphire eyes, she had seen, for one fleeting moment, something which turned her world upside down, and made her tremble with a feeling which was beyond her experience and knowledge, but which gave a curious comfort to her troubled mind.

But now that the moment was over, and Philip, still smiling slightly, was looking at her intently, and she tilted her chin a fraction as she looked back at Rokeby, now in complete control of himself once more.

" *Señor*? I do not understand you. Why should my presence cause you such surprise? Did you not think to find women in the Court of Spain?"

She was conscious that her voice was unnecessarily sharp, and wondered if the King would rebuke her for her discourtesy, but at that moment Philip was called aside by one of his ministers, and she was left to face Rokeby alone.

Nicholas heard the defensive note in her voice and gave a small, unseen smile. She was exquisite; possessed of a beauty which took his breath away, she was oddly and endearingly vulnerable as she tried to stare down his admiring gaze.

" Indeed, yes. I had expected to find women, even in the cloistered Court of Valladolid, but though I was told of the fairness of the daughters of Spain, I am now bereft of speech, for your loveliness completely overwhelms me."

"Bereft of speech, sire?" The slender white hand flicked the fan in quick disdain. " It seems to me, Sir Nicholas that you have a tongue of silvered sweetness, and have no lack of words to aid you."

Before Nicholas could reply, the King turned back to them, and was joined almost immediately by Don Cristóbal, who made his bow to Catalina and then to Rokeby.

Philip smiled gently. " Sir Nicholas, I would have you know Don Cristóbal Lanuza, the Marqués de Avila y Manrique; Don Cristóbal, Sir Nicholas Rokeby from England."

The two men bowed again, but now Don Cristóbal's brows had risen and his voice was cool.

" From England, your Majesty?" The amber eyes narrowed faintly. " We are indeed honoured."

The King inclined his head. " Sir Nicholas and his friends seek refuge with us, Don Cristóbal, until such time as it is possible for them to return to their own land in freedom." He smiled a little more warmly at Nicholas. " Mayhap, sire, 'twill not be too long before that day cometh. And now I pray you, excuse us, for we must leave you for the moment. Don Cristóbal and his betrothed will entertain you for us."

Nicholas was hardly aware that he had bowed at the King's words, for they had struck a chill, deadening note into his heart.

Betrothed? This girl, who was little more than a child, with a heart-breaking beauty which made him feel fiercely protective, betrothed to this man who stood looking down at her with something just stopping short of contempt. Nicholas's face was guarded, and his manner had lost nothing of its assurance as he glanced at Lanuza.

" My lord; my felicitations. You have been greatly favoured by the gods, and I could feel it in my heart to envy the good fortune which is yours."

Don Cristóbal bowed again, his self-possession as polished and serene as that shewn by Rokeby.

" Indeed this is so, *señor*, and I am most conscious of my *fortuna*." For a moment the amber eyes licked hungrily over Catalina's body, and Nicholas felt his muscles tense warily, for the Marqués was making little attempt to conceal his intentions. " Soon we shall be wed; the Lady Catalina and I. Then shall I take her to my *palacio* in Castile, where life is truly civilised, and where a man is free to mould Fate to his own pattern. There I shall see that the Lady Catalina learns all that she needs to know to fulfil her rôle as my wife."

Nicholas shot a swift look at Catalina and saw the sudden pallor of her face. Even whilst he watched, he saw the look of hatred in her eyes turn to one of fear, for she had not mistaken the promise under Don Cristóbal's lightly spoken words either. He looked back at the Marqués and his own face was unreadable.

"The Lady Catalina is also fortunate, my lord that she has so experienced a tutor, for I am sure you will lay your considerable knowledge unstintingly at her feet."

For a brief second the eyes of the two men met, and Catalina held her breath.

She had watched other men confront Don Cristóbal; seen them face him, and then wilt and cringe before him, but this man was unmoved. She felt her mouth dry, and realised her hands were clenched at her side, but she was incapable of speaking or breaking into the silent clash of wills which was as fierce as any duel. The Marqués's mouth was ugly and the cat's eyes were narrowed to dangerous slits, but Nicholas held his gaze with quiet determination, his lips curved in a faint, unamused smile.

It was Don Cristóbal who looked away first, and Catalina watching him closely, knew instinctively that this refugee from England had made a bad and dangerous enemy, for the Marqués was unused to failure of any kind. She was hardly aware of Rokeby's murmured excuse as he withdrew with a low bow, for her eyes were still on Lanuza, but now the golden eyes were no longer like a cat's. Now they burned with the ferocity of a tiger, and she almost cried out as he took her hand in a savage grip to lead her back to the King.

That night, Peregrine Grey and Greville West found Nicholas strangely preoccupied. They had joined him in his chamber, when the royal household had settled down for slumber, with the intention of exchanging notes on the progress of their enquiries, but Nicholas, clad in a robe of heavy velvet, seemed almost indifferent to their reports.

Finally Peregrine stopped his pretence that all was as usual, and gave Nicholas a straight look.

"What is it, Nick? Something troubles you?"

Rokeby, staring into the fire, did not appear to hear him at first, but when Grey repeated his question, he looked up and gave a bleak smile.

"It is nothing, Peregrine; nothing of importance, for it does not affect the reason for our coming here, nor the undertaking we have shouldered for the Queen."

"But it is of concern to you, Nick," said Peregrine softly, "and thus 'tis of moment to us too. What is it, my lord; the Marqués de Avila y Manrique?"

Nicholas frowned sharply and gave Grey a hard look.

"Why do you say this? Why should Lanuza be of importance to me?"

"Perhaps because he is the one who sent the spy to England," said Peregrine lightly, "and then again, perhaps not."

Rokeby's eyes were chilly. "You speak in riddles, sire," he said coldly. "Perhaps the Marqués was the man responsible; I do not yet know."

Grey smiled affectionately at the irate Rokeby, and since anger of this kind was so foreign to Nicholas's nature, he laughed a little and said quietly:

"But this you know, Nick; Lanuza is a dangerous man. A dangerous one, and an unpleasant one, and no fit husband for Catalina de la Vega."

Rokeby's face hardened and when he spoke, his voice was clipped and terse.

"That is not my responsibility. The Lady Catalina is not my ward, but his Majesty's. In his infinite wisdom, the King has chosen Lanuza for the girl's marriage partner; it is not for me to criticise this."

"Nor yet to approve it, Nicholas," said Greville suddenly. "I have been watching this man, Lanuza, and Peregrine is right. He is not only dangerous, he is evil. He has in him a malevolence which chills the blood, and the Lady Catalina is frightened of him."

Nicholas took a deep breath, but his voice was still under control.

"Then surely she has but to beg the King to release her from the engagement."

Peregrine laughed shortly. "God a mercy, Nick, and do you think he would listen? This girl is Philip's ward; she is also virtually his prisoner. His word is law, his every action sacrosanct. No one dares to question his judgement or defy his edicts, least of all a girl of such tender years as Catalina. No, she will not escape the misery of a union with Lanuza that way."

"We cannot know that the union will be so unwelcome," said Nicholas coolly. "He is a man of great wealth and position. His forebears were of the purest of Castilian blood, and this counts for much in this accursed country, Peregrine. The Lady Catalina will be the wife of one of the great nobles of the land."

"Christ's blood, Nick!" Peregrine was done with tact and careful words as he strode forward to stand in front of Rokeby. "Will you stop this folly! You know as well as I do what kind of a man Lanuza is; you are not blind, nor are you a fool. Would you condemn this girl to imprisonment with him for the rest of her days? Would you stand by and let him take her, without lifting a finger to stop him?"

Rokeby lay back in his chair, and now he was smiling slightly. A small, cold smile, which took the heat from Grey's words like a shower of ice.

"This is not my task," he repeated, and his tone brooked no further argument. "I have not come hence to rescue defenceless maidens from distasteful marriages. I have come to find out whom Philip of Spain has sent to England to kill the Queen."

He sat up abruptly. "This task is sufficient to fill my waking hours, and those of the night as well. I have no time to turn aside to question the authority of the King on a matter which is none of my business."

Peregrine's mouth tightened. "I see, my lord. Then the

Lady Catalina is to be pitied, and so is Antonia Ruiz."

Nicholas looked up quickly, hearing something unexpected in Grey's voice.

"Antonia Ruiz?" His eyes narrowed slightly. "What of her, Peregrine? How is she concerned with this matter?"

Peregrine slumped to a low stool beside the fire, and when he spoke it was without heat.

"Have you not seen the fear in this girl? Seen the terror in her eyes when Don Cristóbal looks at her?" His mouth twisted slightly as he glanced at Nicholas. "Perhaps you have not, sire, for I think your eyes have seen little but the predicament of the Lady Catalina." His gaze went back to the fire. "But she is not alone in disaster, Nick, for the Marqués is not satisfied with his beautiful bride-to-be, and would have Antonia also, though not with honour."

Nicholas regarded Grey thoughtfully, and now all anger had left him.

"No, I had not noticed," he said gently, "and I am sorry, Peregrine, for my apparent indifference. This is a matter of importance to you?"

"It is." Peregrine did not look at Rokeby, and his words were without emphasis, but Rokeby nodded slowly.

"I see." He rose and took a pace or two across the chamber, turning suddenly to look back at Grey.

"Then, my lords, let us consider what knowledge we have gained so far, and what our next step shall be, for when we have achieved success in our mission, maybe we shall have left to us a little time. A small measure of days, or perhaps hours, to put right this unfortunate error of the King's."

He came back to Peregrine, and for a brief second rested one hand on his shoulder.

"Fear not, Peregrine. We will make time for the unmasking of Philip's emissary, and for the destruction of Don Cristóbal as well, for I do confess I would derive much pleasure from his undoing."

# 6

As THE weeks passed, Nicholas, Peregrine and Greville slipped easily into the design of life at Court. They had ample opportunities of talking with the King's counsellors and advisers, and took these opportunities with an eager caution, using subtlety and guile to probe the secrets of their enemies.

It was clear that the preparations for the invasion of England were moving rapidly to a climax. Odd snatches of conversations between those closest to the King revealed something of the strength of the fleet which Spain was arming under the unlikely leadership of Medina Sidonia, and once, Peregrine was able to slip into the private apartments of Don Ramón de Cantos, the minister responsible for the supply of guns and small arms, and with wry face imparted to Rokeby the startling quantity of cannon and powder which was already in Medina Sidonia's hands.

Rokeby was worried by the passing of time, although he shewed no sign of this to his companions. They had been in Spain for five weeks, yet not a whisper had come to their ears of the identity of the man who had spent the last two years in Elizabeth's Court. He was painfully aware of the pattern which was being worked out before him.

The Armada was almost ready; this was certain. The men, the arms, the ships were gathering strength day by day, and only the weather held Philip back, but once the spring was upon them, there would be no reason for delay, and when the fatal day came for the fleet to sail, that would be the moment for the death of Elizabeth, for her murder would throw England into panic and confusion. And whilst this chaos reigned, Philip's fleet would approach the Channel to sail brazenly along the south coast to link up with Parma's troops which were known to be waiting in the Netherlands.

There had been moments too when Nicholas had had the opportunity of speaking with the King himself. Philip appeared to have a genuine liking for Rokeby. His initial welcome had been followed up by a kindly interest in his guest's welfare, and an assurance that when he was master of England, he would ensure that Nicholas's confiscated estates would be returned to him.

Rokeby found Philip something of a puzzle and even more of a surprise, for what he had learned of him in England, had not prepared him for what he found in the quiet reserved man with a soft voice and gentle smile.

One day he had met the King returning from his private chapel through the long picture gallery. Characteristically the King was alone, for he needed no aides or familiars to worship God, and when he saw Rokeby admiring the paintings on the richly panelled walls, he stopped to tell him something of their history.

This done, the King welcomed him into his chamber, and poured wine with his own hand into goblets of priceless value and indicating that Nicholas should sit in a chair set before the desk.

Seeing Rokeby's faint surprise, the King gave a small, ironic smile.

" The ceremony of our Court is rigid, I agree, Sir Nicholas, but we are alone now, and it is our wish that you should be seated. We would like you to tell us more of England, for our stay there was but a brief one."

He made another gesture towards the chair, and with a low bow, Nicholas accepted it, conscious that many of the

Spanish nobility would be both shocked and envious at the granting of such a favour, for few were honoured with the privilege of sitting in the presence of the King.

"Now, my lord," said the King, when Nicholas had tasted the wine. "What resistance may I expect to find when my soldiers land upon your shores?"

Rokeby did not make the mistake of accounting the King a fool, and he gave a rueful smile.

"Resistance you will find, your Majesty, as I am sure you know, for it is well understood that there are those in my country now, who send you such intelligences."

Philip nodded. "That is so, my lord, but you are recently come from England, and will therefore be more aware of the determination of your people to resist me than most. Well, sire, what may I expect to find?"

Nicholas, noting the King had dropped some of the royal formality, hesitated, choosing his words carefully.

"You will find some support, your Majesty; this is certain. There are still those in England who do not accept that Elizabeth is the rightful heir to the throne, for she is the bastard of her father's mistress, yet you will find many who are prepared to overlook this, and who have embraced her cause with vigour and enthusiasm."

"This I have never doubted." Philip stirred slightly in his chair. "She was a remarkable girl; she is doubtless no less remarkable in her maturity. She had in her a certain quality which could stir the hearts of men strangely. Has she still got this power, my lord?"

Rokeby's caution increased. "She has, sire. She has not lost this ability to bind men to her, for all that her youth has now fled."

Philip picked up his goblet and for a moment studied the perfectly cut rubies in the stem without speaking. Then he took a sip of wine and looked back at Rokeby.

"Hers was not a magic of the flesh sire; it was something quite different." He gave a small sigh. "Then, my lord, it must be by force that I take your small island home, for I should be foolish to underestimate the strength of support the Queen will receive from her followers."

Nicholas's finger moved slowly round the golden rim of his goblet, and in the silent room, his voice sounded almost harsh.

" This is true, sire, but if she were no longer on the throne when you were prepared to move, then . . ."

His voice trailed off in the unsaid words, and Philip, as calm and imperturbable as ever, raised his brows.

" Not on the throne, Sir Nicholas? But how could such a thing come to pass? She is England's Queen, no matter by what manner of mischance this came about. You tell me she is loyally supported by her people; how then, could she lose her throne in so short a span of time?"

Noting the confirmation of his own belief that Philip's plans were reaching finality, Nicholas shrugged a little.

" She could not be overthrown, sire, that I grant; but there are other ways."

" I cannot think of any," said Philip smoothly, " but I would be interested to know what passes through your mind."

" She is not strong, sire." Nicholas's voice was as cool as the King's. " Her constitution is not of the stoutest."

" And you think she might succumb to some disease?" Philip sounded faintly amused as he took another sip of wine. " You think she might die, most conveniently, of some fever, as my ships leave port?"

Nicholas stopped fencing, and his voice was blunt.

" I think she might die, sire," he said, " but not necessarily from the ravages of a fever."

Again there was a strange stillness between the two men, and Nicholas watched the King's lids drop to veil the expression in his eyes. Then Philip's mouth moved in a barely perceptible smile.

" You hate her that much, Sir Nicholas? You feel no loyalty to this woman who is your Queen?"

" I do not accept that she is my Queen," said Rokeby, feigning quick indignation. " She is a usurper and pretender, and has no business on the throne of England. Yes, sire; I hate her that much."

Philip sighed. "Such passion, Sir Nicholas, is dangerous. What if someone should overhear you? Are you not afraid of this?"

"Not in your Court, your Majesty," replied Rokeby, and saw the gleam of amusement in the King's eyes again.

"You think there are no spies within my walls?" asked Philip with gentle irony. "Oh come, my lord, you are not that naïve." He considered the goblet stem once more with increased attention. "No, there will be those in Spain, sire, who have been sent to plumb my strength and my weakness, just as I, my lord, have sent to England those whose task it is to keep me informed of England's plans."

It was a chance of a lifetime, and Nicholas took it boldly.

"To give you information, your Majesty, and perhaps a little more?" His voice was light. "Perhaps there are other duties they have to fulfil apart from probing secrets from the Queen's counsellors? One man, at least, sire, who has the task of ridding you of your enemy."

He waited with tensed muscles for the King to reply, and it seemed to him an eternity before Philip spoke.

"I trust you will be present at the ball tonight," said the King finally. "It is to be a great occasion, and you will be a most welcome guest."

He rose to his feet, and Nicholas followed suit, his heart leaping within him.

So there was no doubt. There was such a man at Elizabeth's Court. A man sent by Philip, not to uncover her State secrets, but to wrest from her her life, for the King had now confirmed this beyond all shadow of a doubt when he left unanswered Nicholas's tentative enquiry.

Rokeby had framed his question in words, and the King had answered him clearly with silence.

Peregrine Grey, a trifle encouraged by Rokeby's promise concerning the future of Don Cristóbal, made a point of seeking out Antonia Ruiz at every opportunity.

At first she had tried to avoid him, making quick excuses to slip away from him whenever they met, and covering her grey eyes with long feathery lashes so that he should not read her thoughts. But Peregrine was grimly persistent, and gradually he managed to get Antonia to pause as she went about her duties, persuading her to exchange a word or two with him, and although their moments together were few, gradually and imperceptibly something began to grow between them.

Antonia was intensely aware of this tall, bold looking Englishman, and when she dared to look into his warm hazel eyes, she felt her senses swim in a most alarming manner, for she read in him something she had never seen before.

She realised the dangers of those brief minutes they spent, when words were all that were available to them, for Don Cristóbal had sharp eyes and many spies, but so strongly was she attracted to Peregrine, that she risked the Marqués's fury in order to steal the precious fragments of time with this man to whom her heart had opened.

In the privacy of her chamber at night, when she waited for sleep to come, she dwelt lovingly on the words Peregrine had spoken, and treasured anew his smile and the feel of his strong hand upon hers. She even allowed herself to dream a little, and to pretend that this was something more than a passing encounter; that in time, the words might be exchanged for something else, and trembled with quiet delight as her imagination led her down forbidden paths.

But then the soft, happy smile would fade as the remembrance of Don Cristóbal returned to her, and the tremor of ecstasy became a shiver of fear.

She remembered the first day she had encountered the Marqués; a bright, sunny morning in May two years before, when she had recently come to Court to serve the *Infanta*, who was now in Madrid. The Court was at Toledo at the time, and Don Cristóbal, newly returned from a visit to the Netherlands, had ridden into the courtyard with his long retinue and stalked boldly into the palace to make his bow to the King.

Antonia had watched him, and from the very first moment, had seen something terrifying in him. When the King had withdrawn, and Don Cristóbal had moved amongst his fellow nobles, greeting them with that slow, secretive smile of his, she had drawn back, trying to conceal herself in the throng.

But her attempts at anonymity had been useless, and her hope that she would not be noticed by the Marqués was short-lived. Two days later he found her in the gardens with two of her companions, and she had felt the colour drain from her cheeks as his eyes moved slowly and comprehensively over her body. Flight was impossible, for he was a favourite of the King; such discourtesy would not be forgiven or excused, and she was forced to stand before him whilst he completed his deliberately insulting survey. Then he had snapped his long white fingers, sending her companions packing, as he had moved forward to take the basket of flowers from her hand.

She did not know why he had selected her from amongst the women at Court, for she was wholly unaware of her beauty, but with a curiously adult comprehension, she wondered if it were because of the fear he saw in her. Fear which she could not conceal, and which made his smile grow wider and more fearful.

On that first occasion he had done no more than talk to her, questioning her about her presence at Court, and asking something of her family history, but all the time she was bitterly conscious that he used his questions merely to mask his real purpose. He was not interested in her answers, but in the contours of her body which he studied with a practised gaze, and she had prayed for the courage not to wilt before the power of those terrible yellow eyes.

Don Cristóbal had not wasted time. It was the same night that he had sent two of his men to her chamber to fetch her. She had caught up her wrap, pulling it tightly about her as the men walked boldly towards her, unmindful of her loveliness and indifferent to her fear. When she had protested and had tried to withstand their demands, they had seized her roughly by the arms and thrust her from the room, warning her in harsh whispers not to call out or to make a sound.

She had been too frightened to scream or to call for aid, and when they opened the door of the Marqués's chamber and pushed her inside, she could do no more than stand transfixed, her eyes growing darker as Don Cristóbal came slowly forward to meet her.

It was then that the terror really began. At that moment, when he stretched out a hand and pulled her towards him. From that moment her life had assumed the proportions of a nightmare from which she never awoke, for the demands that Don Cristóbal made upon her were no ordinary ones.

He was not satisfied with the possession of her body, for his appetites were not normal, and it had not taken her long to understand what was necessary to sate the hunger and greed which burned in him like a fierce fire.

She was powerless to resist him. There were none to whom she could go for help, for no one would have listened to her. The Marqués, beloved by the King, was too powerful for any to seek to cross his will.

And so she had been forced to submit to him and to his outrageous demands, and as she lay sobbing at his feet, she had been helpless to do more than pray to the Blessed Virgin for release from the torment he inflicted upon her. But despite her prayers, there had been no release, and the Marqués shewed no signs of tiring of their relationship, not even when the Lady Catalina arrived at Court, and the King announced her betrothal to Don Cristóbal. When Antonia had first heard the news, her heart had lifted thankfully for she saw at last the opportunity of freedom from his tyranny, confident that once the enchanting Lady Catalina was his *novia*, he would have no further time for their nocturnal encounters.

But her hopes and prayers had been in vain. The promise of Catalina de la Vega's hand had pleased and flattered the Marqués, but it had not quenched his appetite for other things, as Antonia had soon discovered when, on the very night of the engagement, he had sent for her as the hour of midnight approached, and the whole palace rested quietly in slumber.

That night he had made her a promise. After he had indulged the monster within him, he had bent and pulled her to her feet, the golden eyes burning into her tear-filled grey ones and his voice had been a soft, caressing whisper.

"Do not fear, Antonia," he had said, and now his touch was almost gentle on her trembling flesh. "This marriage will not change what I feel for you. You are the Senorita Catalina's lady-in-waiting, and this is most convenient for it will simplify things for me. When she leaves here as my bride, you will accompany her. I will not leave you behind, my dear; on this I give you my word."

And so Antonia's world grew blacker and more hopeless until she met Peregrine Grey, and even though she was still forced to obey the summons of the Marqués, something of her misery and fear lifted when she was with her gay English gallant.

Peregrine, however, was less patient than Antonia, and one evening when Antonia was hurrying towards the Lady Catalina's chamber, Peregrine, who had been lying in wait for her, stepped out from the shadows of the corridor and barred her passage.

Antonia gave a gasp of fear, but when she saw who it was, a tremulous smile touched her mouth as she curtsied deeply to him.

Peregrine bowed and raised her to her feet, but this time he did not release her hand, but kept it fast in his, and her colour grew warmer.

"M . . . m . . . my lord," she whispered. "You must not. It is wrong for us to be seen together."

Peregrine's eyes were searching her face hungrily and his grip tightened.

"It is not wrong," he said gently. "We do nothing shameful. Our meeting here at Valladolid was a fortunate accident. It was not of our designing, and thus we are blameless. No guilt attaches to those who are the playthings of Fate."

He pulled her gently towards him and felt her trembling. "Why do you fear so, Antonia?" he asked quietly, dismissing the rigid code of manners for which he had such scant patience. "You do not tremble like this simply because our paths have crossed, nor is it only our chance meeting this night which makes your eyes fill with dread. What is it which troubles you? Tell me, for perhaps I can lift from you this distress which vexes you so."

"No!" She was violent in her rejection, pulling her hand free from his, and backing away, her cheeks growing whiter. "No, my lord, you must not! You must not! I beg you, leave me, for you can do nothing to aid me. I need no help; I swear to this."

Peregrine regarded her steadily for a few moments, then he caught her by the shoulders and forced her to look at him.

"You lie, Antonia; you lie, and with little skill. Something is tearing you apart, for I read more than normal fear in your eyes. There is something else there; something which is making you sick of heart and distraught of mind. What is it, *querida*? What ails you, love? Tell me, so that I may kill your dragon for you."

Antonia's eyes closed as slow tears trickled down her cheeks. Peregrine's firm hold, and the gentle strength of his words filled her with a strange, unexpected weakness. Used to the contempt and cruelty of Don Cristóbal, she had almost forgotten that sometimes a man laid hold on a woman for reasons of love, and not simply to gratify lust and other ugly cravings. Peregrine's hands were strong, but they were also compassionate, and his voice washed over her in a tide of blessed comfort.

"It is nothing, my lord," she repeated finally. "Nothing at all, and now I must go, for my presence will be missed."

"By the Lady Catalina?" he asked softly. "Or by the Marqués de Avila y Manrique?"

Her frightened eyes flew to his, confirming what he had already feared, and his hands tightened on her shoulders.

"Antonia, dear love; tell me what is wrong. If it is Don

Cristóbal who causes you to fear like this, tell me, for I will call him to task for his impudence."

"No!" Now there was panic in her voice, and her eyes pleaded with him as she spoke. "My lord, no, no, no! You can do nothing; nothing. I am in no need of help, and even if I were, you could not withstand Don Cristóbal. He is too powerful, sire. None can stand against his wishes."

"You think not?" Peregrine released her, his smile grim. "You will find that you are wrong, Antonia, and so will Don Cristóbal, for I will not stand by and watch you live in torment like this. Dearest, do you not understand what was happened to us?" His anger was gone, and now his smile was warm and encouraging. "This is love, dear one; do you not recognise it? It is love which makes my heart beat like a drum when I see you; which makes my voice unsteady when I speak your name, and makes me tremble when my hand touches yours. Do you pretend it is not the same for you?"

Antonia opened her mouth to protest, but his eyes held hers and the denial died on her lips. Gradually the grey eyes lost their habitual look of fear, and the gentle flush returned to her cheeks.

"I . . . I . . . do not deny it, my lord," she said finally, and she gave a faint laugh. "I am a fool, sire, for naught can come of this feeling between us, yet I would not deny it, for in truth it is as strong in me, as it is in you."

"Then accept it gladly, sweetheart," said Peregrine, and his voice was a little husky. "Do not gainsay it, but welcome it with joy, for it is the most precious thing on earth."

"But it is not for us, my lord." The sadness began to creep back into her face. "There is no future for our love."

"This I will not accept," said Grey calmly. "Our love is strong enough to endure, no matter what obstacles stand in its path. Fear not, Antonia. Have a little patience and faith in me, and I will take you away from this place, and away from Don Cristóbal."

Now her dread was strong again, and she backed away from him, holding out one small hand in protest.

"No, my lord, no! This is not possible," she began, when he lost patience and caught her in his arms.

As their lips met, she felt the world stand still, and all the tremors of fear and apprehension were gone as his arms tightened about her. Time ceased to exist for them, and only their passion was a real and lasting thing, but even as Peregrine bent to claim his second kiss, Ruy de Guaras, Lanuza's sly and watchful body servant, moved quietly out of the shadows and made his way back to his master's chamber.

Catalina de la Vega was in her sister's chamber that afternoon, reading to Margarita. The child was curled comfortably in an armchair, unmindful of the magnificence of the tiny dress of blue satin, her mouth open with wonder at the tale her sister unfolded.

She was a sweet-tempered child, and sharply intelligent, for all that the wide brown eyes could give her no aid with her understanding of the world, and she was greatly beloved by the servants who tended her, and by her sister who gave her devoted and unstinting care.

When the tale was finished, Margarita clapped her hands in glee, begging for another story, but Catalina laughed and rose to her feet.

"No, sweetest, no more now, for the time has come for you to rest. Come, let me help you, for Maria is busy with other things."

Gently she removed the crumpled gown and smoothed the silky hair from the small white brow.

"There, niña, that is better, is it not? Now come, let me help you to the bed."

Margarita sighed, but recognising the inevitability of the enforced rest, allowed her sister to settle her beneath the covers.

"Stay with me, Catalina," she begged, her small hand reaching out to find her sister's. "Stay until I am asleep, I pray you."

Catalina smiled, and took the tiny fingers between hers.

"Very well, sweet, I will stay, but you must close your eyes and rest."

Catalina sat back in the chair by the bedside, Margarita's hand still clasped in hers, and watched the child slowly relax and slip into slumber. As Margarita's steady breathing told her sister that sleep had come, she gently freed her hand but made no move to rise.

There was much to vex her mind at this time, and the opportunities for considering the things that perplexed her were few, and Catalina welcomed this quiet moment alone to dwell upon the situation confronting her.

First there was her growing distaste for the proposed marriage with Don Cristóbal, for her dislike of this man waxed stronger as time passed, and the thought of a union with him made her shudder.

Secondly there was this Englishman who had come so unexpectedly into the tranquil, formal atmosphere of Court and breathed into it something vital and demanding, and who smiled at her in a way which made her heart quail. She had not known how to deal with him; this gallant who bowed low and talked to her in light, mocking tones, whilst his eyes spoke of something entirely different. She had taken the only course open to her and had adopted an air of disapproval and disdain when they met. She kept him at arm's length and was frigidly polite, uncomfortably aware that under his respectful smile and bland words, he was laughing at her for her pretence.

She wondered if the King would listen to her, were she to lay before him a plea to be released from the engagement, a thought which she had hitherto dismissed as impossible, and for all her courage and spirit, she once again set aside this course, realising the futility of rejecting the King's proposals.

She gave a deep sigh and wished, not for the first time, that her brother, Don Manuel, would return to Spain, for to him she could turn for help and advice, and to him, and only to him, could she confide her dread of her forthcoming marriage.

But Manuel was not in Spain, nor likely to return for a while, and now Catalina's fear grew stronger as she permitted herself to remember where her brother was at this time.

When she had first been told of his mission to England, she had paled in horror, but Manuel had laughed at her, holding her hands in his, and begging her to forget her fears.

" It is a great honour, *querida*," he had said, and raised her hand to his lips. " Do you not understand this? I have been chosen to serve the King in this way, and you should rejoice that I have been selected for the task."

She had trembled a little, but she understood that Manuel was held in high regard by the King, for he was constantly on the move to foreign countries, and it was for this reason that Catalina was left to manage the estate with such advisers as the King saw fit to give her. She was completely unaware that Philip was merely pursuing his normal course of keeping his richer nobles away from their own lands, and assumed that her brother was of great importance to Spain.

" But Manuel," she had whispered uneasily, her hand tightening on his. " What is this task? Why do you have to go to England?"

Manuel had grown serious, and his smile had faded.

" It is better that you should not know this, Catalina," he had said soberly, " for what I have to do is not a pleasant thing, but it is necessary for our success."

Catalina leaned forward in her chair, remembering as if it were yesterday instead of two long years ago, how she had clung to her brother's hand and begged him to tell her what his mission was to be, but he had steadfastly refused her, and it was not until she had met Don Cristóbal, that she had learned the truth.

She had entreated him to ask the King to postpone her wedding day until her brother had returned to Spain, and Don Cristóbal had laughed scornfully at her plea.

" Madam, I am in no mood to wait until your brother returns, if, indeed, he returns at all."

She could still recall the spasm of fear which shook her at

his words, but she had held her head high, and had not let him see the dread in her.

"Why should he not return, Don Cristóbal?" she had enquired, and her voice was as steady as his. "This is his home; why should he not return to it?"

"He may not be given the opportunity, my dear." The Marqués was mocking. "When a man undertakes a mission such as this, his life is of little worth, for he risks all when he attempts what Don Manuel has sworn to do."

Perhaps pride was a besetting sin of the Castilian aristocracy, but it stood Catalina in good stead on that occasion, for her tone had not altered as she met his eyes, and her bearing was as cool and haughty as his.

"And what has my brother sworn to do, Don Cristóbal?" she had enquired calmly. "What task is this, which you fear may keep him from coming back to us?"

Don Cristóbal's smile had grown broader, his white teeth gleaming in momentary amusement.

"*Dios*, Catalina, I thought you were apprised of the errand on which the King has sent him. I thought you knew he had been sent to kill the English Queen."

Catalina buried her face in her hands, living again that petrified moment when the Marqués had broken the truth to her, and because the pain of remembering was too great, she rose quickly from her chair and slipped out of the chamber to seek relief from her own black thoughts.

It was perhaps unfortunate that it should be at this precise moment that Nicholas Rokeby had chosen to pass along the wide corridor, for as Catalina rushed blindly from her sister's room, she found herself in Rokeby's arms.

He held her for a second, quietly and without moving, and as he looked down at her, she saw no amusement in him, but only that odd look which made her pulse race furiously.

"Your pardon, Lady Catalina," he said finally as he released her. "I am a clumsy fool, and would crave your forgiveness."

She tried to keep her voice free from emotion as she made

her own apologies, but that queer feeling which beset her whenever they met, drove her back, as always, to defensive hostility.

She would like to have hastened away from him, back to the sanctuary of her own room, but that would have been childish, and would have proved that she was no match for him, and so she walked slowly by his side, and used the small fan fastened to her jewelled belt to give her flushed cheeks some protection from his ironic eye.

" And when do you return to England, *señor*?" she asked with forced politeness as they reached the picture gallery. " Are we to lose you soon?"

Rokeby stifled an impulse to pull her back into the privacy of the corridor and take her in his arms, but with a commendable measure of self-control, he gave a slight off-hand shrug.

" Not yet, madam, for the King is still preparing for invasion. When he is ready to sail for England, then, *Señorita* Catalina, so shall I be."

Catalina stiffened slightly, for although he had run from an enemy State, something in her recoiled that he denied his country and his monarch, and her voice was colder as she spoke.

" I see." The fan flicked more sharply. " Do you not miss your own home, Sir Nicholas?"

" It was no longer mine," he returned briefly, and she shot him a quick glance.

" The Queen . . . the Queen took it from you?" she asked finally, and he nodded, hating the need to lie to this girl who made him feel something strange and rare which he had never experienced before.

" Yes," he said, and his tone was still serene. " She took it from me, and thus, madam, since I have no home in England, what better place could I choose to make my new abode than here in Spain?"

" But you will return when our soldiers land in England?" She was still doubtful, and now his smile was cruel.

"Indeed I shall, for then I shall wreak vengeance upon those who robbed me of my birthright. As they took from me what was mine, so I will wrest from them with my sword that which they possess, and as for that she-cat who sits upon the throne . . ." His voice dropped to a low whisper. "I pray to God that she may be destroyed. That her power may be taken from her, and her miserable, decaying body stripped of the gaudy rags and jewels she wears, and thrust into a bottomless pit."

Catalina drew away from him, her face paling under the torrent of his hate, one hand touching her cheek in uncertainty and distress.

"You can say this?" she asked finally through stiff lips. "You could wish your Queen dead?"

"I would that my own hand could plunge a dagger into her heart," he retorted viciously, and watched the revulsion in her eyes. "But I believe I shall be too late."

"Too . . . too . . . late, *señor*?" The hand dropped from her cheek. "I do not understand you."

Nicholas's smile was savage. "I think, Lady Catalina, that the King has already taken steps to encompass her end. I think she will die, this Tudor witch, whose birth was such a tragedy for my nation. I think she will be destroyed as the Armada sails; slain by the man whom Philip has sent to her Court for this very purpose."

She was ashen, and now she could not conceal her shaking hands as she stared at Rokeby, and had no control over her words as they tumbled from her in bleak agony.

"Ho . . . h . . . how did you know that the King had sent Ma . . ." She bit the word off, but she was too late, and Nicholas's eyes narrowed.

So she knew who it was; this delicate, fragile girl with the dark, beautiful eyes and a mouth which threatened to drive all else from his mind. She had been entrusted with this most precious and dangerous of the King's secrets. He frowned a little, not understanding why this should be, a trifle startled that the bait he had used many times before on Philip's nobles should have been grasped by this girl, but the brief interval had given Catalina a chance to compose herself, and when he glanced back at her, her face was as cold as stone.

He could not make her speak now, for she was on her guard. She had already said too much, and she knew it. The time was not ripe now, for he would get no more words from her at this time, nor, he fancied, on any other occasion unless he were able to force her tongue in a way which she could not resist. He saw the resolution in her and bared his teeth fractionally; he had seen this kind of determination before. It was the look of the martyr; the stubborn courage which kept men silent when their bodies were racked with pain, and when the meaning of life itself was no longer important.

He gave a faint, resigned sigh, and raised her hand to his lips.

" I pray you, madam, not to let this matter vex your mind, for it is but a trifling consideration. Soon my most ardent desires will be fulfilled, for I read in his Majesty the most inflexible purpose which will serve me right well. Now, Lady Catalina; I beg that I may be allowed to escort you to your chamber."

Their eyes met once more. The jewel-bright eyes of clear blue, which gave no hint of what thoughts passed through Rokeby's mind in that moment, and the dark, sad eyes which tried to sustain contempt and dislike as the tide of longing washed through them.

Then Catalina laid her hand lightly on his arm, iron-hard under the misleading softness of dove-grey velvet, and was led back to her room without further ado.

As the door closed behind her, Luisa came forward with a wide smile. She was a plump, comfortable woman of respectable birth, who had cared for Catalina since her childhood, and who could not have loved her more dearly had she been of her own flesh and blood.

" *Niña*." The firm, warm hands took Catalina's small, cold ones in a comforting embrace. " What is it, pretty one? Why do you look like this? Is it . . ." Luisa hesitated, reluctant even to mention the name of the man Catalina was to marry, for she recoiled from him as a rabbit from a snake. " Is it Don Cristóbal?"

Catalina smiled a trifle wanly and shook her head.

" No, Luisa, no. I have not been with the Marqués." Her mouth drooped slightly, and anger began to flicker in her eyes. " I have been with the Englishman. The Englishman who has fled from his own country to seek refuge here."

The anger grew a little more, and Luisa's quick, intelligent eyes saw something more than indignation in her charge's lovely face.

" He is very handsome," said Luisa casually, " and most gallant of bearing."

Catalina pulled her hands abruptly away from Luisa's and said coldly:

" He is a traitor, this *visitante ingles*. A betrayer, who runs from his country when it most needs his help; a coward who would rather hide behind the cloak of King Philip than face his Armada in the Channel. Pah!" Catalina almost spat the monosyllable in her anger. " What do his looks and bearing matter, Luisa? What of his pride and his honour?"

Luisa was unmoved by her mistress's fury, for she was watching with increased interest the unusual passion this man's name had aroused in her beloved, and saw the small white hands clenched with an emotion no man had ever engendered before.

" There, there, sweetest one," she said soothingly. " Do not enrage yourself over the man if he is as worthless as you say. Come, it is time we began to prepare for the banquet."

" If he is as worthless?" Catalina looked indignantly at Luisa. " How can you say this, Luisa? Can you not see what manner of creature he is?"

Luisa remained entirely unruffled as she began to unfasten Catalina's jewels. " Perhaps, my love, perhaps. But he remains true to his faith. You forget why he came to Spain; that he might worship God and remain true to the Catholic Church."

" There are other things in life," said Catalina shortly, and then Luisa did look a trifle alarmed, glancing over her shoulder, and raising one hand in protest.

" Hush, *niña*, hush! Do not say such things, lest they should be overheard and misunderstood. You forget how diligent and watchful are the familiars of the Holy Office, even in the King's palace. Come, let us forget this man, for, as you say, he is of no account, and there is no need for you to think of him again."

Slyly she glanced at her mistress as she spoke, and for one unguarded moment saw the expression in Catalina's eyes. Her normally steady hands trembled a little as they wrestled with the golden fastenings on the bodice of the dress.

Catalina was in love. For the first time in her young life, Catalina's heart had been roused, and by an Englishman, without home or money and precious little honour. Luisa bit her lip and went on with her task, but as she did so, her eyes were worried, for she was thinking of Don Cristóbal.

If he should ever see that look on Catalina's face, and realise that it was not for him, the English knight was as good as dead.

# 7

It was at this time that the King received a visit from Don Pedro de Valdez, who came as the emissary of his Commander-in-Chief, the Duque de Medina Sidonia.

Don Pedro was one of Spain's most distinguished leaders; a knight of Santiago, who had held the rank of Admiral of the Gallician Squadron when Portugal was brought to her knees in defeat under Spain's iron heel. He lacked some of the experience of his fellow squadron leader, Don Juan Martinez de Recalde, second in command of the fleet, and had less dash and *élan* that Don Miguel de Oquendo, but he was a thoughtful, dependable man, with a good measure of initiative, and furthermore, had one paramount virtue which fitted him well for his present task.

He knew the English well. He understood them, as well that is as it was possible for an *aristocrata* of Spain to understand the apparent madness of the English sea lords for he had clashed with Drake and his men on more than one occasion, and had had cause to feel some bitterness when his own men had succumbed to the light-hearted insolence of *El Espectro* off the coast of San Sebastian two years before.

Don Pedro was not looking forward to his interview with the King, for he was well aware that the plea his Commander had sent to the monarch would not be well received, and it was with no small reluctance that he followed the equerry along the corridor to the audience chamber.

When he had made his obeisance to the King, he stood quietly, waiting for Philip to complete the letter he was writing, not stirring so much as a muscle as he watched a secretary shake sand lightly over the parchment and humbly make his bow as he removed the letter from the desk.

Finally Philip leaned back in his chair, waving his two secretaries from the room, and looked up at de Valdez.

"Well, Don Pedro," he said in his cool, unhurried voice. "What brings you to Valladolid at this time?"

Don Pedro took a deep breath and tried to infuse some confidence into his voice.

"Your Majesty, I am sent by the Duque de Medina Sidonia to lay before you his most earnest plea." He looked anxiously at Philip, but the King's face was like a mask.

"So?" The King tapped his quill lightly on the desk. "And what is this boon the Duque seeks? More ships? More men?"

De Valdez gritted his teeth. This interview shewed every promise of being as difficult as his worst fears had led him to expect, and he gave a slight bow, shaking a reluctant head at the King.

"Your Highness, it is not that. I think you know that the Duque is not happy with the arrangements which have been made for the Enterprise."

Philip glanced up from his pen to meet Don Pedro's eyes.

"I do not ask him to be happy, my lord. He is merely required to be successful."

With an imperceptible grimace, Don Pedro tried again.

"The Duque fears, sire, that were the Armada to sail now, or in a matter of a few weeks, when the weather is more favourable, it would meet with nothing but defeat. He is convinced we are not equipped for our task for we have insufficient men, ships and provisions, and our guns and powder are scarcely enough for a minor skirmish."

For a moment Philip said nothing, and his eyes were expressionless. Another man confronted by such a comment from one of his leaders would have exhibited anger and indignation, or at least some concern that the Enterprise which was so near to his heart, and on which he had spent so much time and money, appeared to be in jeopardy, but Philip shewed no reaction at all.

Finally, when the silence grew to a length which made Don Pedro squirm, the King leaned forward slightly and drew towards him a parchment, spreading it out calmly with one well-cared for hand, and eyeing it thoughtfully.

"A minor skirmish?" The King's voice was as emotionless as if he were enquiring the hour of day. "I find this difficult to understand, Don Pedro."

A long white finger began to run down the list on the parchment.

"The Duque complains that he has too few ships. He has sixty-five greatships and galleons, and thirty-two small ships. There are four galleasses, four galleys, and no less than twenty-five urcas for his stores. What manner of skirmish would this be, sire, which needed a fleet of this size to quell it?"

Don Pedro moved uneasily. "Sire, I am aware of the number of vesels at our disposal, but they are not all in the best of condition, and they are not as swift or mobile as those which the English sail."

"They have been carefully serviced," said the King, unmoved by de Valdez's criticism, "and they are well fitted for the task they have to undertake. They are not required to engage in a game of hide and seek with the English navy, but to sail through the *Canal de la Mancha* to join forces with the Duke of Parma and his troops."

De Valdez shifted once more, acutely uncomfortable in his role of messenger. "Then, sire," he said, trying to avoid Philip's steady gaze, "we are short of men."

The finger moved again, and Philip said gently, "You have more than thirty-thousand men, my lord, and the Duke of Parma will provide the troops for invasion. Your next complaint?"

Don Pedro flushed, but he had no choice but to continue, for the brief from his Commander had been very precise.

"The guns and powder, sire," he said reluctantly, and waited for the finger to move again.

When Philip had recited in the same toneless voice the weight of guns and the quantity of powder available to the fleet, he put aside the scroll and looked back at Don Pedro.

"Sire," he said, and still there was no anger in him. "Go back to the Duque and tell him that I have provided him with all that is needful for this undertaking. I have given him the ships, the men, the weapons, and the provisions of war. Now it is for him to obey my commands, and when the winds are propitious, for him to sail in the name of God against the English."

The King leaned back in his chair and his gaze became a little sterner.

"And I bid you to tell the Duque this also, Don Pedro. I am not a fool, and I do not embark upon foolish endeavours. The Armada is the greatest fleet ever sent by one nation against another, and of its success there can be no doubt, but I have taken other steps to seal the achievement of my will. My orders regarding the passage through the Channel I have made clear many times. You will not pause nor hesitate in your course, nor will you turn aside to engage the foe on the south coast of England, but will sail straight way towards the place where Parma will await you. Then, when his men are embarked and you turn again to the coast of England, you will find that she is not so well prepared as you had thought, for by then, there will have been a small incident which will have thrown your enemies into confusion."

Don Pedro was staring at the King, seeing for the first time some glimmer of emotion under the quiet words; some hidden, secret gleam in the blue eyes which fastened upon his own.

"I . . . I . . . do not understand, your Majesty," he said finally, and the King gave a faint, mirthless smile.

"You are not required to understand, Don Pedro, but merely to take my word that when my troops land upon English soil, they will find their task is the easier because I have already taken steps to bring about the downfall of my enemies. Tell this to the Duque, and bid him send me no more pleas to abandon this Enterprise, for this I will not do. Bid him to remember also that he is an officer of Spain, and sails in the name of Almighty God, and thus he cannot fail no matter the depths of his own uncertainty."

De Valdez, seeing the King's final word had been spoken, bowed low, murmuring his excuses and contrition for his visit, and withdrawing from the King's presence as hastily as courtesy permitted. And when he had gone, Philip put aside the list he had been consulting, setting it carefully down on one corner of the desk and laying gently and reverently upon it a small crucifix fashioned in polished ebony and beaten silver. Then he picked up his quill and began to write again.

Whilst Philip was interviewing Don Pedro de Valdez, Catalina was sitting in her chamber with Antonia Ruiz, working on the fine embroidery at which she was so skilful. She cast a sidelong glance at Antonia, her face softening as she watched her lady-in-waiting ply her needle with patient but indifferent ability. The dark green dress which Antonia wore seemed to enhance the pallor of her face and to make her eyes seem larger and more haunted, and Catalina's slight smile faded as she allowed her work to drop into her lap.

"Antonia," she said quietly. "What is it that troubles you?"

Antonia gave a slight start, as if her thoughts had been many miles away, and she looked at Catalina, a faint flush colouring her cheeks.

"Nothing, *señorita*; nothing, I assure you."

"It is not good to lie," said Catalina calmly, and picked up her needlework again. "And it is not necesary to pretend to me, Antonia, for you must know by now that I have great affection for you, and would do nothing to harm you."

"Oh, I do, I do." Antonia's face took on a shadow of anxiety. "*Señorita* Catalina, it is not that I do not trust you, but . . ."

"But you will not speak to me of Don Peregrine, is that it?"

Catalina smiled warmly at her companion and laughed a little at Antonia's stricken expression.

"Dear Antonia; did you think I did not know? Did you think I was so blind that I had not noticed how you looked at him and, indeed, how warm his gaze is when he comes upon you?"

Now the lovely colour in Antonia's face was deeper and she bowed her head to conceal the expression in her eyes.

Catalina leaned forward a little and touched the girl on the arm. "Tell me about him; tell me about this Englishman who makes your eyes like stars, and lifts your heart towards heaven."

Antonia, blushing harder still, raised her head.

"*Señorita* Catalina, I do not know what to say. I had not meant to . . . to . . ."

"Had not meant to fall in love?" Catalina smiled a trifle wryly. "One seldom means to fall in love, but it happens nevertheless." For a second Antonia saw her mistress's face grow sad, but then the look was gone and Catalina smiled encouragingly.

"Well, will you not tell me of him? He is a bold one, this Don Peregrine, no? And handsome too."

Antonia's face was alight with something which made Catalina want to cry.

"Oh, *señorita*, yes, yes! So strong, yet so gentle and kind. I did not know it was in the nature of man to be so tender and compassionate, but in Don Peregrine there is such warmth and sympathy that I do not know how to repay him."

Catalina felt tears prick behind her lids as she looked at Antonia's radiant face, and prayed hard to the Virgin to send her the right words to use.

"I am glad," she said finally. "Glad that he is such a man, for it is good that you should learn not all men are as Don Crist . . ." She broke off abruptly, but Antonia's face had lost its glow and had grown pinched and white again.

" As Don Cristóbal," finished Catalina firmly, and put the embroidery aside again. Listen to me, Antonia." She took Antonia's hand in hers. " It is clear that you have much affection for this Englishman, and although I am not wise enough to see what may come of this love you have for one another, I feel that there is risk for you both. Now that you have opened your heart to me about Sir Peregrine, will you not tell me why you tremble when Don Cristóbal passes by? What is it between you and the Marqués? Why do you draw back and grow pale when he enters a room? What hold does he have upon you that makes you fear him so?"

Antonia was shaking and her face was buried in her hands, but Catalina pursued her questions with undaunted resolution.

" I beg you to tell me, Antonia. What is it between you and the Marqués, and have you talked of this matter to Don Peregrine?"

" No! " Antonia gave a little cry, and her hands fell from her face. " *Señorita* Catalina, no! I could not; I could not. I pray you do not mention this to him, for if he were to learn . . ."

" If he were to learn what, Antonia?" asked Catalina softly, but Antonia continued to shake her head, growing more distressed as she saw the determination in her mistress's face.

" *Señorita*, I beg you not to question me further. I can tell you nothing, for there is nothing to tell. If I have seemed to fear Don Cristóbal, it is simply because he is a man of great power, and I am overawed by his presence; it is no more than that, but I would not have his name mentioned to Sir Peregrine."

" No," said Catalina bleakly. " This I can understand, for if Don Peregrine should learn the truth, you would not turn him aside as easily as you do me. He would not accept your excuses and falsehoods as I am forced to do, for he is not that kind of man. *Niña*." She leaned forward again and laid a hand on Antonia's cheek. " I beg you to take care in what you do. If you cannot tell me what is wrong, I must accept this, but I would not have harm befall you, or your English-man. I am to marry Don Cristóbal." For a moment Catalina's face was hard. "And I think I understand a little of the manner of man he is, and I tell you, Antonia, you must use caution."

Antonia nodded, silent for a moment as the two women shared the common fear of the man they could not bring them-selves to discuss more openly. Then Antonia touched Catalina's hand with her soft lips and smiled.

"You are kind, *señorita*; kind as Sir Peregrine is kind, and I love you for it, but I pray you, do not worry for me. Life is not always easy, and sometimes we are forced to accept the heavy burdens which God sends to us to bear, but when it is given to us to meet one who makes our mere existence a blessed and holy thing, then, *señorita*, we must thank the Almighty for his generosity and learn to treasure each minute of the time we are thus given."

"You love him greatly," said Catalina slowly, and watched the joy rise in Antonia again. "You are fortunate, Antonia, no matter what your burden may be; you are fortunate."

"Indeed, yes, for were I to die this very day, I could truly say that my life had been most fully lived. If I were never to see him again, nor feel his hand upon mine, still I have been given the greatest gift a woman can receive."

As Catalina tried to blink back her tears, Antonia looked at her and smiled gently.

"And you understand me, *señorita*, do you not? You know what I am saying is true, for you too have been given this gift."

Catalina looked up quickly, and now it was her turn to blush a little. "I do not understand you," she said a trifle coldly. "I am fortunate indeed that the King has selected for me so noble a bridegroom, but . . ."

"That is not fortunate," said Antonia, and for a second her voice was bleak. "But I did not mean this." The smile returned. "It is strange that we should both find happiness in men not of our own country, is it not? Odd that I should love Sir Peregrine, whilst you . . ."

"Whilst I?" Catalina was sitting up very straight, and was at her most haughty. "I do not see . . ."

"But I do, *Señorita* Catalina. I see." Antonia gave a little chuckle. "Those in love have acute perception, sweet mistress. I have seen you watch Don Nicholas when you believed you were unobserved. Your eyes sparkle with something I have never seen in you before, and there is a new aliveness and awareness in you since he came to Court."

"This is nonsense!" Catalina was curt. "You are foolish, Antonia, for you imagine these things. Love for Don Peregrine has made you see that which does not exist."

Antonia's smile grew deeper. "Deny it if you will, but whilst your words fall like empty echoes on the air, your heart is telling you a truth which cannot be gainsaid." She sighed. "Oh, I pray that for you there may be true happiness, but I am afraid, for Don Cristóbal . . ."

Again there was silence between them; grey, frightened eyes meeting defiant black ones as yet again they paused for a moment to consider the Marqués. Catalina was shaken to find her heart was beating rapidly at the mere mention of Nicholas's name, and not for a moment would she allow herself to admit that Antonia's words had any truth in them, for she still clung doggedly to her contempt for him.

But as the moments ticked away, something of her rigid poise relaxed, and Antonia saw the merest shadow of a smile touch her lips. Perhaps the future seemed a little dark, and perhaps the thought of marriage with Don Cristóbal was no matter for rejoicing, yet suddenly, even Catalina had to admit that life did not seem quite so hopeless, nor the world quite so formidable a place, for now it contained Nicholas.

He was an Englishman, a traitor, and a coward, but when he had held her hand in his, for that small moment of time, nothing else had been of any importance.

With a sigh Catalina threaded her needle with a strand of lilac silk and gave a rueful smile.

"We are neglecting our labours, Antonia," she said, "and letting ourselves dream of things which may not be ordained for us. Come, we must forget such delusions as dazzle our minds, and apply ourselves to our task again."

She gave her companion a quick smile.

"But I will pray for you, dear Antonia, and for your Peregrine, but most of all," her face sobered. "Most of all, I will pray for your safety, for in truth, I am sore afraid for you."

In the early hours of that morning, Peregrine Grey, Greville West and Jacob Blount made their way to Nicholas Rokeby's chamber and gathered round the fire. April had come to the land with cold, biting winds and driving rain as sharp as needles, and they were glad enough to take advantage of the warmth of the flames as they drew closer together.

Presently Nicholas moved away from the fire and paced up and down the room, his face unusually sombre, for time raced by on winged feet, and still his task was undone.

He turned to his companions and raised his hands in a gesture of helplessness.

"I confess myself confounded," he said finally. "I have lost no opportunity of turning my conversations with the King's counsellors and advisers to the wisdom of destroying the Queen before the Armada sails. They have nodded and their eyes have smiled secretly, but not one has let a word escape him."

"Save the King," reminded Greville, thrusting another log upon the fire. "In his Majesty you found some confirmation of his intent."

"But not in words." Nicholas laughed shortly. "Yet you are right, Greville, for by his silence, Philip did in truth confirm our fears. There can be no doubt; there is such a man at our Court."

"But we do not know his name, nor do we know any who will tell us." Peregrine was frowning. "Nick there is not much time left. It is April now, and when this month is at its ending, the elements will not rage so loudly. Then will the King set loose his ships upon us and then . . ."

"And then will his spy kill the Queen. Yes, Peregrine, I

know there is but little time. Yet there is one who knows the name of the man in England sent to do this foul deed, and who might be made to reveal this to us."

Peregrine and Greville exclaimed quickly, but Jacob Blount was placidly still, standing like a stone sentinel by the carved fireplace, watching his master with alert, unblinking eyes.

"You know someone, Nick? Who is this? One of the King's men?" Peregrine's voice was sharp.

Nicholas's smile was not pleasant. "In fact, no, Peregrine; one of the King's women. The Lady Catalina."

"What!" Peregrine stared at Rokeby unbelievingly. "Nick, you cannot mean this? Why should the Lady Catalina be privy to such a plot as this? In the Court of Spain the women are more sheltered than in a nunnery. Who would take a girl of her scant years into their confidence in such a matter?"

Rokeby shook his head slowly and his eyes were troubled.

"This I do not know, Peregrine, but she knows the man's name, for she all but let it slip from her. Alas, she recalled just in time that this information was not for my ears, and I knew 'twould be useless to question her further, for she would have said no more."

"Could you not persuade her, Nicholas?" Greville smiled a little. "You do not normally have trouble in bending the fair sex to your will. Can you not coax the lovely Catalina to confide in you?" ·

Greville saw Rokeby's lips twist slightly, and watched the lines harden at the corner of his mouth.

"No," he said bleakly. "I cannot, for the Lady Catalina has nothing but contempt for me. She believes me a traitor to my country and to my Queen, for to trick her into a betrayal of her secret, I had to speak harshly of Elizabeth. Harshly and cruelly, and this greatly angered Catalina." Suddenly his face relaxed. "She is made of fire, my little Catalina," he said softly. "She turned on me most roundly for my spiteful words, and berated me sharply for my disloyalty. I think the Queen would approve of her, Greville."

Greville, knowing Elizabeth's narrow-mindedness where her

favourites' love affairs were concerned, rather doubted this but he nodded.

" It is good that she has spirit, Nick, and perhaps she doe not honour you for what she thinks you have done, bu even so, could you not get her to reveal the man's name?"

Nicholas's face grew cold again. " It is the only way we shall ever know who the man is," he said shortly, " but persuasion will not do. She will hold her tongue no matter what words I use. No, Greville, I must take another and less happy course to gain my ends."

They watched him silently as he paced the room again, all very conscious of the tension in him, all wondering in their several ways why this should be, for he normally shewed no such emotion.

Then he turned and looked at them, his eyes as bright and as cold as the sapphires they resembled, and when he spoke, it was in a tone both terse and unemotional.

" There is only one way to force this girl to speak," he said, " and that is by attacking the one she cares for most. She would not fear for herself, and even if I were to lay about her with my whip, she would not speak, but if I were to threaten the life of her sister, that would unlock her stubborn tongue."

Peregrine got slowly to his feet and his voice was hushed.

" Threaten the life of her sister? Margarita? Nicholas, you cannot be serious."

" I have never been more serious in my life." Rokeby shot him an unfriendly look. " Do you imagine I would choose such a moment to jest, Peregrine? The child is the key to our endeavours. I shall take her from her room one night when the time is ripe, and Jacob shall spirit her through the palace to the side door where Jorge Delgardillo will be waiting with a horse."

" Delgardillo?" Peregrine's voice was still hushed and incredulous. " Who is he?"

" A man in my pay," said Rokeby briefly. " He will take the child to his home some ten miles hence, and keep her safe. Then shall I send a message to Catalina, bidding her to meet me in the chapel which stands on the edge of the palace grounds, for this is seldom used, and furthermore our rendezvous will be at night."

His mouth was a thin, hard line, and Peregrine said faintly:

" Nick; there must be some other way."

Rokeby said something softly under his breath; then he began his pacing once more. " There is no other way. We have been here too long already, as you yourself have said. Time is slipping through our fingers like sand, and day by day Philip strengthens his ships and adds more men to those who sail in her. Only yesterday he received a visit from Pedro de Valdez; some last minute preparations to be discussed no doubt. I have told you, I am baffled, for none of my approaches to Philip's nobles have borne fruit. No; there is no other way. I shall send Catalina a message, and when she meets me, as she most assuredly will do, I shall tell her that to save her sister's life, I want the name of this man Philip has sent to England."

" Nick! You cannot do this." Greville rose to his feet and came to stand by Peregrine. " Peregrine is right; there must be some other means. You cannot take the child like this. Nick; she is blind."

Rokeby stiffened slightly, but his expression did not change.

" That I know," he said coolly, " and it makes no difference. I have told you; there is no other course open to us."

" I will not be a party to this," said Peregrine hotly. " God's death, my lord, what are you thinking of? Has so short a stay in this bedevilled country soured your soul and warped your mind?"

" No." Nicholas stared straight into Peregrine's angry eyes. " I am neither troubled of soul nor of mind. And you have no choice, sire, for I am ordering you to take part in this undertaking, and those orders you will obey."

The stillness was frightening. Blount, as mute and motionless as ever, watched the two men as their wills clashed in violent silence. Then Nicholas said through set teeth:

" You will obey me, my lord."

Grey's eyes fell, and he clenched his fists hard against his side, but he did not speak again, and Rokeby, giving him one last look, turned to Blount.

"Jacob. You have sent the message to Jorge as I ordered?"

Blount nodded, feeling the slight relaxation of the atmosphere. "I have, sire. I have warned him that we shall take the child within the next two weeks. He will come daily to the palace and will await my signal."

"Good." Rokeby glanced at West. "Well, Greville, have you no words of stricture for me?"

Greville shook his head. "I do not like what you do, Nick, but if you say there is no other means to gain our ends, then I will accept your word."

Rokeby gave an ironic bow. "I thank you, Greville, for your trust. And you, sire?" He turned back to Peregrine. "Have you now overcome your feeble scruples sufficiently to give me aid?"

Peregrine looked up, and Nicholas saw his face was white and strained.

"Forgive me, Nicholas. I did not mean to doubt you, and I know that what we have come to do must ride above all other concerns, but it was because of the child. She is so small and helpless. She cannot see, and will be frightened, and . . ."

Nicholas smiled, and now his smile was warm again and the hand which gripped Grey's shoulder was comforting.

"I know, Peregrine, I know. God! Do you think I am enjoying this? But we will not frighten her; this I promise you. She shall be spared fear; I pledge my word on this. Now come, Peregrine; we need all our wits about us."

Peregrine raised his shoulders helplessly. "Very well, Nick; I am yours to command as always, but . . . but . . ."

"But?" Rokeby watched him struggle for words. "But what, Peregrine?"

"Nicholas, she will not forgive you for this; the Lady Catalina. She will not find it in her heart to forgive what you do."

Nicholas's expression did not alter, but his voice was very quiet.

" My life is not my own. If it were, I would cut off my right hand before I would lay it upon the child, but I have to measure the censure and hatred of Catalina de la Vega against the life of the Queen, and, Peregrine, there is no margin for choice in that. I would to God I had met Catalina in other circumstances; in another place, in another time, for when I look at her, I confess she makes my heart rejoice, but I did not meet her in another place; I met her here. Here in Philip's Court, whence I have been sent to save the life of England's monarch, and perhaps to save the life of England itself, for were Elizabeth to die as Philip's ships bore down upon our coast, God knows what might be the ending of that day's mischief."

Whilst Nicholas ate his heart out at what he had to undertake, and made clear his purpose to his companions, Don Cristóbal Lanuza was making his way to Antonia Ruiz's chamber.

His servant had told him of her meeting with Peregrine Grey, and had cowered away when he saw the latent fury in his master. The Marqués had no affection in his heart for Antonia, for he was wholly incapable of such emotions, but he regarded her as his property, and would tolerate no other man's attentions being paid to the girl whilst his interest in her lasted.

He strode quickly through the silent corridors, his black robe mingling with the mysterious shadows of night, and under the torches set on the walls, his eyes glowed fierce and bright with the rage in him.

He walked with fluid ease, despite his haste, as if he were tuned to some inner rhythm. He never made a clumsy movement, and the grace of his smallest gesture was a pleasure to the eye. In his tall, slender body was all the hauteur and dignity of his race, and in his heart, all the biting savagery of which man was capable.

A man comely to look upon, and terrible to understand. Shrewd, capable and completely without fear, he was tainted with a degeneracy which made his reputation a tarnished thing. He was brave and valorous and utterly decadent, wielding his sword with honour, and his thin, pliant stick with a viciousness which reduced him to the level of a brute.

His was not the impartial, fanatical cruelty of Philip, who burned and tortured the bodies of those who denied the faith he upheld so devotedly, in order to save their immortal souls. His was the highly personalised cruelty of one who satisfied his degraded appetites with no other justification than that it fulfilled an urgent need within him.

His servants feared him, and his companions were never wholly at ease in his company, for something in him set him apart from them. His exquisite manners never completely hid the animal in him, nor did the soft turn of phrase and gentle words he used entirely muffle the growl of the untamed monster in his heart. Yet the King had great affection for him, apparently blind to what others saw, welcoming him to Court, and showering untold favours upon him, and because of this royal patronage, none had ever dared to stand against him. Thus he grew stronger and more dangerous as the years went by.

When he entered Antonia's room, she sat up abruptly, still dazed by the much needed sleep which he had disturbed, but when she saw who it was who crossed the floor and lit a candle by her bedside, she came sharply awake, and despite her firmest efforts, began to tremble a little.

Don Cristóbal turned to look at her, standing in the uncertain, dancing light of the candle, one jewelled hand resting casually on his hip. In his other hand, a short cane flicked idly to and fro, and Antonia, bitterly familiar with the slender cane and what it could do, shivered as she drew back against the pillows.

The Marqués saw the movement, slight though it was, and his eyes narrowed.

" That is no way to welcome me," he said softly, " and this is not the first time this day you have shewn me discourtesy."

Antonia's lip quivered, and her huge grey eyes searched his face, her spirits sinking as she saw his expression. It was an unmistakable look, and her heart began to thud in cold dread.

"My lord . . . I . . . I . . . do not understand. I have not . . ."

"Oh, but you have." The Marqués moved a pace nearer to the bed, and his mouth curved in a smile of humourless mockery. "When I spoke to you this morning, you did not heed me."

"Sire . . . my—my—my lord . . . I—I . . . did not hear you."

Antonia tried to still the panic which threatened to overwhelm her. "I would not insult you so; this you must know."

Her terrified eyes moved involuntarily to his right hand, and in spite of his warning, she shrank back a little further.

"But I think you would." He was still frighteningly calm, none of the sick rage which so often shook him yet apparent. "I think you would, for is it not an insult to me that you exchange words, and more, with this English *perro* who speaks our tongue with such remarkable fluency?"

He took a final step to the bed, and her mouth dried unpleasantly for she saw no mercy in him, and the strange brightness of his lambent eyes gave clear warning of what was to come.

"My . . . my . . . lord—I—I do . . . do . . . not understand . . ."

He bent towards her, his free hand biting into her shoulder.

"You understand me well, Antonia," he said, and his voice was barely above a whisper. "I was told of your meeting with the Englishman, Grey. Of the words you exchanged with him, and of the caresses you bestowed upon him. Did you think I would not learn of this?"

He released her and she fell back against the pillows, stunned by the knowledge which was his, and desperately trying to conjure up the face of Peregrine to give her courage.

"You are mistaken, my lord," she began, when he slashed the stick hard across the bed.

"Do not lie to me, Antonia," he said, and now there was

145

some feeling under his words for all their softness. Now the layers of sophistication and control were beginning to peel away.

"You were seen, my dear; did you think you would not be? You and your English lover. And how long has this been going on? How long?"

He spat the last two words, and she flinched as he caught her arm between steely fingers. "I would have you tell me, *amada*, how long you have made sport of me by casting these languishing looks at this man. How long have you enjoyed his kisses, and made me look a fool?" The fingers bit deeper. "Well, Antonia; how long?"

She was only vaguely conscious of the pain he was inflicting by the pressure of his fingers, for under his terrifying gaze she had lost the momentary sense of comfort that the mention of Peregrine's name had brought to her.

She struggled to see in her mind's eye the warm, hazel eyes; the mouth which smiled in that special way for her, and the way his hair curled back from his brow, but she had lost him. She could not remember his face, nor the way he had held her in his arms, nor the strength and passion with which he had kissed her.

All she was conscious of was Don Cristóbal and his tiger's eyes, which burned into her like a sharp stab of pain; all she could remember was what had passed between them on other occasions, and now the agony of his fingers penetrated her stunned mind and she whimpered as his grip tightened.

"You will answer me, *querida*," he said, his voice dropping back to a whisper. "You will tell me what I want to know, and when you have made a clean confession, I will help you to purge yourself of your sins."

She made an effort to pull herself free from him, but his hold was like iron, and in her blind terror, she tried to deny her love for Peregrine, conscious, even as she did so, that her heart was crying out in condemnation of her cowardice.

Don Cristóbal listened to her stammered excuses and pleas, the same frightening half-smile on his lips, and when her voice

146

finally trailed off into stricken silence, he relaxed the hold on her arm and straightened up.

"You have been foolish, Antonia," he said, and something flickered greedily behind his eyes. "Foolish and wanton, my dear. You are greatly honoured that you have been chosen to serve my future wife, but you must learn that such privileges bring obligations with them. I must help you to see what those obligations are, and to ensure that in future you do not behave like a slut with this English pig."

Antonia shut her eyes tightly as she felt him strip the bed-covers away, and her heart cried out in voiceless agony to Peregrine for the help he was not there to give her.

# 8

By the following day, Peregrine and Greville had become reconciled to Rokeby's plan, and whilst not favouring such means to gain their ends, appreciated that the ends in question were of such importance that nothing else could be allowed to stand in their way.

During the morning Peregrine tried hard to catch a glimpse of Antonia. He had seen little of her for two days, but his urgent longing to hold her in his arms was only one reason for his concern. Loving her as he did, he had a heightened perception for things which affected her, and under the carefree and gay front which he assumed, he was bitterly conscious that something was very wrong with Antonia.

She was young; not more than eighteen, yet the sadness and knowledge in her eyes was frighteningly mature. He knew she was afraid, but since she would not talk of what troubled her, he was still not entirely certain of what it was that caused those flashes of panic in her clear grey eyes.

Certainly it was not the Lady Catalina, for he had seen the warm affectionate smiles the two women had exchanged, and knew Nicholas well enough to realise that he would not have lost his heart to a girl who was capable of terrorising another human being. It was unlikely to be the King, for he lived in a remote void, and was hardly to be expected to know the names of the ladies-in-waiting at Court, and certainly would not have had any dealings with them.

Peregrine's mouth became a thin line as his thoughts turned once more to the man whom he suspected as the author of this fear, and his eyes were hard.

From the first he had disliked Cristóbal Luis Lanuza, with a quick, instinctive revulsion which had nothing to do with intelligence or common sense. Something about the man had made Peregrine's hackles rise with all the involuntary fierceness of an animal which scented its enemy at hand. It was not the reaction of a cultured and civilised man, but the raw, basic instinct of the jungle, and Peregrine respected it.

Yet what could the Marqués do; here in the palace at Valladolid, in the very presence of the King? Antonia was Catalina de la Vega's lady-in-waiting, not a scullery maid. She was well protected and well cared for, and would have no cause to cross the path of the Marqués, save on a few occasions when the Court came together, yet when he had mentioned his name, her face had taken on a new pallor and there had been something in her eyes which had made him sick at heart.

Slowly Peregrine made his way to the long gallery. It was mid-afternoon, and the winds blew mercilessly outside the tall diamond-paned windows. Inside, servants had built high the four great fires which heated the gallery, and here the Court had gathered to pass away the hours until it made ready for the evening meal.

When Peregrine entered the gallery, he saw Nicholas and Greville at the far end, and began to wend his way towards them, but before he had gone many paces, he saw Antonia, standing a little behind Catalina who was engaged with one of Philip's chamberlains.

Quietly he went to Antonia's side, and with no fuss or commotion, drew her away to a seat running along one wall under the heavy oil-paintings which adorned the gallery. moment he said nothing, studying her face, colourless and pinched, with eyes pink and swollen from weeping, despite the light cosmetics she had used to conceal her grief.

At that moment he would have given all he possessed to have been alone with her. To have been able to take her slender body in his arms and whisper comfort in her ear and kiss the pain from her lovely mouth, but since there were at least a dozen people within earshot, he could not even stretch out his hand to cover hers in gentle reassurance.

She tried to smile at him, but the sadness in her was too deep, and he was filled with a sudden gust of primitive fury. He wanted to catch her by the shoulders and shake the truth from her so that he could put a quick end to the evil that beset his love. But all he could do was to look at her and use words to fight his battle.

" Antonia. You have been crying. What is wrong?"

He saw her swallow hard and brace herself as she began to lie to him.

" Nothing, Peregrine; it is nothing. I have a headache, no more."

He controlled himself with an effort, knowing that anger would not help him now.

" Antonia, *amada*; it is more than that. You would not cry for so small a reason, nor would your face be filled with such misery. Is it that you do not trust me, *querida*?"

" Oh, Peregrine, no!" He saw anxiety flare in her eyes and she half-raised her hand towards him, then let it fall to her lap again. " No, my lord, it is not that."

Grey cursed silently, and looked around again at the assembled nobles and their ladies, finely clad and immeasurably satisfied with themselves, and wished them all to perdition.

Then he glanced back at Antonia. " I asked you once before, Antonia, why you feared the Marqués de Avila y Manrique, and you would not answer me. Now I ask you that question again. Why are you afraid of him?"

He saw his thrust go home like the jab of a rapier and felt rage rise like a choler inside him. So, his instinct had been right. Whatever tore at the heart of Antonia had something to do with his infernal nobleman.

"Tell me," he said in a dead, expressionless voice. "I want to know, Antonia, and if you will not tell me, I shall ask him myself."

"No!" Despite the growing assembly, Antonia laid a quick hand on his wrist. "No, Peregrine, no! I beg you not to do this. If you have any feeling for me at all; do not do this."

With equal disregard for what might be seen by the sardonic and prying eyes of the Court, he covered her hand with his, but his mouth was still hard.

"Then tell me yourself," he said curtly. "For I will know the truth of this matter one way or the other. Is he your lover? Is that it? A jealous lover who has seen my love for you and resents it? Is this it, Antonia?"

She gave a stifled sob and rose to her feet, giving him one last agonised look as she stumbled back to Catalina's side, and with a bitter heart, Peregrine left the polished bench and threaded his way through the chattering crowds to Nicholas.

Rokeby saw his face and frowned a little, excusing himself to the small group of people to whom he had been speaking, and drawing Grey to one side.

"Peregrine? What is it?" The blue eyes were watchful. "What has happened?"

Grey's face was set in granite hard lines, and when he spoke it was in a voice both harsh and furious.

"I am sensible, my lord, to what is our task in Spain, and I am ready to obey your commands concerning the undertaking before us, but no longer will I tolerate the situation which exists between Antonia and Lanuza."

Nicholas drew a deep breath. "Situation? What situation is this, Peregrine?"

Grey shot him a quick glance. "I do not know: faith, I wish I did. I know only that Antonia is afraid. She is sick with fear, Nick, and when I look at her face I want to weep, but she will not tell me what is wrong."

Rokeby studied the emerald on his index finger and said

casually: "Why do you assume her distress is caused by Lanuza? Has she said that this is so?"

"Not in so many words, but by her evasions and lies, I know he is the one, and I will keep silent no longer. When Lanuza comes hence this day, I shall charge him with this and let my sword speak for me in my fury."

"You will do no such thing," said Rokeby curtly. "Our mission cannot be disturbed by quarrels of this nature. You came to Spain to save the Queen's life, not to make a fool of yourself over a woman. If Antonia is afraid as you say, then she has only to confide in Catalina. What can Lanuza do to the girl whilst she is under Catalina de la Vega's protection?"

Before Peregrine could answer, there was a slight commotion at the doors, and the throng moved aside leaving a passage through which Cristóbal Lanuza strode with his customary arrogance, followed by four of his men. He wore an elegant riding habit and tall boots of softest leather, and in his hand he held a whip which he swung gently back and forth. As he passed Antonia, he slashed the crop with careless unconcern against her skirts, not brothering to look at her ashen face as she shrank back from his path.

Nicholas felt Peregrine tense and caught his arm in a vice-like grip.

"Be still," he commanded in a whisper which was not to be disobeyed. "I forbid you to speak to this man; it is not the time for such an encounter."

Grey was white with rage, but Rokeby felt the first surge of his passion die, and after a moment or two, the Marqués strolled over to Rokeby and made him an ironic bow.

"Well, my lord," he drawled, casting a scornful glance in Peregrine's direction. "You must find time hangs heavily upon your hands. Doubtless you are anxious to know when the King intends to invade your homeland and return your stolen possessions to you."

Nicholas, returning the Marqués' bow, smiled blithely upon him and gave a light shrug.

"I am content to wait upon the King, my lord; I am in

no particular hurry, for your Court is a pleasant enough place to spend the time of waiting."

Don Cristóbal looked at him disdainfully, his thin lips barely concealing the sneer of contempt.

" Yes, doubtless you are not anxious to return to England, sire, for were you to do so, you would have to take up arms against your own countrymen."

Again Nicholas shrugged, and still his blue eyes were lazily amused. " And why not, my lord, for did they not take up arms against me when they stole from me my home and my fortune?"

Lanuza cocked an eyebrow. " Say you, my lord, that you will in truth fight with us when we land upon your shores? *Madre del Dios!*" He turned to laugh at his companions. " *Señores*; this will indeed be a sight to see, and I look forward to it with great interest." He turned back to Nicholas, apparently unaware of Peregrine's thunderous face. " And what weapon will you use, sire, to fight your own comrades? A club; an axe; a bludgeon? For there is no Englishman born who can handle a sword or rapier with skill."

Lanuza might just as well have drawn off one of his fine gloves of scented leather and slashed it across Nicholas's face, for the insult was no softer for being couched in words, but still Rokeby smiled benignly upon the Marqués.

" Alas, sire, I fear you may be right. I am conscious of my own lack of skill, practise though I may. Yet I hope perhaps that after a sojourn in Spain, where the true masters of the sword are to be found, I might improve sufficiently to defend my life." He cast a bland look over the Marqués. " Come, sire, you could aid me in this. What say you to a lesson in the art of swordsmanship, for I am told you are the ablest of Philip's blades? A contest with you would doubtless polish my poor endeavours and fit me to give assistance to your King when the time is come."

Lanuza was staring at Rokeby, his eyes narrowing, but when he saw that Nicholas was in earnest, his mouth moved in a faint, ugly smile.

"You would have me teach you something of my skill, Sir Nicholas?" The Marqués's long white fingers caressed the hilt of his sword with the gentle tenderness of a lover stroking the soft flesh of his mistress. "You wish to learn a little of the art of the *duelo* from me? Is this not a risk?"

Nicholas adjusted a fold in his cloak and laughed.

"For whom, my lord? No risk to you, for your ability is beyond question. And for me? Well, it is but a lesson after all; no more. What harm could come to me in your capable hands?"

Cristóbal's eyes were shining with some inner satisfaction, but his voice shewed nothing of the hate in him.

"And when shall we see the measure of your ability, Sir Nicholas? When may I have the privilege of testing your sword against mine?"

By now, those close at hand had grown still. For all the lightness of the tone of the two men, the intent behind the invitation and its acceptance was not misunderstood, and the quick whispers which had passed between those assembled had now died into a breathless silence.

"Why not now?" Nicholas's smile was still as untroubled as ever. "It is a dull afternoon, and we have several hours to kill. This gallery is long enough, my lord, for our purposes. What say you to my first lesson here and now?"

Lanuza's fingers unclasped the diamond fastening of his cloak, flinging it at one of his men as he nodded slowly.

"Why not indeed, my lord," he said softly. "Why not indeed?"

As Nicholas removed his own cloak, the crowds fell back, and Catalina and Antonia drawing nearer, paled a little as Don Cristóbal drew his sword from its sheath with one quick practised movement.

"*Dios!*" Catalina's voice was shaking. "He will kill Sir Nicholas, for none can match his skill. Antonia; we must stop this!"

But even as Catalina moved forward to protest, Rokeby drew his own sword and made his ceremonial bow to his adversary.

Now the long gallery was utterly still and silent. The length of the room had been cleared for the two men, and all were pressed back against the walls, waiting with eager eyes and bated breath for the destruction of this brash and impudent Englishman.

Suddenly the Marqués made a lightning move; a quick, expert slash of the steel which would have destroyed his opponent had that opponent been as inept as Rokeby had claimed to be, but even as the shining blade fell, Nicholas leapt aside with a speed and agility which drew a quick gasp of admiration from the crowd. A split second later his own sword struck down hard on Cristóbal's blade.

Wrenching his sword free, the Marqués met Nicholas's eyes for one startled, unbelieving moment; then his white teeth shewed in brief comprehension. Disliking Rokeby from the first, Lanuza had been delighted to have this opportunity of shewing him how a Spaniard used a sword, and further, he had grasped most readily the chance to inflict a wound, perhaps a fatal one, on this upstart for whom he had conceived so much ill-feeling.

Now, as he met Rokeby's sardonic gaze, belated understanding came to him. Rokeby needed no lessons in swordsmanship. The Englishman had enticed him into this duel for exactly the same motives as he himself had acquiesced in such a course, and gripping the hilt of his sword, the Marqués smiled grimly as he abandoned the proposed lesson and prepared to fight.

Lanuza's grace and superb control stood him in good stead, and he had a sinewy right arm, most strenuously tutored in the art of the duel, but Nicholas was more than a match for him. As light on his feet as a cat, Rokeby's reactions were as swift as the mind which controlled his sword arm, and when he struck, it was with a deadly, remorseless strength which caused his opponent to stagger more than once.

The Court watched in dazed awe. It was certainly a lesson, but the master was not the favoured Marqués, for he had nothing to teach this man who had pleaded lack of polish and experience.

Nicholas moved like quicksilver, first to the left, then to the right, jabbing and feinting and parrying the Marqués's thrusts. He took risks which made the crowd catch its breath in horror, and made Catalina's hand fasten on Antonia's wrist in quick panic, but just when it seemed that he could no longer avoid the nemesis of cold steel, he twisted away in a movement so swift and elegant, that the Marqués was left cutting through empty air and looking a trifle foolish in the process.

If Nicholas had set out to ridicule Cristóbal Lanuza, he could not have chosen a better way, for the Marqués was the acknowledged maestro of the sword, and Rokeby had reduced his reputation to naught in a matter of some ten minutes.

Peregrine watched with sour triumph. He envied Nicholas his ability, for it would have salved and soothed the anger in him to have been the one to make a mock of the Spaniard, but he knew he had none of the brilliance which made it possible for Rokeby to achieve his ends. Instead he had to be content with watching the Marqués publicly stripped of his pride, and made to look a fool.

When Rokeby, moving so fast that even Peregrine did not see the stroke coming, spun Cristóbal's sword out of his hand and sent it hurtling the full length of the gallery, Grey saw the expression on the Marqués's face. For one brief, terrible moment there was a look of such concentrated hatred and fury on Lanuza's face that Peregrine felt his heart leap.

Nicholas might have won his duel, but equally his success could well prove to be a Pyrrhic victory, for in defeating the Marqués de Avila y Manrique, he had rendered his own life less valuable than the merest speck of dust.

When Lanuza sent a message to Antonia commanding her presence in his chamber that night, she felt a numb hopelessness creep over her. Like Peregrine, she had rejoiced with fierce gladness over the reduction of Don Cristóbal, and although she had not seen the look he had cast upon Rokeby, she knew that there would be a dear price to pay for his defeat.

She wondered momentarily whether she dared to seek

Peregrine's help. Whether she could go to him and confess her relationship with Don Cristóbal which made her feel degraded and unclean, but even as she considered the idea, she dismissed it. There was no future for her love for Peregrine, no matter what his courage and determination might be. It was a doomed and cursed thing, for once he learned that she was not the innocent maiden he believed her to be, but the plaything of a man who had not hesitated for a moment to possess her, he would turn from her in disgust, and that look of gentle devotion which she loved so much to see in his eyes, would be gone for ever.

She thought again about turning to Catalina for aid, but, as on previous occasions, could not bring herself to burden her mistress with a secret such as this, nor to sully Catalina's ears with the details of Don Cristóbal's unpleasant practices. And since there were none to whom she felt able to turn for help, she had no choice but to obey the Marqués's orders, and when the palace had settled down to sleep, she went slowly to his chamber and entered with leaden feet to face what was to come.

The outer chamber was empty, but as she closed the door behind her she saw the inner doors were slightly open, and on drawing closer, heard the Marqués engaged in conversation with two of his men.

Don Cristóbal's voice was low, but he bit off the words with such crisp, concentrated venom that none were lost to Antonia as she hid behind the door, and she felt her palms grow damp with apprehension as she listened to his spite.

" Miguel, this man must be destroyed. I will not tolerate his presence at Court so much as one day more. You know his chamber?"

Miguel Alcalá's gruff voice gave Don Cristóbal the assurance he needed, and the Marqués said coldly:

" Then when you are sure he is sleeping, you will enter his chamber. You have the knife; the one you took from the man Grey?"

Again Alcalá assented and the Marqués gave a terse laugh.

"Then plunge it hard into his back, Miguel, and let us be done with this *bastardo*. Let his blood cleanse the shame I have suffered this day."

"My lord, will there not be questions?" It was Carlos Gomez who spoke, his voice unsteady with the fear he had of his master, and of what his present plan might bring about.

"Oh there will be questions," agreed Lanuza, and his tone was grimly satisfied. "But those questions will be laid at the door of Peregrine Grey, not at mine."

"But will they believe this, sire?" Gomez was unconvinced and his voice pleaded for reassurance. "Why should West kill Rokeby, for he is his friend?"

"They quarrelled," said the Marqués smoothly. "Over a woman. Grey is known to have succumbed to the charms of Antonia Ruiz; Rokeby was jealous and so they argued as to whom should claim her."

"But, sire," Gomez sounded bemused. "Sir Nicholas has shewn no interest in the girl Ruiz. I do not understand for . . ."

"No, indeed he has not," said the Marqués curtly, "for he seems more interested in Catalina de la Vega, but this fact has been observed by few I fancy. And Antonia Ruiz will confirm my story, for she will tell those who ask her that she was plagued both by Rokeby and Grey, and will assure her questioners that she feared their anger would turn to violence."

"And she will say this, my lord?" Alcalá sounded doubtful, but Lanuza laughed again. A low, ugly sound which made Antonia stiffen with fear.

"She will say this, and all else that I tell her to say. Have no fear of this, for I have already sent for the girl, and when she comes, I will instruct her in what she has to do. Have no fear, Miguel, I am well versed in tuition such as this."

As he began to repeat his instructions to his men to ensure that they understood the parts they had to play, Antonia crept soundlessly from the chamber and when she had reached the safety of the corridor, her legs were trembling so that they could scarcely support her. With characteristic thoroughness, the Marqués had found a way to rid himself of Sir Nicholas, who had made him the laughing stock of the Court, and of Peregrine, who had dared to love her whilst she was still desired by Lanuza. Antonia put a shaking hand to her mouth, wondering whether to take refuge in her room, or to seek asylum in some hidden corner of the palace. Then she straightened her shoulders as some of her courage returned to her. She could do neither, for she could not run away from this duty which had been thrust upon her. Not only was Rokeby's life at stake, but also Peregrine's, and their only chance of survival was a warning before Miguel Alcalá set forth on his errand of death.

She reached Rokeby's chamber without meeting anyone and when she tapped on the door, he answered immediately, rising to his feet as she came into the room.

Since a visit to a man's room, unaccompanied and at night, was so foreign to the nature of the strictly-raised Spanish women, Nicholas hardly needed to look at Antonia's face to know that something was seriously wrong, and he wasted little time with conventional courtesies as he came forward to meet her.

" My lord . . . my lord . . ." she began, and could not go on.

Rokeby took her hands in his, and although they did not make her tremble with delight as Peregrine's did, they were cool and strong and comforting and she clung to them as she blurted out the conversation she had overheard.

Rokeby's fingers tightened over hers.

" You have much courage, *Señorita* Antonia," he said quietly, " and I thank you for coming to tell me this. I thank you also in Peregrine's name. He will be proud of you for what you have done."

" But what can you do, my lord? How can you escape Don Cristóbal's anger, for if Miguel Alcalá should fail this night, Don Cristóbal will try again."

Nicholas smiled down at the frightened girl and she saw no trace of fear or concern in him. Rather, he seemed amused as if he welcomed the opportunity of another bout with the Marqués.

159

"Do not worry, *querida*," he commanded gently. "I will deal with Alcalá when he comes."

She hesitated, for it seemed foolish to warn one as strong and able as Rokeby, yet somehow she managed to put into words her fear for his safety.

"Miguel is dangerous, my lord; very dangerous, and he uses his knife with skill. He has killed many men this way, and it is for this reason that Don Cristóbal keeps him by his side."

Nicholas released her hands and a moment later a slim knife lay on the palm of his right hand, winking with malicious satisfaction in the candlelight.

"It was made for me by a Spaniard," said Nicholas considering it reflectively. "It is a beautiful thing; balanced to perfection, with an edge so sharp that even the air seems severed as it cuts through it. It is fitting, *Señorita* Antonia, that I should protect myself against the onslaught of a Spaniard with a blade of fine Toledo steel. I hope he will appreciate its quality, and savour the justice of its bite as I plunge it into his heart."

Antonia swallowed convulsively, but the blade had vanished as quickly as it had appeared, and Nicholas took her arm and led her back to the door.

"You must not be found here," he said quietly. "You have taken enough risks for me already. Go back to your chamber and lock the door."

"But I cannot for Don Crist . . ." She broke off in a panic, fearing she had said too much, but he affected not to hear her words, repeating his order in a firm voice which left no room for arguments.

"Lock your door, and stay within your room this night, no matter what may come. And Antonia," he caught her shoulders and turned her to face him, "I do not know what it is which troubles you so, nor will I try to force secrets from you which you do not even feel able to entrust to Peregrine, but I would say this to you. No matter what it is, and no matter whom is involved, when you are ready to seek aid, my sword

160

is at your disposal. For you, I would use it, most readily and with right good will. Remember this."

When Carlos Gomez reported the discovery of Miguel Alcalá's body in the woods beyond the Palace, Don Cristóbal's face whitened and he raged like a wild beast. The control which normally veiled his naked violence was completely shattered, and for five minutes Gomez shrank back against the wall and shivered under the intensity of the Marques's passion.

When the fury died away, Lanuza sent Gomez for three of his other men, questioning them closely as to any who could have overheard his instructions to Alcalá, for he knew Miguel to be silent of foot and swift of action and only if Rokeby had been waiting for him, could Alcalá have failed.

When one man, stammering a little under the Marqués's piercing gaze, confessed that he had seen Antonia Ruiz hurry away from his master's chamber the night before, but had not waited to see which direction she took, Don Cristóbal flung himself into a chair and closed his eyes.

"Yes, of course," he murmured, half to himself. "Of course, for the girl did not come to me last night as she was ordered. I received word that the King required my presence, and I forgot that I had sent for her. Of course, I should have known. She must have come to the outer room and heard me speak with Alcalá, and then run like a scared rabbit to warn Rokeby of my intent."

His men watched him cautiously. True, the first black anger had now passed off, and his voice was calm and controlled, but there was a fine line of perspiration on his brow, and his fingers were clenching and unclenching convulsively on the arm of the chair.

"Shall I fetch the girl, sire?" ventured one man finally. "Will you question her?"

Don Cristóbal closed his eyes again and after a moment said softly:

"No, Domingo, no. I will not question her, but there will be others who will. She shall be punished for what she has done, but not by me, for I am tired of the girl, and would be done with her. She no longer affords me amusement, and thus I will rid myself of her in a way which none can question."

They watched, still half-tearful, knowing that under that deadly calm some devilish scheme was brewing, and when Don Cristóbal rose to his feet and crossed to the desk, they waited in hushed silence for him to unfold his plan.

Quickly he unlocked a drawer, taking from it a packet of letters, some pamphlets and a small book which he thrust into the hands of Domingo de Mañara.

" Domingo. See that these papers are hidden amongst the belongings of the girl Ruiz. Hide them well, for I do not want her to find them; this pleasure I reserve for others. Do it now, for I want no delay in this matter."

De Mañara glanced down at the papers and when he saw what they were, he paled in renewed fright.

" Dios, my lord! These are . . ."

" Those are pieces of evidence," said Don Cristóbal calmly. " Evidence that Antonio Ruiz works against the faith which she professes to embrace. Take them, and conceal them well, Domingo, for when the Holy Office sends its emissaries to search, I want them to find them undisturbed.

With that he left the room, flinging on his cloak as he went, and calling to his groom to saddle his horse, and in a few moments he was riding through the palace gates as if the devil were at his heels.

When he reached the offices of the Inquisitorial Council which adjoined the *casas santras* in the centre of the town, he was immediately shewn into the sparsely furnished chamber of the Grand Inquisitor of Valladolid, a tall, gaunt, Dominican, with a yellowed face and heavily lidded eyes of inscrutable darkness.

Their courtesies exchanged, the monk, Father Bernardo Almirez, indicated a stout wooden chair in front of his table, and the Marqués sank into it with his casual, easy grace.

The patricians of the Court of Spain were fervent upholders of the Inquisition, and fought eagerly for the privilege of becoming familiars of the Holy Office, none more anxiously than the Marqués de Avila y Manrique. Don Cristóbal had served the Holy Office well, and had been recklessly generous in the payments he had lavished upon its officers for the furtherance of their work, and since he was also a close companion of the King, he was held in high regard and respect by those placed in charge of the Holy Office at Valladolid.

Dom Bernardo listened carefully to the Marqués's words, and since Cristóbal's voice was filled with hushed concern and regret at his findings, he shook his head sadly as the Marqués finished his tale.

"And so you see, Dom Bernardo, it is important that the girl should be removed from the palace with speed and discretion. His Majesty is most anxious that this matter should not be made public, and in this he does me much honour, for he is thinking of my future wife, Catalina de la Vega, who is served by this wretched creature who spurns the Holy Church in this lamentable fashion."

The monk nodded gravely. "It is a serious charge, Don Cristóbal," he said slowly, "and we must investigate it well. Perhaps in a week or two . . ."

"No!" The Marqués's voice took on a sharp note and the Dominican looked up quickly, startled by the violence he heard behind that single word.

"No," repeated Don Cristóbal, controlling himself as he saw the surprise in his host's eyes. "Not in a week or two, Father, for this is not the King's wish. Now, at once. He wants the girl taken, no later than tomorrow, tried and punished before the week is out."

Dom Bernardo's brows came slowly together, and he rubbed his chin thoughtfully.

"Punished, my lord? But what if she is innocent?"

"She is not," said the Marqués shortly. "I would not have wasted your time, Father, had I any doubts at all. She is guilty, as you will find, and she must be dealt with swiftly and with prudence. What date is fixed for the *auto-da-fé*?"

Dom Bernardo hesitated; there was something about the Marqués's manner which made him uneasy. This man was powerful and rich, and had the ear of the King, and even officers of the Inquisition had been known to fall foul of the monarch over matters of faith, and none were so safe and secure that they could afford to quarrel with the King.

"At the end of the week," he said finally. "In five days time, but that is a public gathering, my lord, and you said . . ."

"It matters not once her guilt is proven. She will be dealt with then." Don Cristóbal rose to his feet. "You will take her tomorrow, and this will give you time to question her and satisfy yourself that she is guilty as I say. Bid your men search her chamber well, Father, for you will need evidence. Then, when you are thus convinced, she can be dealt with with the others who have fallen so far from grace."

Dom Bernardo stood up, and for a moment his gnarled fingers touched the crucifix fastened to the rope around his waist.

"Are you acquainted with this girl, my lord?" he asked quietly. "Do you know her well?"

Don Cristóbal fastened his cloak, and his eyes were cool and untroubled.

"Not well, Dom Bernardo; not well. I have seen her for, as I say, she serves the *Señorita* Catalina, but I know no more about her than this. That is, of course, until this sad tale was brought to me and I had cause to investigate its validity." He bowed low. "And now I must return, but I pray you to lose no time, nor to forget that I bring the King's express orders to you in this matter."

He turned to the door, and Dom Bernardo sank back in his chair, still rubbing his chin with a worried hand.

He had held this office for some years, and was markedly successful in the manner he filled it. He had been responsible for bringing many suspects to a proper understanding of the faith, but something about this case troubled him greatly.

He was not a man who liked to be rushed. He preferred to work slowly and painstakingly, ensuring that the man or woman brought before him was given every chance of answering the questions posed, and had every chance of repenting of their sins and making peace with God before bending to the punishment meted out for the salvation of their souls.

Sometimes this resulted in the suspect being confined in the holy house as long as two years, but this was of little concern to the Inquisitor General, for whilst the prisoner lay helpless in captivity, every fact and rumour could be sifted and the truth laid bare before sentence was passed.

To take a woman, question her, pass judgement upon her and consign her to the flames within a space of five days was unheard of, and Dom Bernardo wriggled uncomfortably inside his harsh black robes. But even as he fidgeted uneasily in his chair, he knew that he would have no choice. It did not occur to him for a moment that the order had not come from the King, and even if he had realised that the mischief was one born solely in the tortuous mind of Cristóbal Lanuza, it is doubtful whether it would have altered his decision, for he could neither risk angering the Marqués, nor could he shew any shred of compassion or leniency for one accused of heresy, for were he to do that, his own life would be inevitably forfeit.

When Catalina de la Vega found Antonia was missing, she sent servants to search in all the likely places her lady-in-waiting might be found. When they returned to her with hands raised in helpless defeat, she frowned a little, but did not begin to worry immediately. She had seen the sadness and anxiety in Antonia's face and wondered if she had sought refuge in a quiet corner in the servants' quarters, there to compose herself and seek respite from whatever it was which troubled her so. After two days, however, when there was still no sign of Antonia, Catalina grew really concerned, and when she encountered the Marqués in the long gallery, she made it her business to question him, for it occurred to her that Don Cristóbal might well know what had become of Antonia.

The Marqués, kissing her hand with gentle lips, gave a faint exclamation of dismay when she posed her question, and raised a self-condemning hand to his head.

" *Dios*, Catalina; yes, of course. I crave your forgiveness. I should have told you. The girl came to me two days ago with a tale of illness in her family. She begged me to seek the King's permission for her to leave the palace to visit her aunt who lives a few miles from here. Alas, *querida*, I forgot to mention it to you. How stupid of me to be so forgetful."

Catalina was watching the Marqués's face with unblinking eyes. Behind the self-reproach and expression of contrition, she read something else; something hard, cold and exulting and her heart missed a beat. What could he have done with Antonia? How could he have taken her from the palace without a soul knowing? She drew a deep breath, and gave him a straight look.

" I did not know Antonia had a family near Valladolid, my lord. She has never mentioned it to me, and if she sought leave to visit a sick aunt, why did she not come to me? Why to you, Don Cristóbal?"

He shrugged idly. " Who knows, *querida*, how a woman's mind works? Perhaps she thought I had readier access to the King."

" The King would scarcely be concerned with the absence of one of my ladies-in-waiting," said Catalina sharply, her anger rising as the conviction that the Marqués was lying grew stronger.

" But he would be concerned in this instance, my dear, since he appointed Antonia Ruiz himself to care for you. Come, you make too much of this. The girl is well enough, and will be back in a day or two."

" I do not believe you," snapped Catalina, and saw the spurt of anger in his eyes. " You are lying to me, my lord. Why? Where is Antonia Ruiz? What have you done with her?"

" You dare to say this to me? You accuse me of lying?"

He caught her wrist and she felt the rage running through his finger tips, but she kept her voice icily calm and met his angry eyes with contempt.

" Take your hand from my arm, my lord," she said steadily.

"I am not Antonia Ruiz; I am Don Fernando de la Vega's daughter, and a ward of the King. I pray you not to forget this."

Lanuza's mouth curled in fury, but after a moment he gave a harsh laugh and withdrew his hand.

"And soon you will be my wife," he reminded her softly, "and then, my dear, you will learn not to address me in that tone of voice."

"Do you think so?" Catalina's wrist was aching, but she did not glance down at it. Instead she held the Marqués's eyes locked with her own, and her voice grew colder still.

"You may not find it so easy to terrorise me, sire, nor is our marriage as certain as you think."

"Oh?" The Marqués was suave, his anger muffled beneath the quiet monosyllable. "Why do you say this, *señorita*? All is settled; only the day has to be named."

"I may not name it at all, my lord," she said, refusing to back down under his menace.

"You will not be asked to do so," he returned smoothly, and now his manner was calm again. "For that is the privilege of the King, and I have already made known my wishes in this matter." He smiled unpleasantly. "His Majesty has been gracious enough to agree to my suggestion. We shall be married in two weeks' time, before I sail for England. You would do well, Catalina, to make your preparations accordingly, and to remember that before long, you will be answerable to me, and not to the King."

Catalina choked down her ire and tried not to let her voice betray her.

"But still you have not answered my question, *señor*. Where is Antonia Ruiz? What has happened to her?"

The Marqués let his eyes flicker over her in a calculating and insulting fashion; then his lips moved in the faintest of smiles.

"I had hoped to spare you, my dear," he said lightly, "but, alas, if you persist in questioning me, I have no choice but to impart the truth to you, unhappy though it may be."

Catalina felt a sudden shiver, and now her eyes were frightened.

The Marqués saw the fear in her and his smile deepened.

"Yes, I regret, my dear, that Antonia Ruiz has been taken to the headquarters of the Inquisitorial Council, there to answer questions concerning certain evil practises against the Church. He shrugged in regret. "I am afraid you must face it realistically, Catalina. You will not see the girl again, for she is clearly guilty."

Catalina was staring at him in horror. "Guilty? Of heresy? Is this what you are saying? My lord, you cannot mean this! No one is more devout and pious than Antonia. This cannot be; there has been a mistake; a terrible mistake. My lord, you must make them see that . . ."

"There was no mistake." Cristóbal was relishing her distress, and the tawny eyes shone with unbridled pleasure. "The representatives of the Holy Office found evidence; irrefutable evidence, my dear. No, clearly the girl has sinned greatly, and will be punished accordingly."

And with that he made a low bow and left her, smiling coldly and in satisfaction as he made his way to the King, there to make the final arrangements for his marriage to Catalina de la Vega.

# 9

ANTONIA RUIZ crouched against one wall of her small, dark cell, her spirit broken, her eyes dull with pain. It was doubtful, in that moment, as she looked up at the dim ray of light falling through the grating at the top of the tiny square dungeon, whether she had any true cognisance of the circumstances which had revived the most dreaded organisation the civilized world had ever known; the Sanctum Officium, or Holy Office, which was popularly called the Holy Inquisition. The terrible scourge of the Middle Ages, which had once again stretched out its cold, fearful fingers to chill the blood of mankind.

It was unlikely, as she shivered and felt her heart thud in cold dread, that she remembered the start of the new reign of sacred terror in Spain which had now held men locked in fear for over a century.

She was more conscious of the seeping cold and the scuffling of the rats, than of an understanding of the rebirth of the system which now had her firmly grasped in its sorrowful, un-relenting arms.

It was in 1477 that Cardinal Pedro Gonsalez de Mendoza, then Archbishop of Seville, had first tried to re-kindle the Inquisition as a method of keeping the Catholic faith pure from the taint of the Jew and Infidel. He had met with opposition; much opposition, for one of the outcomes of his obsessive plan was the confiscation of the property of those who had worked against the Archbishop's proposals. But Isabella and Ferdinand, seeing in it not only a way of upholding Catholicism in such a manner that its stability was ensured, but also a way of reducing the power of the nobility and enriching the royal coffers at the same time, nodded approval, and gave their support to Mendoza's plan, and so, in Seville in the year 1481, the *Inquisicion Suprema* had first seen the light of day.

In 1478, Isabella and Ferdinand, in their determination to see the Inquisition succeed in its mission, appointed Fray Tomás de Torquemada as the first Grand Inquisitor.

Prior of the Dominican Convent at Segovia, and Father-confessor to the Archbishop, Torquemada had been a worthy pioneer in the work of keeping pure and unsullied the Catholic faith. He had grasped his opportunities with eager hands, scarcely stopping to sleep or eat as he pursued his path of devastation through the land.

He had no less than two hundred familiars, mostly noblemen, and a strong guard of fifty soldiers to watch over him, but all his food, meagre though it was, was thrice checked by a venom taster, for he had no illusions as to his popularity, and spent the latter years of his life in fearful expectation of a sudden and violent death.

The Inquisition had flourished, as was to be expected. Any court of law, be it sacred or secular, which was born of fear and raised in bloodshed, was assured of success, for the secrecy and dread with which it surrounded itself made everyone its slave.

No one was safe. One never knew from day to day when there would be a rap on the door which heralded the *familiare* of the Holy Office. There was no warning and no redress, and one never knew one's accusers. There was a certain inevitability about the manner of the working of the Office which bred a frozen defeat in men, even before the icy hand of the Inquisition had reached out to touch its latest victim on his quivering shoulder.

The *casas santras*, the Inquisition's prisons, had grown in number, and although the supreme tribunal had its head-quarters in Madrid, many off-shoots and branches had sprung up, and gradually the destructive weed of religious fanaticism had spread like a sick decay over the land.

But Antonia had had no time to recall these things, for her bewildered mind could only absorb the stunning blow which had befallen her, and as she watched a grey rat burrowing hastily back into its hole in the corner of the cell, she tried to remember again exactly what had happened that night when she had heard the quick, decisive knock upon her door.

She could remember fastening her robe about her, and taking a candle in her hand; she could feel again the coldness of the handle of the door as she turned it, and the sudden chill premonition which had cut through her like a knife as she opened the door and found herself confronted by two noblemen accompanied by four guards in bold, resplendent uniforms.

She could remember the quietness of the corridor, in shadow save for the two flares held in the guards' hands, and she could remember the silence splintering into a thousand fragments as the elder of the two men spoke.

" In the name of the Inquisition," he had said, and Antonia had felt the strength drain from her, her mouth opening in disbelief as she stared at him. She knew these men. The elder was Don Rafael de Reyna of Toledo; the younger, the Conde de Ibanez, Don Antonio Diaz.

The Conde was young, not more than twenty years, and his face was composed and stern above the fine linen ruff, held rigidly in position by the pickadils of silver cloth on the edge of his upstanding collar. His cloak was black, its heavy folds half-concealing a velvet doublet with peascod belly and ties of silver and gold cord.

In contrast his companion, Don Rafael, was a stout, florid man, nearing his sixtieth year, his bulk majestically filling the violet brocade doublet, and providing a broad shoulder from which to hang the Dutch cloak of matching purple and silver.

His face was deeply tanned and lined against the goffered ruff, and his small blue eyes were at once condemning and worried as he stared at Antonia in hostile silence.

She had been oddly aware of every detail of their elaborate dress as they stood there in the quiet darkness. Of the bom-basted, paned trunk-hose of Don Rafael, and the tightly fitting cannions of purple brocade which clung like a second skin to his solid thighs. She could almost feel the delicate crispness of the Conde's hand-ruffs of finely made lace, spilling over falling-bands of silver cloth, and the great, glowing ruby which he wore on his slender forefinger.

That moment had seemed a very long one, but finally Don Rafael cleared his throat and repeated the dread words in a slightly louder voice.

"We have come," he said gravely, "in the name of the Holy Inquisition, and we require you to accompany us to the *palacio inquisidor*, to answer some questions, for certain accusations have been made against you."

Antonia's face had felt stiff, and for a moment it had been difficult to breathe, but finally her dry lips parted and she managed to answer him.

"My ... my ... my lord? *Señor* ... accused ... of what? And by whom?"

Don Rafael frowned quickly, and Antonia had taken it as a mark of his anger that she should presume to question his authority, but, in fact, for once the nobleman was out of countenance.

Normally he found a certain smug satisfaction in his work as a familiar of the Holy Office, and was untiring in his efforts to preserve the *sangre limpia*, and to bring to a sense of their failings those who had sinned against the law of the Church. But in this instance he had been uneasy from the beginning. All those now assembled in the *casas santras* in the centre of the town, had been there for many weeks; some indeed for several months. They had been most thoroughly questioned and investigated. The most refined tortures had established their respective shades of guilt, and now they awaited their various punishments at the *auto-da-fé* which was to take place in a few days' time.

But this girl; this slim, lovely creature who stared at him with the innocent eyes of a child. There was to be no such preparation for her. True she may have sinned, and thus might require a measure of corrective treatment to make her see the error of her ways, but in fact her fate had already been decided, and he felt a small murmur of distaste worrying at his conscience, for she would have no time to repent and reflect upon her transgressions in the way that her fellow prisoners had had.

He had not been told a great deal by Dom Bernardo, but even as the ageing Dominican had given him his instructions, he had been aware of a similar reluctance in the Superior. Furthermore, he had heard odd rumours; quiet, wary whispers which had filtered through the barriers of secrecy which seemed to be building up about this girl. A murmur of the King's personal intervention, and a hint of the name of Cristóbal Lanuza. Rafael de Reyna did not like the Marqués, sharing the other grandees' unexplained distaste for this man who walked closely with the King, but whose name caused men's eyes to fall in discreet withdrawal.

Yet the grip of fear which the Inquisition had upon men was too strong, and Don Rafael had dismissed his uneasiness with a brisk shrug and gave his curt orders to the guards.

Antonia stirred a little on the hard wooden bench which was the only furnishing in the cell, and pressed shaking fingers against her temples. That had only been the beginning. A frightening beginning, but only the start of the real ordeal to come.

She had spent the remainder of that night in the tiny box of a prison, her stupefied mind hardly able to comprehend what had happened to her. She had prayed to God, and to the Blessed Virgin, for their aid and had thought longingly about Peregrine, wondering if he had been told of what had taken place.

When dawn's pearl-white fingers stole slyly through the

grating overhead, she heard the rasp of a bolt being drawn and through a small aperture, a piece of coarse bread and a mug of water had been passed to her, but she could not swallow, and put the food aside for the rats to gnaw upon in their rabid hunger.

The time seemed to pass with unbelievable slowness, but, in fact, in obedience to the commands of the Marqués, Dom Bernardo wasted no time, and sent for Antonia as the hour of ten struck.

She was taken to the *audiencia* by two stalwart guards with faces like the masks of the dead, and as the wide doors of the chamber were flung open, she somehow managed to force her legs to carry her to the centre of the room where the soldiers held her fast.

It was a wide, empty chamber with high barred windows and a stone-flagged floor. Along one wall, a table was placed, covered by a cloth of black which reached to the ground, and behind it sat Dom Bernardo in his black and white habit, flanked by two *calificadores*, three scholarly looking notaries, who were shuffling their papers about in leisurely fashion, and a sharp-eyed secretary, who was neatly trimming his quill with a small curved knife, and who paused in his task to cast a quick but penetrating glance at Antonia.

There were candles on the table, next to a white bone crucifix and a Bible, and on the wall behind Dom Bernardo's head was a large wooden cross. On either side of the room the Inquisitorial guards stood stiffly at attention, their faces blank and impassive under the glare of the torches fastened in iron brackets above their heads.

It seemed to Antonia as though she had already reached hell, for the atmosphere was as chill and menacing as the grave itself. She tried to moisten her lips, but her mouth was too dry, and she felt a wave of faintness pass over her as Dom Bernardo finally raised a hand and beckoned her closer.

She made an attempt to concentrate on what he was saying but her alarm made it difficult. She heard him, but could hardly understand the accusations which had been made against her, and although she tried to speak, the words would not come to her defence.

Dom Bernardo looked at her severely, and his mouth turned down forbiddingly.

"Come, come, girl," he chided bleakly. "Have you no answer? You have been accused of practises contrary to the teaching of the Church; of sedition and heresy, and of consorting with Jews and Infidels. Furthermore." He frowned and his voice grew graver. "There is evidence before us that you have corrupted the minds of others with boasts of miracles, and have claimed to have power of life and death over other souls which belong to Mother Church."

"No!" Finally Antonia managed to get the denial through her ashen lips. "No, no! Father, this not true . . . not true. I have done nothing . . . nothing . . ."

Dom Bernardo rapped sharply on the table with a bony knuckle.

"We have proof," he reminded her tersely. "We have the list of those whom you have met; a note of remedies and false cures with which you have blinded the reason of those unfortunates who have sought your aid, and this book, which is the work of the Devil, and most strictly forbidden to the children of the Church." He picked up the book and regarded it with acute disfavour.

"But they are not mine." Antonia tried to take a step nearer to the table, the better to convince the sceptical friar, but the grip on her arms tightened. "Father, they are not mine; I swear, they are not mine!"

"They were found amongst your possessions," he said coldly. "Hidden, 'tis true, but they were there. If they are not yours, how is it they were found in your room?"

"I . . . I . . . I . . . do not know. I cannot explain this, but Father, I am innocent. I have never once said a single word, nor committed one act, against the Church. I have not practised evil, nor spoken it, but have been faithful in my prayers and diligent in my duty to God."

Dom Bernardo shook his head regretfully and glanced at his companions.

"Good Fathers," he said sadly. "This unhappy child is not penitent, and is unwilling to make a full confession of her sins. She will not admit her guilt, but adds contumacy and defiance to her other trangressions. What are we to do?"

The plump friar on Dom Bernardo's left shrugged. "There is no help for it, Father. We must aid her and enable her to see the path of hell which is stretching before her. We must try to save her soul, though she resists us to the last. It is our duty to wrestle with the devils in this girl and to drive them out, for 'tis clear to me that she is a witch, and has been possessed by Lucifer for his own black purposes."

"No!" Antonia's voice rose in panic. "No! No! It is not true; I am not a witch. I have done nothing . . . nothing. Oh, Reverend Fathers, believe me . . . good sires . . . heed my words, for I do not lie. I have been truly devout and faithful to my Church. I have prayed for guidance from the Blessed Virgin, and made my confession regularly. I have not spoken one false word, nor done one act which was against the teaching of the Holy Father. Oh, I beg you; hear me . . . hear me . . ."

The monk on Dom Bernardo's right compressed his lips and stared at her with hostility.

"She lies," he said in a hoarse, grating voice. "The girl is lying; that is obvious. But Dom Pablo is right; we must not shirk the duties laid upon us. It is for us to save her from her sins and wrest this soul back from Satan's grasp. Thus, Father, let her be questioned under torture that we may drive the devils from her body and send her soul clean and pure into God's hands."

Antonia gave a little moan and sagged in the guards' hold, but as they dragged her forward and tied her to the wooden bench in front of the table, she had no strength to resist them, nor could she muster any further words to fight off the blanket of despair which was smothering her. She was dimly conscious of the bite of the ropes on her wrists and ankles and the rough hands of the soldiers as they ripped open her gown, but the room was swimming round in a strange, misty fashion as a tall black-robed figure came slowly towards her and bent to lay one cold hand upon her shoulder.

Two days later she had been dragged before the tribunal once again, but this time the guards had to carry her, for she was too weak to walk by herself and needed their strong arms to support her as her mind, now painfully lucid, absorbed with wild disbelief Dom Bernardo's strictures as he pronounced sentence upon her.

" It is now clear, my child," he said sadly, " that the devil still has a hold upon you, for despite our efforts, you have not confessed your guilt, nor sworn to abjure the works of darkness. There is no choice left to us, for you have thrust away mercy and charity and have wrapped round you the cloak of darkness and evil. Thus, you are condemned to die at the stake, nor will the mercy of the garrotte be yours, for you have shewn yourself unfitted for such clemency. The purity of the fire shall cleanse you of the base wickedness in which your body is clothed, and thus will your soul be released from the prison of sinful flesh which you have fashioned for it."

He made a brief sign of the cross, and dismissed her, and she was taken back to the cell, there to await the terrible salvation meted out to her.

Now she moved her head a little, and watched the light dying through the meagre grating above. It was hard to believe, and still harder to understand, but at last a kind of hopeless resignation was beginning to overcome her, and she no longer screamed inside at the outrageous injustice which had been done, nor pressed herself violently against the cold stone floor, praying aloud to a God she had once worshipped with loving faith, and who now, with incomprehensible indifference, had turned away from her in her hour of need.

She just sat on the bench, her face turned to the damp stone walls and watched the rats running about like dark shadows in the corners. She could no longer think of God, or of death, and even less of life, and of Peregrine. Her body was one aching, throbbing bruise, but she hardly felt the pain any longer, for the mortification of her flesh had dulled her senses, and she simply lay still against the wall, waiting numbly for death. Death which would come in the guise of a blessing, with the fierce roar of flames licking amongst the sulphur-soaked timbers to ease her torment.

Whilst Antonia resigned herself to death, Peregrine grew increasingly frantic as he tried to find her. Forced to conceal his anxiety and interest, it had been difficult to question the servants, and impossible to gain access to Antonia's companions, and so the terrible days of uncertainty had passed in slow torture until finally he could stand the agony no longer and sought the ear of Catalina de la Vega.

He met her in the gardens, accompanied by her ladies-in-waiting and by a small escort of guards, but when she saw Peregrine, her colour faded a little and she signalled to her companions to remain where they were, whilst she moved slowly forward to Peregrine's side.

For a long minute they looked at one another without speaking, then Peregrine said quietly:

"You know where she is, do you not? You know where Antonia is. If you have any pity in you, Lady Catalina; tell me. For the love of God, tell me! Where is she?"

Catalina did not shirk the pain in his eyes, nor did she attempt to conceal the wound she had to inflict upon him, but for a moment her small hand hesitated as if to rest upon his arm in comfort.

"She has been taken," she said in a whisper. "The Inquisition has taken her and . . . and . . . she is held as its prisoner."

He heard the tears in her voice, but violent shock made him rough and he had no time to comfort her. Catalina's words had momentarily drained the strength from him, but now his anger burned him to life again.

"The Inquisition? What are you saying? Why should the Holy Office seek her. She has done no ill; you must be mistaken."

Catalina shook her head. "No, Don Peregrine, I would to

178

God there were some error, but it is not so. She was taken five nights ago, without warning and without reason. I know no more than that, save that she is held in the holy house at the Inquisitor General's Palace."

"But have you not tried to obtain her release?" Grey was curt, and his eyes were coldly furious. "Have you done nothing? Have you simply stood by and let them . . . let them . . ."

"No." Catalina was not angry, for she understood his bitterness and grieved for him. "I have talked to the King myself. I went to him when I learned what had happened, for he is the highest authority I could reach."

"And what did he say? Did he promise you his aid? If so, why is Antonia still held? In the name of Heaven, *señorita*; why, why?"

"The King would not help me," said Catalina in a toneless voice. "I begged him; I pleaded with him to intervene, but he said it was not within his power, and he could do nothing. Then I tried the Archbishop, but he would not even listen to me, and chided me for my interference."

"But why did you not tell me?" Peregrine checked the savage fury in him, and gripped the hilt of his sword hard to prevent himself taking Catalina by the throat and shaking the life out of her. "In God's name, girl, why did you not tell me?"

Catalina's lashes fell, and he saw the sparkle of tears on them.

"What could you have done, Don Peregrine? What can you do now? Nothing. We are all helpless in the hands of the Holy Office."

"Be damned to the Holy Office," he snapped and gave her a look of pure hatred. "I will do something about it, and without delay. If you are content to accept its dictum without a murmer, I am not. Your pardon *señorita*."

And with that he turned on his heel and left her to cry quietly and unseen into her small scented handkerchief.

When he arrived in the town, he found it thronged with

excited people milling, pushing and shouting to one another as they thrust their way forward. Finally, bewildered by the obvious purpose of the mob's passage, he stopped a man and enquired what the commotion was about, and why so many had gathered in the town that day. The man stared at him in astonishment, then grinned and shook his head.

"You must be a stranger, *señor*, for all who live here know that this is the day of the *auto-da-fé*. For weeks now the flag of the Holy Office has flown over the Inquisitor's Palace to give warning of this occasion, and now the time has come for the procession, and for the fire to be lit in the *quemadero*."

"The *quemadero*?" Peregrine's voice was suddenly very quiet. "The place of burning?"

"That is so, *señor*." The man tipped his hat back on his head and chuckled. "But before the final burnings, there will be the lesser punishments to watch, for some have recanted and made their peace with God and with Dom Bernardo. For them there will be the lash, and the sentence of banishment, or a term in the galleys, but when these are done, then, *señor*; then comes the burning!"

Peregrine reeled away from him like a drunken man, and pushing against the crowds, made his way to the nearest church where he enquired about the *casas santras* and the prisoners. It took him some time to reach the prison, and when he did, he found a few guards on duty, for the condemned and accused had already left and were even now making their way to the *plaza*, where the judgements were to be pronounced and the sentences carried out.

He fought like one possessed to get through the thickening crowds, but it was a losing battle, for all were impatient and greedy to witness this spectacle, and none were willing to give way to this man who tried to thrust his way past them, a violent oath on his lips.

Finally he reached a flight of steps leading to one of the *palacios* near the square, and took them three at a time, lurching desperately to the balcony to try to locate the procession.

At last he saw it; like a long, sinuous snake, it wound its

way towards the square below him, accompanied by the sound of trumpets and the muffled note of the slow drum. He saw the white banner overhead, and the brilliant robes of the familiars; the line of soberly clad *calificadores*, followed by members of King Philip's Court, and the more notable of the clergy.

His hands gripped the stone edge of the balcony until his palms were raw, and he felt his heart thud with the frightening roar of thunder in his ears.

Then he saw the prisoners. A sad little column of men and women wearing the *sanbenito* and *corazo* of shame. Some had the Cross of St. Andrew painted on their yellow scapulars to indicate that they had repented, but others had heads of devils amongst the flames on the breast and back of the *sanbenito* which meant that they were to be consumed by fire whilst still alive.

In front of the prisoners who still clung grimly to life were the coffins of those who had died in sin, and whose remains were to be purified on the bonfire of righteousness, and with them were the effigies of those who had been wise enough and lucky enough to escape from the ruthless hand of the Church's implacable justice and mercy.

Just as Peregrine was about to turn away to make one more effort to force his way through the press, he caught sight of Antonia. She moved very slowly and had to be aided by one of the guards, and her long blonde hair, now matted and discoloured, fell over her cheeks as her head bent beneath the weight of the tall cone-like cap which denoted her disgrace.

Her saffron-coloured tabard boasted no Cross of St. Andrew, but flaunted devils and flames which spoke of her continued defiance, and for a moment Grey thought he was going to faint.

With an effort, he thrust down his all absorbing fear, and rushed down the steps to try to reach her. But he was too far away, and too many people stood between him and the procession, and fight as he might, he could not shift the solid bulk of roaring, screaming, hating humanity which lusted for the sight of the blood of the cowering victims.

He pushed and kicked and beat with his fists, but he was hemmed in, and found himself thrust first this way and then that, but never nearer to the procession. The world had become a black nightmare and he could not think or speak or feel. He could only fight and strike helplessly with his hands whilst he felt time slipping away from him as frenzy raced through the endless corridors of his mind.

Finally he found himself on the edge of the crowd again, but as he tried to force his way back into it, a man rounded on him in snarling anger and struck hard at him. Grey fell backwards, hitting his head on a nearby wall, and all the noise and horror was wiped out in a single, brief second.

When he regained consciousness, he had no idea how long he had lain by the wall. He could still hear the shouting and the cries of the excited crowd, but now the trumpets were silent and the drums had stopped. He groped to his feet, holding his aching head and trying to stop the world spinning round him in helpless chaos, and when his vision had cleared sufficiently, he staggered forward and began to circle unsteadily round the crowd.

Now the people were on the move again, and he mingled with them in their jostling, not realising where his steps were taking him until he suddenly became aware of a strange acrid smell in his nostrils. Even then, the truth did not dawn upon him until he glanced up and saw the pall of smoke rising into the clear air a short distance away.

He heard himself cry out, and now nothing could stop him.

He fought his way like a madman through the mob, now strangely quiet and absorbed, and after a minute or two, reached the front ranks which were held back by the civil guards who had taken over from the officials of the Inquisition, for once the time came for the execution of the sentences, the Church primly washed her hands of the matter and left the secular arm to carry out the work for which she accepted no responsibility.

Peregrine raised his eyes, blank and unbelieving, to the pile of faggots and kindling, and saw the greedy flames curling their avid fingers round the smouldering wood. Slowly his gaze moved upwards, and the roar in his ears grew louder and louder as he saw Antonia's slight body chained to the stake in the centre of the pyre. Her long hair was now brushed over her shoulder, falling down her back like a cloud of tangled silk, and as he watched in paralysed silence, he saw a yellow tongue of fire reach up and suck the end of her tresses into its rapacious mouth. Her eyes were open, and despite the smoke which was now beginning to obscure her face, he saw her pallor and the look of blind helpless fear which made her look like a small, trapped animal.

He tried to move, but his limbs would not obey him, and he tried to shout, but his tongue was locked between teeth clenched hard down. He saw the smoke thicken and grow darker, and was dimly aware that the crackle of the fire was growing fiercer as the pall of grey mist burned suddenly orange bright as it caught the thick sulphur smears alight.

He could hear screaming, but he did not know whether the cries came from Antonia, or from his own aching throat. He tried to cover his ears with his shaking hands to shut out the awful sounds, but they hung like deadened lumps by his side and gave him no succour. He felt himself sway, and hoped that death had come to claim him, but just as his senses began to slip from him, he felt an arm go round him with iron strength, and a voice cut through his numb horror, thrusting demandingly into his stunned brain.

"Peregrine!" Nicholas Rokeby, his face white and tense, gave Grey a little shake. "Peregrine! Can you hear me? Peregrine!"

Grey staggered and would have fallen, but now Greville West was at his other side, and between them, Rokeby and West managed to draw Grey away from the assembled on-lookers.

He tried to fight them off, but he had no power of resistance left, and as he was forced into the saddle by a grim-faced Rokeby, he could only mumble in a slurred undertone the same words over and over again.

" They are burning Antonia . . . they are burning Antonia. They are burning her . . . they are burning Antonia . . . Antonia . . . Antonia . . ."

That night Rokeby took Margarita de la Vega from her chamber. He had planned to wait a little longer, but the death of Antonia Ruiz had forced his hand, for he feared for Peregrine's sanity if left in Spain too long.

Peregrine had lain for some hours in a coma, but when he arose from his bed, he was coldly sane and icily remote. Wisely, Rokeby made no attempt to comfort him, nor to plague him with words of sympathy. Instead, he merely told him in a calm matter-of-fact voice what he proposed to do, and then went off to make final arrangements with Jacob Blount, leaving Greville West to keep a wary eye on Peregrine's set face.

When Nicholas entered the child's chamber that evening, she was alone, for he had awaited the moment when her maid-servant had slipped out to get her nightly meal. He stole quietly to the bed and looked down at the small face, endearingly like her sister's, and for a moment his mouth twisted in self-disgust. Then he put a gentle hand on Margarita's shoulder and laid a soft finger on the child's lips as she started awake.

" Sweet love," he whispered. " Do not cry out or be afraid, for there is naught for you to fear. I have come to take you away from here, but I will not harm you, and no ill shall befall you."

Margarita's sightless eyes were now wide open, and one small hand groped towards his face. For a moment he allowed the butterfly fingers to explore the contours of his cheek and brow; then he kissed the little hand and held it tightly in his.

" Come, moppet," he murmured, and pulled her dressing-robe from the end of the bed. " Come, and do not be afraid."

Margarita smiled suddenly, and again Rokeby saw the likeness of Catalina and felt his heart contract.

" I am not afraid," she said, " for I can feel you are a kind man. Your cheek is gentle and your mouth is good. Why do you take me? Is this a dream I am having?"

Nicholas laughed a little and wrapped her warmly in the robe, lifting her into his arms and holding her closely to him.

"Perhaps it is, *niña*; perhaps it is. Can you believe this for a while? Can you pretend that you are a princess; an *infanta* who is being rescued from a dragon by a prince?"

Margarita nodded vigorously. "I can pretend that," she said eagerly, "for Catalina read me such a tale not long ago. The prince was a handsome one. You are handsome, *señor*; this I know, for my fingers tell me so."

"Then we have all that we need to contrive a romance," he said, and moved silently towards the door, "but we must make no sound, *querida*, for now we leave the safety of the princess's chamber for the dark woods outside. Can you be as silent as a mouse; as still as an owl on a branch of a tree? Can you hold your breath in muteness, little one?"

Margarita nodded and clung to him with two small determined hands. "I can," she breathed in his ear. "I can, *señor*, but hold me tightly."

"I will, dear one," he assured her as he closed the door behind him. "I will hold you most tightly, love."

When he reached his own room, Jacob was waiting for him, and Margarita was ceremoniously but quietly introduced to him. Now thoroughly awake and entering into the spirit of her nocturnal adventure, Margarita cuddled into Jacob's arms as he slipped down the servants' staircase to the side door, and Rokeby, his smile fading, went to the desk and began to write a note to Catalina de la Vega.

When her ladies told her of Margarita's disappearance, Catalina nearly fainted. By now she had learned of Antonia's end, for Don Cristóbal with an unerring sense of cruelty had regaled her with each last detail, and in her sudden panic, Catalina, with illogical fear, had associated her sister's disappearance with that of Antonia's.

She managed to control herself, for a public display of emotion was not a luxury which her strict upbringing had permitted, and when she had taken a sip of the wine which one of her women had rushed to get her, she began to ask, in a voice commendably calm, what steps had been taken to find Margarita.

That day the palace was in an uproar, for the loss of a child of Don Fernando de la Vega's was a very different thing from the abduction of a lady-in-waiting, and the King's servants and guards scoured the palace and grounds with great thoroughness, questioning all, and leaving no stone unturned in their efforts to satisfy the King's peremptory commands.

But by evening, none had seen her, nor found the slightest clue to the child's whereabouts, and Catalina's face grew paler and more drawn as each long hour passed by. She retired to her room at nine, only Luisa by her side, for she could bear no other company, and together they sat by the fireplace, hardly able to meet each other's eye. Then Catalina rose and picked up her missal from the table by her bed, murmuring something about further prayers to the Holy Mother, but as she took the book in her hand, a paper fell from between the pages and fluttered to the carpet at her feet.

Slowly she picked it up, opening the folded note and reading it with widening eyes of fear.

"Luisa!" Her voice was like the harshness of tearing silk. and Luisa came quickly to her side and took her arm.

"*Querida?* What is it? What is wrong?"

"This note . . . Luisa . . . it is from the man who has taken Margarita."

Luisa paled, but she patted Catalina's arm encouragingly.

"Do not be afraid," she whispered. "I will call the guard, and we will . . ."

"No!" Catalina's fingers were frantic on hers. "No! You must not call the guard, for this note warns us that if any should be told of this, Margarita will die. Be still, Luisa, and listen."

In silence Luisa listened whilst Catalina read the note aloud, and when she had finished, the maid said hesitantly:

"He bids you to meet him tonight, at twelve, in the chapel of Santa Maria. *Señorita*, you . . . you cannot . . . you cannot go alone as he commands you. It is not safe; he might kill you."

"If I do not obey, he will certainly kill Margarita, for this he makes plain."

Catalina folded the note and tore it into shreds. Then she turned to look at Luisa.

"Luisa, you have served me most faithfully and well, and I owe you much. Will you now give me your aid once more in this, the most difficult thing I shall ever ask of you? Will you help me to get to the chapel of Santa Maria this night? Will you help me to do this, and thus save Margarita's life?"

Luisa began to cry, but even as the tears rolled down her plump red cheeks, she was nodding and holding Catalina's hand tightly in hers.

"I will help you, *querida*," she said and her hand was warm and solid over Catalina's cold fingers. "Never fear; I will help you."

And she was as good as her word, for by eleven, she had managed to procure the brown habit of a friar and had smuggled it to Catalina's chamber.

Catalina's face lightened. "How clever you are, Luisa, for this is the perfect disguise. If any should now see me on my way to the chapel, it would cause no surprise, for where else would a Brother go, but to the chapel to pray for peace to bless his sleep."

At eleven-thirty, Luisa managed to create a small diversion by engaging in conversation the guards on duty in the corridor, leaving Catalina free to slip noiselessly down the back stairway and into the garden.

The night was crisp and cold, and she was glad of her enveloping robes as she hurried along the terrace and down to the lawns. It seemed a very long way to the chapel, and by the time she reached its door, midnight was already striking from the clock in the small steeple overhead.

The chapel was deserted and strangely peaceful, lit only by two branches of candles on the high altar, and she closed the doors apprehensively behind her, taking quick, tentative steps down the aisle.

Before she had gone half-way, she heard a faint sound and whirled round, and there in the gloom, saw another robed figure, tall and dark and frightening as it moved from the pew to stand before her.

"You need go no further," it said, and the voice was muffled in the hood which shrouded its face. "This is far enough. Now sit here, for we have a bargain to make."

She found herself sitting on a pew, and felt the man slip into the seat behind her.

"Do not turn your head," he said in the same muted whisper, "for if you do, you will find that I have gone, and your sister will be lost to you for ever."

Obediently she sat staring straight in front of her, her heart beating rapidly and her hands damp with fear, but she managed to speak with the same rigid control which had come to her aid earlier that day.

"My . . . my sister? She is well? You have not harmed her?"

"She is both safe and well, and I will not harm one hair of her head, provided you do as I bid you."

Catalina relaxed a fraction and felt a wash of relief flood over her.

"I will . . . will do as you wish," she promised, trying to stop her voice trembling. "What is it you want? Money, jewels? I have both. You may have what you want; merely tell me what you need."

"Information." The man stirred a little in the seat behind her. "I want neither gold nor gems, for these I have."

"Information?" Catalina almost turned her head, but just in time remembered his warning, and forced herself to concentrate on the altar cross. "What information do you need, señor?"

"A name. No more. Just a name." The whisper grew a little louder. "I want to know the name of the man the King of Spain has sent to England to kill Elizabeth. Tell me this, and your sister is safe. Refuse me, and she will die."

Catalina felt her heart pounding unbearably, and the altar was tilting oddly as if it were falling, but somehow she managed to sit still and retain her self-control.

"I . . . I . . . cannot . . . cannot . . . tell you this; I do not know." Her voice was not so steady now, and he heard the agony of indecision in her whisper.

"You know." He was cold and determined. "And I too will know, or your sister will die. If you keep silent and refuse to tell me this man's name, I will kill the child, but slowly and without mercy, so that her death will be a lingering torment."

Then Catalina gave a whimper of pain. All the years of training and tuition could not stifle that one small cry, and Nicholas cursed soundlessly and bowed his head in the darknes, loathing himself and the cruel circumstances which forced him to torture this girl so brutally.

"Tell me," he repeated finally, for love her though he might, he remembered with painful clarity his own words to Peregrine, and had no choice but to abide by the rules he had himself decreed. The Queen's life was at stake, and that could be his only concern.

"If . . . if . . . I tell you . . ." Catalina's voice was hardly audible, but it was filled with such hopelessness that Nicholas felt physically sick. "If I tell you, will you release Margarita? Will you return her to me?"

"Immediately." He waited tensely, wondering fleetingly why she hesitated to save her sister's life by withholding this unknown agent's name for even one second, but before he could dwell on this, she began to speak again.

"He is my brother," she said softly, and he knew instinctively that she was crying although it was too dark to see her face. "Manuel de la Vega, but in England he is not known thus. In England he has another name. He is called Dyke; John Dyke."

She rose suddenly, half stumbling over the long robes as she fled down the aisle to the door, and Nicholas slumped back against the pew, thrusting the hood from his face and holding his head in his hands. Then, after a moment, when he dared wait no longer, he rose stiffly to his feet and made his way back to the palace, there to set about the destruction of Manuel de la Vega, and thus putting from him for ever the chance of gaining the love of the girl who held his heart in thrall.

# IO

Nicholas returned to his chamber where Peregrine Grey and Greville West awaited him, and flung off his borrowed habit with an irritable hand.

West saw the unusual whiteness of his face and glanced at Peregrine, but Grey was slumped back in his chair, turning an empty goblet round and round in his hands, apparently unaware of the tension which Rokeby had brought with him.

Greville moved to the table, pouring wine into a silver beaker and handing it to Rokeby, his eyes perturbed.

" Drink this, Nick, for by the faith, you look as though you had seen the devil."

Rokeby nodded his thanks and downed the wine in one gulp.

" Perhaps I have," he said, and even Peregrine glanced up as he heard the note in Rokeby's voice.

" What is it, Nicholas?" Instinctively West adjusted the hilt of his sword, for he scented trouble. " In what guise have you met Satan?"

Rokeby gave a bleak smile. " Perhaps it would be more accurate to say that I have uncovered one of the tricks he plays upon mortals. One of the malicious little ironies he designs to destroy man's soul and plunge him into the sulphur pit where everlasting damnation awaits him. Give me more wine,

Greville, for perhaps this will stiffen my courage for the task I have to do."

With a worried glance, West obeyed, and Nicholas relaxed a fraction as he saw Peregrine's eyes upon him. For the first time since he and West had brought Peregrine back from the *quemadero*, there was a semblance of an expression in his eyes. At first they had been blank and sightless like a blind man's, and later, when he had risen from his bed, they had been cold and expressionless, but now Rokeby saw the first flicker of something, and controlling his own despair, he gave Grey a warm smile.

"'Twill not be long now, Peregrine, and we can return to England, for now I know what I came to discover. Now I have learned the name of the man who threatens the life of the Queen."

West turned quickly. "Nick! It succeeded? You know the man? Who is it? De Vere? Blandford?" He took a pace forward, gripping the beaker as if to snap it in two. "Nick?"

"It is Dyke." Rokeby took the wine from West, but shewed none of his regret, for this was not the time for it. "But this is not the jest the devil held in store for me." He smiled, but now the smile was not warm, but coldly bitter. "Oh no; 'tis a far merrier joke than this."

Peregrine stirred slightly in his chair, yet still he said nothing, but West caught Rokeby's arm and said sharply:

"Nicholas! Speak plainly. What jest is there in this?"

Rokeby took a thoughtful sip of wine and met West's eyes over the rim of the goblet.

"His true name is Manuel de la Vega," he said quietly. "Catalina's brother. That is what I forced from her when I threatened to kill the child. That is the prize I have earned myself by my endeavours. A rich irony, do you not agree?"

West released his arm, his face stunned, but Peregrine rose from his chair and came to Nicholas's side.

"We must return to England," he said quietly, "and without delay. Have you made arrangements for our passage? Will the ship be ready when we reach the coast?"

Rokeby nodded, and despite his inner anguish, felt a spasm of relief at the calmness of Peregrine's tone.

"It will be ready," he said. "For Jacob has done all that is needful. The horses will be brought to the small copse beyond the west gate of the palace tonight; there is nothing to hold us now, and we have work to do in England."

"You will go straight to London?" Peregrine was watching Rokeby carefully. "You will ride to Westminster to give Lord Burghley the news?"

For a moment there was a pause, then Nicholas looked into Peregrine's eyes and slowly shook his head.

"No, I shall not do this. I shall go to Blandon Point and send a message to Manuel de la Vega, ordering him to come to Devon without delay. I shall tell him I have further instructions from King Philip, and I shall tell him also that his sister is with me and that if he does not heed my words, her life may be endangered."

Peregrine frowned. "You will send for him? But why? Why do you not unmask this man without delay? What is the point of bringing him to Devon, when Whitehall has so well furnished a dungeon ready for such a man?"

Rokeby was silent for a moment, then he said softly:

"That is exactly the point, Peregrine. If I reveal his true identity to my lord Burghley, he will not be content with taking his life to secure Her Majesty's safety. He will want more information, more facts, more names. And, as you say, Whitehall's dungeons are well equipped for extracting such details."

"Nick!" West sounded a trifle breathless. "You do not think to let this man go? You will not aid his escape?"

Rokeby's mouth twisted slightly. "No, this I will not do, but I will give him a swift and clean death. This much I will do for Catalina, for now 'tis the only way in which I can serve her."

Peregrine's face was suddenly white and drawn, and Rokeby winced at the look in his eyes.

"It is more than the King of Spain was prepared to do for his own subjects," he said bitterly, "for he shewed no spark of mercy or compassion when an innocent girl was wrongly accused."

"Would you have me behave so?" asked Nicholas gently. "Please God, Peregrine, the manner of my life has not led me to such depths. Well I understand your anger and your hatred, but I beg you to allow me this one indulgence. I have lost Catalina as surely as you have lost Antonia, though in a less fearful fashion, for whilst I take her to England with me as a surety of Don Manuel's obedience, I shall merely hold her prisoner. I cannot hope for her forgiveness for what I must do to her brother."

Peregrine looked at Nicholas and for the first time since Antonia's death, he smiled slightly.

"I think you are unduly fearful, Nick," he said, and the note of affection was in his voice again. "She will be sorrowful and will grieve for her brother, and, at first, she will blame you for this, but if she is in love, and I believe she is, then in the end, nothing else will matter."

Rokeby raised his hands helplessly. "I do not know, Peregrine; I pray to God that you are right, but I dare not hope. That is a risk I am afraid to take."

"What of the child?" asked West suddenly. "Where is she now?"

Nicholas laughed, some of his worry leaving him. "She is with Jacob and greatly enjoying herself, for Jacob has discovered in himself a hidden talent. A gift for making a world of magic for a child's delight, and will not be parted from his infant for a single moment."

"And she is not afraid?" West still looked a trifle concerned, but Nicholas chuckled again.

"She is not in the least afraid, for she has much courage that little one; as much as her sister." His voice softened. "No, she is revelling in each moment as she dictates Jacob's every move, demanding of him a new tale of wonder each hour. He is in truth her prisoner, and her slave; you need have no fear for her, Greville."

"And the Lady Catalina?" Greville looked soberly at

Rokeby. " You can weave no such wonderland for her, Nick. How will you get her to come with us? And must you take her? Her brother will not know that your claim is untrue, and in any event, if your message purports to be from the King, he will come in any case." He frowned. " It is a risk to take them to England. Can you not leave Catalina here?"

" To marry the Marqués de Avila y Manrique?" It was Peregrine who answered him, and now the venom and rage was back in his voice. " God, Greville, would you condemn the girl to this? I would not consign the meanest bond-woman to that creature who calls himself a man, but who is completely without soul or spark of godliness. For it is he who brought about Antonia's death; of this I am sure. It was said by the officers at the prison when I questioned them that evidence had been found in her chamber. Evidence which proved her a heretic. She was not a heretic. She was true; humbly devoted to her Church and to God, and if evidence was found, it was hidden there by some other hand. And I know whose hand that was."

His eyes were blazing. " No; you are right, Nicholas. You must take Catalina away from this barbarian, but I crave one boon from you before we go."

Nicholas bit his lip and his eyes were troubled.

" No, Peregrine," he said finally. " I know what boon it is that you seek; but no. There is no time now, but your opportunity will come, for we shall meet again; Cristóbal Lanuza and I. We are not yet finished with the dons, Peregrine; this is only the beginning. Soon Philip will send the ships from his harbours like a flock of vultures to swoop upon our fair shores, but we shall be waiting for them, and then . . ." He caught Peregrine's shoulder. " Then, my friend, you may give your answer to this man who stole the most precious part of your life away."

West rubbed a thoughtful hand over his brow. " Nick, you have learned the name of the man sent to Court, but what news of the Armada? Has any word reached you of the time at which it will sail?"

"I cannot be certain." Rokeby shook his head. "At least not as to the exact date, but from my probings I have gleaned this much. The King has grown impatient for all his apparent calm, and has commanded the Duque de Medina Sidonia to make ready for his Enterprise at the beginning of next month." He grimaced. "We have little time, for April moves on apace, but it will be time enough."

"You have still not said how you hope to persuade Catalina to accompany us," reminded Greville. "Since she does not yet know the identity of the man she met in the chapel, she may well incline an ear when you seek to speak with her, but when she finds what your purpose is, she will not listen further."

"I shall tell her 'twas me." Nicholas was definite, and his companions saw a new hardness in him. "I would have told her then, but she rushed from the chapel before I could say more to her. But now I shall tell her, and if she will not come willingly, then I shall take her by force."

"This will not be easy," said Peregrine musingly. "The palace is still abuzz that the child has not been found, and new searches are made every hour. How are we to encompass this, Nick, without the forfeit of our lives?"

"By the same method as before." Rokeby's lips thinned. "What succeeded once, can succeed again. I shall send her a note, commanding her to silence, and requiring her to meet me once again in the chapel, there to have her sister restored to her."

"It is a risk." West frowned. "What if she tells the guards? Or Lanuza, or even the King?"

"She will not do that." Rokeby was calmly confident. "I made clear to her the manner of Margarita's death should she disobey me. She will not have forgotten that."

Peregrine gave him a wry smile. "You have done little to endear yourself to the Lady Catalina, Nick."

"That I know," said Rokeby curtly. "But there is no choice left to me. When she comes to the chapel, I shall take her to the west gate, where you will meet me with the horses."

"And if we meet the guards?" West was pouring himself a much needed goblet of wine. "What of them?"

"We will kill them," said Nicholas coolly, "for there will be no time to stand upon ceremony, and our good English blades can put paid to the impudence of Spanish steel. Now come, we must get rest, for there is much for us to do this night, and Elizabeth's life is in our keeping. We must not put this most precious charge in hazard for lack of sleep. Get you to your rooms, sires, and fit yourselves for what lies ahead, for in this small moment of time, England's future rests in our most unworthy hands."

Catalina received the second note with mixed joy and apprehension. The promise of the return of Margarita made sudden hope leap into her eyes, but the manner of the proposed reunion filled her with fear.

She had waited all that night and morning for her sister to come back to her, and as each minute ticked away, her heart had grown heavier. She had paid a terrible price for the safety of the child. She had sacrificed Manuel's life to keep Margarita safe, and as each hour dragged on, it seemed that this sacrifice had been in vain.

She had had to school herself not to think of what she had done. She dared not let one thought of her beloved Manuel escape from her frozen mind, for were she to remember his gentleness to her and his grave good humour; his warm sympathy and the ready ear he bent to her girlish problems, and the way his eyes had smiled at her in loving reassurance, her heart would have broken beyond repair.

Despite her resolution she found herself wondering if Manuel would understand. Whether he would forgive her treachery and see that she had no choice. She tormented herself with speculating as to Manuel's decision had he been faced with a choice between her own life and that of Margarita's, and had to press her fingers to her lips to stop the sob that was rising in her throat.

Dimly she wondered who the man had been. She had not

recognised his voice, for it had been dull and muffled, and his habit had concealed his identity too well for her to hazard a guess as to who he was, but she had felt the determination and strength in him, and shivered a little as she sat watching the jewelled hands of the clock move slowly round the dial.

When Luisa came to her at the hour of three with the note concealed under her white apron, Catalina opened it with fingers which were unashamedly trembling, and once again the two women held each others' hands and prayed for strength to meet what lay ahead.

Finally midnight came again, and with horrifying repetition, Catalina slipped cautiously from the palace and made her way across the lawns to the chapel of Santa Maria, tucked secretly away behind the tall cypress trees.

The scene which met her eye was uncannily familiar. It was as dark and eerie as on the previous night, and the candles still burned upon the altar, as if time had stood still since she were last there. Slowly she began to walk down the aisle, pausing half-way, remembering the heart-stopping moment when she had heard the sound behind her on that other night, but when she found the stillness unbroken, she continued on her way and reached the chancel where the faint light of the candles made a small pool of brightness in the gloom.

It was then that she heard a slight movement, and every muscle in her body tensed as she peered helplessly into the shadows.

" *Señorita* Catalina."

The voice was quiet, but so unexpected that Catalina spun round with a cry she could not control, and as she stared at Rokeby, her eyes grew wider and more frightened.

" My . . . my . . . my lord," she managed finally. " What are you doing here? Why have you come hence at this hour?"

She glanced round quickly, half-expecting to see the cowled figure she had come to meet, fearful lest the presence of Rokeby were to drive him away.

" I have come to meet you," he said and watched the dis-

198

belief leap into her great dark eyes. "You received my note did you not?"

Catalina felt as if the world were slipping away, and one hand groped out to seek support but none was to be found, and he saw her sway slightly on her feet.

"Your . . . your note?" She was incredulous. "You sent me the note? The note about my sister? I . . . I . . . do not understand. How are you concerned in this matter? How did you know where my sister was?"

Nicholas kept his eyes blank and his hand gripped his sword. He longed to move forward and catch her in his arms and to whisper comfort and assurance in her ear. He wanted to kiss the unhappiness away from her beautiful mouth and to brush the shadows from her eyes, but all he did was to bow slightly and to raise one brow.

"Is that not obvious, madam? I took your sister. Thus, of a certainty, I know where she is."

"You . . . you . . . took her?" Catalina's whisper was lost in the shadows. "You took Margarita? But . . . but . . . why . . . why?"

"You gave me the answer last night," he returned in the same light tone. "It was not the answer I expected, but it was the one I wanted."

"But . . . but . . . why did you want to know this, *señor*? Why did you need to know that my brother had gone to England to . . . to . . ."

"To kill my Queen?" he finished, and now there was the slightest trace of emotion in his voice. "Because that is why I came to Spain, Lady Catalina. For that purpose and for no other, save perhaps to see how Philip's Enterprise was faring, for Sir Francis Drake is always interested in news of this."

He gave her a brief, unamused smile and moved a little nearer to her. "We knew, you see, that there was such a man at our Court, but we were not certain what manner of disguise he had adopted, and since Elizabeth would not suffer the innocent to be questioned, another way had to be found to unmask the man who sought her life. Thus, I came to Spain, for I know your country well, *señorita*, and I have had much to do with your people."

She saw the quality of his smile and shuddered. " I do . . . do . . . not understand. I still do not understand. You said you hated the Queen; that you wished her dead. Is this not true? Did you lie to me?"

" I lied," he agreed equably. " For I would lay down my life for Elizabeth. I would give everything I possessed to save her one moment of distress or worry, for she is not as your monarch, madam. She does not shroud herself in silence, closeted in a mausoleum where the light of day cannot find her, eschewing the company of men. She is alive and warm and vital, and her people love her; and she loves them. She loves them most dearly, for no matter what rumours may have reached you in Spain about our Queen, England is all that she lives for. It is her child, her lover, her heart's treasure and her eternal joy. To England she promised her life, and with England she has kept faith. There is no man who would not barter his soul to serve her, for she holds her subjects firm with a steadfastness and affection which Philip of Spain could not begin to comprehend."

She managed to reach a nearby pew and clung to the polished back with all her might.

" How did you dare to come?" she whispered. " How could you take such a chance; you, and your companions? You walked with death each moment you were here. You are still in mortal danger."

For a brief second their eyes met in complete and naked honesty; all the tragedies and problems fell away, as silently they acknowledged the truth in their hearts.

Nicholas ached to reach out and lay his hand upon her smooth cheek and to rest his lips on hers, and Catalina felt a sudden craving for the comfort of his arms about her, but slowly the precious, intimate moment faded, and Rokeby nodded.

" Perhaps, but danger is not new to me. I have met it

many times before, and, God willing, will meet it many times again."

"What did you mean when you said you knew my countrymen well?" She searched his face, trying to understand him. "Have you been here before?"

"Not to Valladolid, but to other places, particularly on your coast." He smiled suddenly, his white teeth bared in grim amusement. "On your coast, Lady Catalina, and on the decks of your galleons as I stripped them of their treasures. I had not had the pleasure of being in your Court before, but I have encountered your noblemen in many other places."

Catalina's hand tightened on the pew, and her eyes grew wider still.

"You are a pirate? An English pirate?" She half stumbled, but he made no move to touch her.

"A privateer," he corrected gently, "although possibly your seamen have another name for me."

"But . . . but . . . why were you not recognised?" She was bewildered. "There are many at Court at this time who sail the seas. Why did they not recognise you, if, as you say, you have encountered them in the past?"

He laughed gently and she saw the genuine amusement in him as he rubbed his cheek.

"I do not care to shew my face, *señorita*," he said softly, "and thus I cover it so none shall know me."

Catalina swallowed hard. "You . . . cover it? You . . . you mean you wear . . . a mask?" The fear in her was growing. "But . . . you . . . you . . . are not the man they call . . ."

"*El Espectro*." He gave another bow. "The very same, madam, and now we must dally here no longer."

"But Margarita?" She tried to thrust off the shock and disbelief his words had brought. "Where is my sister? You promised that she should be returned to me."

"And so she will be." He came to her side, and now he took her cold hands in his. "She is safe and well and entirely content; do not fear for her. But I cannot leave her here, nor can I leave you to the mercies of Don Cristóbal. Moreover, I need you in England, for there you may render me one last service."

He did not elaborate, but Catalina was hardly conscious of his last comment, for she was still trying to absorb the meaning of his first words.

" You . . . you want to take me to England?" Her hands were gripping his, although she was not aware of this, nor of the strength which his touch sent tingling through her veins. " But I cannot come to England, *señor*; I cannot. It is impossible."

" Nothing is impossible with me," he said, and she heard the depths of assurance in his voice which made her heart beat faster.

" I will not leave you here, for no matter what hazards you may face as we make our way to England, none could be so great as marriage with Cristóbal Lanuza. He killed Antonia Ruiz as surely as if his hands had fastened round her throat and choked the life from her. He would kill you just as certainly, but it would take longer; it would take a lifetime."

Again their eyes met in a strange, unspoken understanding.

" I will not let him destroy you, Catalina," said Nicholas and his voice was very low. " Though you will hate me until your life's end for what I have done, and what I still have to do, yet I will give you this one, most precious gift. I will give you your life, free of fear and hatred."

Suddenly she was aware that her hands were still in his, but she did not realise that as he spoke, her fingers held his the tighter.

" How can you do this, *señor*?" She did not try to assume an anger she did not feel, for if he had tricked her, it was because something stronger than life itself had forced him to do it, and she felt an odd calmness within her as she looked up at him.

He was no traitor, this man with eyes like azure jewels. He did not hate his Queen, nor wish her dead; he loved and revered her and had risked his life for her safety, and Catalina felt tears welling up behind her curling lashes. He was all that a man should be, this daring, impudent Englishman with the smile which made her heart contract in pain. He was bold and gay and courageous, but he was also kind and *compasivo* and he gave her a feeling of security she had never known before.

He was so different from Don Cristóbal that she felt it an insult to think of him in the same breath as her betrothed, yet for all the sudden, unexpected longing she felt within her, she did not forget that she was a Spanish grandee's daughter, and that her country was all but at war with England.

Slowly she withdrew her hands, and with a grave, unconscious dignity she held her head high and faced him with courage.

" I thank you, Don Nicholas," she said, and he recognised the quality of her valour with a small smile. " I am aware of the thought you would give to my welfare, and am grateful to you for what you would do, but what you suggest is not possible. Perhaps your Queen does hold her people's hearts more warmly than does my King, but, my lord, he is my King. For all his faults, he is my King. As you are loyal to your *reina*, so will I be true to my sovereign. I have delivered my brother's life into your hands, and for this I will never forgive myself, but I know what you have to do, and bear you no hatred for the task ahead of you. Manuel would have done no differently had he had to face the same decisions. But I cannot come with you, Sir Nicholas; I must stay here in Spain, for this is my home, and these are my people. And as for Don Cristóbal."

There was the slightest tremor in her voice.

" Perhaps he is a cruel man and a hard one, but he is also a man of outstanding courage and has served Spain's cause without hesitation. When I am his wife, I shall learn to accept the life he makes for me, and do not fear for me, for my situation is not as Antonia's. My father's name protects me, and Don Cristóbal will do me no harm."

" There are many sorts of harm." Nicholas looked down at her, and his smile had gone. " He may not use force as he used force on Antonia, but he will find other ways to make you suffer, for he is pitiless and without mercy. He will find a hundred ways to wound you, using words and silences to torture you as surely as he punished Antonia with his whip. No, Catalina, I do not give you a choice. I am not asking you to consider whether you will come with me; I am telling you of my decision, for this was made when I saw Antonia Ruiz chained to the stake, the flames tearing screams from her smouldering body."

He was deliberately brutal, and when she turned white and shrank back, he caught her in his arms.

"Yes, Catalina, you cringe away from my words, but you cannot undo the mischief done by closing your eyes and shutting your ears. I saw Antonia burnt to death, and I know why she died. She overheard Don Cristóbal plan my murder, and she had the courage to come and tell me of this. Thus, my life was saved, but hers I could not protect, for I was too slow and too witless to see what lay in the heart of this despicable creature you call a courageous man. He did not have the spirit to call me out, for he remembered our fencing lesson and its outcome. Instead, he took his revenge on a helpless girl, and condemned her to the most terrible of deaths to appease his anger and his ruffled pride.

"That damnable Castilian pride, Catalina. If I could ask God for only one concession; one gift alone to help me through this troubled life, then I would pray to Him for the blessing of humility, for I have seen what pride can do, and I want no part of it."

His arms tightened. "I have no more time to reason with you, Catalina," he said quietly. "For each moment that we linger here, the risk grows greater, not only for you and me, but for my Queen who dwells in danger whilst your brother lives. And since you will not come with me willingly then must I take you forcibly, and pray that one day you will find enough mercy in your heart to forgive what I do now."

And with that he swept her into his arms and strode the length of the chapel away from the candles' soft light, and into the darkness of the night.

They reached England without mishap towards the end of April, and Catalina, now united with Margarita, watched with awe as they rode through the countryside to Blandon Point.

Despite the harsh winds of March, spring had thrust its exuberant fingers through the chill earth to touch the fields and hedgerows with a greenness Catalina had not seen before. She had heard that England was a place of grey dampness, with no sun to warm the heart and to kiss the cheek to golden brown, but found to her surprise that this was not so. It was fresh and sparkling and verdant, like a paradise garden, and her eyes were like stars when Nicholas lifted her from her mount.

" Come," he said, and held out his arm. " Come, and welcome to my home, for this will be yours as long as you need it."

She laid her small hand tentatively on his, but her brow was puckered.

" My lord, I thank you, but . . . but . . ."

" But?" He led her towards the house and saw her attention stray and her lips part as she saw it standing defiantly atop the cliff face.

" It is called Monks' Walk," he said gently, " and you will find it contains all that is needful for your comfort."

She nodded, but then her frown returned. " I do not doubt this my lord, but . . . but . . ."

" But? What troubles you, Catalina? Do you not like my home? Does its aspect displease you, or is it that you fear to dwell in it with me?"

She blushed furiously and he laughed. " I have thought of that, *señorita*, and would not insult you by allowing you to stay here without the most severe of chaperones. My aunt, the Lady Caroline Fitzmorton, has come from London for this purpose, and no *camarera mayor* in the Court of Spain was ever more watchful or diligent than my good aunt. She will supervise each breath you draw, never fear, and I doubt that I shall be allowed to see you, once I hand you into her determined care."

Catalina's blush grew deeper. "You thought of this, *señor?* I did not think you would . . ."

He gave a short laugh. "Oh, I thought of it, madam. We may not stand so delicately upon the finer points of courtesy, as in the Court of Spain, but we know well how to protect our women's lives, and their reputations. You will be safer here than in a convent, for there is no Abbess born as vigilant as the Lady Caroline."

As they reached the front door, Catalina paused, and for a moment her hand held his tightly.

"Manuel?" she whispered. "What of Manuel? Have you . . . have you sent word to your Queen? Has Manuel been taken yet?"

He saw the agony in her eyes and cursed the ill-fortune which had sent this torment upon them, but he let no emotion colour his voice as he answered her.

"No, I have not told the Queen. I have sent a message to Don Manuel, requiring his presence here, and the tenor of my missive is such that he will not ignore it, for he will believe it to be from the King of Spain. Also, lest his purpose should be wavering, I have told him of your presence here, doubly to ensure his compliance with my commands."

"You have not told those who sent you to Spain who he is?" The fingers tightened on his yet again. "But why, Don Nicholas, why? And why is he to come here?"

Nicholas took a deep breath and covered her hand with his.

"If my lord Burghley were to learn the truth, madam, your brother would not die easily. Just as in the prisons of Spain there are men well-versed in the loosening of a man's tongue, so in Whitehall are there those with skills no less effective. I cannot give you your brother's life, Catalina, for this is forfeit, as you must know, but I can ensure that the manner of his dying will not cause you greater suffering than that which you already have to bear."

She would have questioned him further, but by then Peregrine and Greville had joined them, together with Jacob Blount who held the small, chattering Margarita in his arms, and with a graceful bow, Nicholas ushered his guests indoors and delivered them safely into the keeping of the Lady Caroline.

Two days later, Manuel de la Vega arrived at Blandon Point and was shewn into the library where Nicholas Rokeby awaited him.

Wise after the event, Nicholas could now see the likeness of this man to Catalina, and as he rose from his chair, his mouth shewed the distaste in him for his task.

" Sir Nicholas! " De la Vega was astonished. " I had not thought to find you here. I received a message from . . . from . . ." He broke off abruptly, conscious of the danger into which he had walked, but Nicholas smiled tightly.

" The message was from me, *Señor* de la Vega, although I signed my missive with a name which I thought you would trust more readily than my own."

Manuel's face whitened and he tensed as Nicholas came towards him.

" You know my name? Ah, but then this you must know, since you claim to have my sisters here with you. Was this a lie? Was it merely a trick to ensure my coming?"

Nicholas shook his head. " No lie and no trick, *señor*. Catalina and Margarita are here, and safe, and it was not only to ensure your coming that I brought them to England with me." He paused and eyed the young Spaniard thoughtfully. " Do you know the man to whom your sister is betrothed? Had you met him before you came to England?"

Manuel shrugged a little uneasily. " I knew him, *señor*, but I do not see . . ."

" Then you should have refused your consent," said Nicholas shortly. " He is not fit to live, far less is he fit to have the honour of becoming Catalina's husband."

" It was not for me to give or refuse consent," returned

Manuel stiffly. " The King made the decision and I accepted it."

" Then you are a fool," said Nicholas irritably. " But I did not bring you here to discuss this. There are other things for you and I to talk about."

Manuel was wary again. " Other things, *señor*? My presence at your Court, perhaps?"

" That, and your reason for being there." Rokeby's hand was resting lightly on the hilt of his sword.

" I was sent to discover the plans for England's defence." De la Vega did not quite meet Rokeby's eye. " Just as you went to Valladolid, my lord, so I went to Whitehall. These things we both accept as inevitable in times of war."

" I did not go to Valladolid to commit murder," said Rokeby softly, " but that is why you went to London. You were not interested in the plans we made to defend our shores; your task was to destroy Elizabeth, when news reached you that the Invincible Enterprise had set sail."

Manuel's face was starkly white and his eyes were startled. " You knew this? And yet you went to Spain?"

" I did not learn who Philip's assassin was until I reached his Court," said Nicholas curtly. " It was to discover your identity, sire, that I went to Spain."

" But now that you know, my lord, why have you sent for me?" Manuel tilted his chin with the same unconscious pride that Catalina had displayed. " Why have you not told Burghley and Walsingham, for surely it is they who sent you, and who now await your report."

" Because of me," said Catalina, and the two men swung round sharply as she came forward into the room. " Because of me, Manuel."

" Catalina!" Manuel made a half-gesture towards her, then checked it, and said stiffly: " I do not understand you, Catalina."

" You should not be here," said Rokeby sharply. " Where is the Lady Caroline?"

" In her chamber," Catalina gave him a quick glance. " I

208

tricked her, *señor*, and locked her in, for I heard of Manuel's arrival, and I had to see him. Oh, Manuel . . . Manuel."

She went to his side and buried her head on his shoulder, unmindful of all that protocol and etiquette had taught her, for her emotions were too strong to stay within the confines of her strict upbringing.

"This is my fault, Manuel; my fault. I told Sir Nicholas who you were. It is because of me that you are here, and in danger. I beg you to forgive me, for I cannot forgive myself."

Manuel stared down at her for one uncomprehending second, then he thrust her away and his eyes were hard.

"What are you saying, Catalina? You told Sir Nicholas of my identity? You? I cannot believe this."

"It is true." She felt a tear coursing down her cheek as she saw the outrage in her brother's eyes, but she did not spare herself. "Manuel, it is true. I told him."

"She had no choice," said Nicholas crisply, and Manuel turned his head to look at him blankly. "I took Margarita from her chamber and held her prisoner; away from the King's palace. I told Catalina that if she did not tell me who had been sent to London to murder the Queen, I would kill the child."

Manuel was staring at Rokeby, unconscious of Catalina's quiet tears as she buried her face in her hands, and finally he said through stiff lips:

"You did that, *señor*? You took the child?"

"I did." Nicholas was definite, and now his right hand was tighter on the sword-grip. "And I took the Lady Catalina from Spain against her will, for she wished to stay there and face what might come with Don Cristóbal, but I would not permit this. I forced her to come with me, and thus she is entirely blameless. Your quarrel is not with her, but with me." He glanced at Catalina. "Leave us, madam, for your brother and I have a dispute which must be settled here and now, and this is no place for you."

"No!" Catalina's hands fell from her face. "No! Sir Nicholas, I beg you; I beg you." She ran forward and caught his arm. "No! No! Please . . . I beg you . . . do not . . ."

"Catalina!" Manuel's voice was like a whiplash. "Control yourself."

Rokeby shot him a quick glance. All the quiet gentleness of the man he had known as John Dyke had gone. There was an unexpected assurance about the way he held his head, a new breadth to his shoulders as he straightened them, and the soft, pleasant tone he had assumed was lost under the decisiveness of his native tongue. He had played his rôle well and convincingly, but it had only been a rôle, and now Nicholas could see what lay beneath the mask which Manuel had worn; a mask no less effective than that which he himself had used so many times before.

Now Manuel no longer aped the gallant English squire, smiling benevolently on his companions, and bowing graciously to the ladies of the Court. Now, as his fingers curled round the jewelled hilt of his blade, Nicholas could see all the arrogance and fire which had lain hidden for two long years, as the son of Don Fernando de la Vega faced his enemy across the wide airy room.

Catalina whimpered, but Manuel ignored her distress.

"Return to your chamber," he said curtly. "Will you disgrace me further by your foolish tears and lack of self-control? Leave us, Catalina, this instant! I will not tell you again."

She stumbled blindly from the room, closing it quietly behind her and groping helplessly towards the stairs. She paused for one second on the bottom step and heard the first clash of steel; then with a sob fled back to her chamber and buried her agonised tears in the softness of the satin bedcovers.

# I I

CATALINA SAT in the small rose-arbour in the garden which
John Rokeby had fashioned so lovingly for his young wife,
and stared down at the fine lacework on which her slim, deft
fingers had been working.

She wore black, unrelieved save for the starched whiteness
of her ruff and the modest pearl and silver billiment which
kept the smooth coils of her dark tresses in place, and her face
was drawn and sad as she gazed at her work unseeingly.

She had been at Monks' Walk for four days, but in some
ways it had seemed a lifetime since she had lain stretched on
her bed in tears, waiting for the step behind her which would
tell her who had survived the execution in the library below.

For that was what it had been; it had not been a light-
hearted challenge to satisfy a point of honour, nor yet a duel
to prove the superior quality of one swordsman over another.
It had been a judicial putting to death, for neither of the men
engaged in that inexorable confrontation had used his blade
for personal reasons, but for something of far greater importance.

Catalina felt the tension in her once again as she remembered
that terrible twenty minutes whilst she waited to learn whether
it was her beloved brother who had died; Manuel, whom she
had betrayed, or whether it was Nicholas Rokeby, the English-

man, who had had sufficient courage and boldness to enter the Court of Spain itself to protect his Queen.

Nicholas, whose smile made her tremble, and whom she loved with all her heart. It was useless to deny this truth to herself any longer, for there could be no other cause for the pure, undiluted happiness which surged through her when he came into a room, or when he turned to look at her in that faintly quizzical way of his.

Her white fingers moved uncertainly against the lace as she recalled the moment when she had heard the door of her chamber open, and had tried to summon up the courage to turn to face the victor. Finally she had been able to do it, for the daughters of Spain's grandees were not brought up as weaklings, and when she had pulled herself up and turned her head, no sound escaped her lips as Rokeby made his bow.

" *Señorita.*" His tone was devoid of the slightest emotion, and his face was blanker than the mask he wore when he boarded his enemies' vessels. " I have to tell you that your brother, Don Manuel, is dead. It might help you to know that he fought with great courage, and died as a Spanish nobleman should. I shall honour his memory, and regret to my life's end that I should have been the one chosen for this unpalatable task."

She could not answer him, although she longed to rush into his arms for comfort. She wanted his strength and a small share of his own courage at that moment, but all she could do was to stare at him with dark, pain-filled eyes.

He paused for a moment, one hand fingering the diamond and pearl medallion he wore around his neck, then he spoke again, in the same expressionless voice.

" I have to go to London, but I shall leave you here with the Lady Caroline. Here you will be safe, for my aunt and my servants will tend to all your needs. I do not ask for your forgiveness, for this, I know, you cannot give, but later, when the wound is healed a little, I would pray for your understanding."

And with that he had gone, closing the door quietly behind

him as if he wanted to shut off part of his life which he could no longer bear to think about, and Catalina had got stiffly to her feet and made her way to Margarita's chamber.

They had not let her see Manuel's body, for those had been Nicholas's orders, but from somewhere they had found a Catholic friar to conduct the requiem Mass, and had lain Manuel to rest in a quiet corner of the garden under a large tree which was beginning to stir to life under the warmth of the spring sun.

Catalina felt a lump in her throat and tried in vain to apply her wandering thoughts to her labours once more, but it was impossible. She grieved bitterly for Manuel, the more because she felt responsible for his death, but she mourned even more deeply because of her inability to tell Nicholas that she understood what he had had to do.

There was a terrible inevitability about what had happened. From the first moment when she had heard what Manuel's task was to be, and Don Cristóbal had told her of the part he had assumed, she had recognised the risks he was taking, and knew that should he be discovered, his life was the price he would have to pay.

Thus, in some strange way, she had been preparing herself for Manuel's death for a long time, and Nicholas had made it possible for that death to be a quick and honourable one. Young though she was, Catalina was not a fool, nor without understanding of the alternative. If Rokeby had not sent for him and drawn his sword against him, Manuel would have been taken in London where the Queen's counsellors and officials would have had scant patience with honour. There would have been no dignity on the rack, and even the fiercest of Spanish pride could crack under the torment of the hoist, but Nicholas had spared Manuel that disgrace and degradation, and Catalina was eternally grateful to him for his charity.

She was still staring sadly at her idle bobbins when the Lady Caroline bore down upon her, her great farthingale brushing callously against the tender green leaves now making their first tentative appearance.

" God's life, child! " she said and threw up her hands in dismay. " What are you doing here by yourself? I have been searching the house for you."

She sat by Catalina's side and searched her white face in silence. Then she clicked an impatient tongue and frowned fiercely upon her charge.

" Lack a day, girl! This will not do. You have been crying again, and this I will not have. Nick has charged me to care for you. What will he say if he finds you weeping when he returns?"

Catalina made an effort to smile, but there was an anxious question in her eyes.

" You think he will return, madam? You believe he will come back?"

" Come back? Mercy, child, of course he will come back. This is his home; why should he not return?"

Catalina hesitated and then her head drooped to avoid Caroline Fitzmorton's piercing gaze.

" H . . . he . . . might not wish to see me again," she said in a small voice. " He might wait until I have left here, for I must remind him of many things he wishes to forget."

Caroline's plump white hand stretched out and lifted Catalina's reluctant chin, and for a moment the two women were silent, but for all their lack of words, each understood the other's thoughts, for suddenly Caroline began to chuckle a little.

" So you love him, eh? Perdition; who would have thought it? I told young Nick he should be wed but he had no time to listen to me then, and spurned the suggestions I made to him. Perhaps 'twas just as well, for it seems that in Spain he found something to convince him more readily than my words."

" Oh no, *señora*; no! " Catalina's hand caught Caroline's. " He does not feel for me in this way. He has been kind and compassionate, but he does not love me. How could he, for my brother tried to kill your Queen. In his heart, Sir Nicholas can have nothing but dislike for me."

"Stuff and nonsense!" said Lady Fitzmorton sharply. "Permit me to know my own nephew better than you, miss. I have had to suffer long lectures on how you are to be treated, as if I had never had to care for a girl before. Do you suppose Nicholas would concern himself so greatly over a woman he disliked?"

"It is an obligation, *Doña* Caroline," said Catalina with a faint, hurt smile. "I am his guest, and as in my country, this is no light matter. Naturally he was concerned to see . . ."

"Rubbish!" Caroline snorted and patted Catalina's hand again. "This is not Spain, girl; this is England, and we are talking about that rapscallion of a nephew of mine, not one of your precise and proper dons. And since we talk of your country, child, what was Nicholas doing there?"

Catalina's eyes widened. "You do not know? He has not told you?"

"Should I need to ask if he had?" Lady Fitzmorton was acid, for her curiosity was eating hard into her. "But since he was so remiss, you shall tell me, young Kate. Now, what was Nick about in Spain?"

Catalina still hesitated, but she was no match for Caroline Fitzmorton in her present mood, and when Catalina got to the end of her tale, she gave a small, miserable sniff into her lace-edged handkerchief.

"And so you see, *señora*; Nicholas was forced to slay my brother, and thus, since Manuel was his enemy, so must I be."

Caroline was staring at Catalina in amazement, but when she saw the sadness in her again, she closed her mouth with a snap.

"Fiddlesticks! I see there was no choice for him but to do his duty and take your brother to task, and it was as well for Don Manuel that he did." Caroline looked sober for a minute. "The alternative would not have been . . ." She broke off abruptly and gave another snort. "Nick, a pirate! I cannot believe it. He never shewed a scrap of interest for anything but the cut of his doublet and the quality of his jewels, or the

215

latest wench who . . ." Again the indignant Caroline broke
off with unusual tact. "But he gave no hint of the other life
he led, the scoundrel, though many's the time I have wondered
about those trips he took of which he would not speak."

Her eyes were warmly approving now, and she adjusted her
ruff with a complacent hand. "Lord preserve us! The boy
has something in him after all. Well, I always suspected it, but
I had not thought of this."

Catalina was not smiling, and now she sighed. "He had
much courage, madam, but his task is not yet done, for soon
King Philip will send his fleet against this country, and it is
invincible, this Armada which my countrymen have prepared.
Though there will be many like Sir Nicholas who will resist
our ships, they cannot hope to turn aside so great a force."

Caroline laughed and her dark eyes snapped with a militant
gleam.

"It is clear that you have fallen into the same error as your
misguided monarch, miss, for he too underestimates the ten-
acity of our English seamen and of Elizabeth's fighting ships.
Do not fret yourself, child; Nick will be back, you will see."

Catalina took a deep breath and tried to keep her voice
steady. "I trust he will, madam, but it cannot, of course, be
of concern to me."

"Oh?" Lady Caroline cocked an inquisitive brow. "How
so, Kate, for I thought you had some tenderness for this
knavish boy of mine?"

Catalina was busy straightening her threads and bobbins
and would not look at Caroline, but she managed to keep the
dejection out of her tone as she answered.

"I am betrothed to another, Lady Caroline; to a nobleman
of my country to whom the King has given my hand. Thus,
when I am free to return to Spain, I shall be wed to Don
Cristóbal, if he will still accept me, and I shall see Sir Nicholas
no more."

"Ah!" Caroline grunted in sudden comprehension. "So
that is it? Well, never fear, child; Nick will not let you marry
this man. Have you not told me yourself, this very morning,

216

that the boy is a pirate, and what other business has a pirate but to steal another man's possessions?"

She rose majestically to her feet and held out an imperious hand. " Come. You have been alone long enough. We will take a glass of wine together and forget these matters for a while. But don't fret." For a moment her voice was soft, with a depth of kindness few people had ever heard. " He will come back for you, never fear. He will not let so precious a treasure slip through his fingers though all the might of Spain should stand against him."

And with that she pulled Catalina to her feet and marched her firmly back to the house.

When Nicholas Rokeby arrived at Whitehall he was ushered immediately into the presence of Lord Burghley and Sir Christopher Hatton, and for the ensuing fifteen minutes none dared venture near the tightly closed doors. This task done, Nicholas went to the Queen, for she was waiting impatiently for his arrival, and when he had made his bow and kissed her outstretched hand, she gestured to him to rise.

" Well, Nick?" She gave him a brief smile, but her gaze was demanding. " What have you been about?"

Rokeby laughed, making another flourishing bow and coming a little nearer to the dais.

" The Queen's business, ma'am; what else?"

Elizabeth nodded. She was in her finest feathers this day, for the warm May sunshine had coursed through her veins with encouraging fire, and it had taken three hours to decide between the black velvet gown with the heavily jewelled fore-part and the delights of the peach-satin brocade, on which two hundred pearls had been laboriously sewn. Finally, she had rejected both and plumped for the new peacock-blue silk, with monstrous sleeves of stiffened and padded satin, criss-crossed with silver thread and studded with miniature diamonds. The great ruff was of the most delicate silver cob-web lace, which matched the wrist frills, and the wired, heart-shaped headrail. She wore her newest wig of bold, defiant red, topped with a diamond and sapphire ornament fit to ransom a king, and round her neck were no less than six ropes of pearls including the fabulous black pearls which Rokeby had brought her as a gift.

She moved her fan slowly back and forth and eyed her courtier with approval.

" A right and proper answer, Nicholas. And you have achieved that which I sent you to do?"

Privy to the answer, she still watched with interest as he paused to consider his reply. She had the feeling that she had not been told all the circumstances of Rokeby's success and was a trifle piqued, but with a curious, unfeminine tolerance, she was not prepared to press him too hard.

" It is done, ma'am." Nicholas was brief, but even the brevity of his response told Elizabeth that her instinct had been right. Something had happened to the boy in Spain; something which had made his face a trifle colder, and the line of his mouth a little harder. The fan swept to and fro unhurriedly, and Elizabeth said lightly:

" I am in your debt, my lord, yet your achievement has not brought you the satisfaction one might expect. It troubles you, Nick; what you have done? Why is this?"

Rokeby paused fractionally, but then he smiled in the way she remembered so well, and his voice was as light and gay as ever.

" I am not troubled, ma'am, for I have done what I set out to do, and may rest easy now, since your life is no longer in danger."

Elizabeth laughed caustically. " No longer in danger, Nick? Odds fish, boy, my life will always be in danger, for no monarch's life is worth a moment's purchase. There will always be those who will seek to bring about my death, but for the moment, praise be to God, and thanks to you, there is no immediate risk."

She closed the fan with a snap and studied the soft egret feathers with care.

" Sir John Dyke is no longer at Court," she said after a

moment. "He left without a word of his going. Will he be returning to us, Nick?"

She glanced up and saw the light change behind the sapphire eyes, and watched the hardness of his mouth in silence. Then Rokeby shook his head.

"No, ma'am, he will not be returning."

"I see." She gave a small, bleak smile. "Yet he was not taken here in London, Nick. Some say he received a message, though none can hazard from whom it came. It is said that he leaped upon his horse and rode as if the devil was at his heels." She turned her head and gazed at the tall mullioned window through which the sun poured its golden light. "It is also rumoured, Nick, that he took the road to the West; to Devon. Think you this might be so?"

"'Tis possible, ma'am." Rokeby was non-committal, and the Queen turned back to look at him.

"Is it also possible he may retrace his steps, my lord, and once more seek to achieve his purpose here at Court?"

Nicholas met the dark imperious eyes without flinching and for a second he hesitated. Then, with a slight bow, he shook his head.

"Not so, ma'am, for he is dead."

The Queen's rouged lips twisted slightly. "And you do not propose to tell me how or why this came about, do you, my lord? Were I to question you all the morning, I should do no more than chase you down the labyrinth of evasions you have built about yourself. Ah well." She sighed and opened her fan again. "I shall not plague you so, Nick. I asked for your help and you gave it without stint; it is not for me to force from you the details of the methods you used to reach your ends. Now tell me, my lord, what of my revered brother-in-law? What made you of him?"

Rokeby turned thankfully from the delicate and dangerous topic of Manuel de la Vega, and laughed.

"He is an interesting man, ma'am, and a little unexpected."

"How so?" Elizabeth was sharp. "Has he grown so much in spiritual stature since I last saw him that makes you speak

219

thus of him. When he was here, in England, he was a narrow-minded, pious, bigot, who spent his days in prayer before the altar, and his nights . . . well . . . sufficient to say that whatever his prowess in other women's beds, he failed to give a single moment of true happiness to my sister, his wife."

"Perhaps we all grow a little in stature as we age," said Nicholas gently. "He is still a man of deep religious convictions, and although he has allowed them to smother his humanity and blind his reason, I believe that to him, they are true enough. He burns and tortures those who would stray from the Church's teaching because he believes it to be his duty, but before God, he is a humble supplicant."

"He does well to be," snapped Elizabeth, "for God will most surely call him to account for the deaths he has brought about by his fanatical zeal. And what else, sire? What of the man himself?"

"A quiet, withdrawn man, ma'am." Nicholas was reflective and the Queen watched him with narrowed eyes. "Almost a recluse, for he has no taste for pomp and ceremony, but a thoughtful man and an intelligent one. He has a great love for music and art and literature, and his palace at Valladolid is a veritable treasure house."

"Of stolen property," said Elizabeth bitingly, conveniently overlooking the fact that much of the wealth and beauty which surrounded her had also been appropriated from the loaded treasure ships from the East and the New World. "But go on, my lord. What else. Did he speak of me?"

"He did, ma'am." Nicholas smiled at the woman in the Queen who could not resist this question. "He spoke of you as he remembered you, and in a way which none could mistake."

"He wanted to marry me." Elizabeth's eyes had lost some of their hardness. "When my sister died, he thought to make me his, for thus could he hold fast to his claim to England, but I would not heed him for I saw his purpose clearly enough."

"Perhaps you did not, ma'am," said Rokeby softly. "At least, perhaps you did not see all that he intended."

The Queen stared at Rokeby, but then she shrugged and gave a brittle laugh.

"Well, 'tis done, Nick; it is long years ago, and who can say now what Philip meant then? Now 'tis clear enough what he intends. Did he speak to you of this?"

"A little, ma'am, but he was cautious. Yet is is clear that we must soon face the dons, for their preparations are all but done."

"It had to come." The Queen was quiet. "From the very day Philip of Spain set foot upon our soil as the bridegroom of Mary Tudor, he hankered after this fair island of ours. It was England he wanted, sire, not my sister Mary, for when he realised how strong was the resistance against him, he soon returned to his own land, there to wait for another opportunity to be our master. He has waited long years, Nick, and will have prepared well for this Enterprise of his, and that he believes he comes in the name of God, will make stronger his determination to succeed."

"We will be ready for him, ma'am," said Rokeby and now the Queen saw the sparkle in his eyes again. "With all our fierce Protestant stubbornness, and all Master Hawkins's fine ships and guns. We have cut our teeth on skirmishes with Philip's nobles in distant waters; now God willing, we will prove our manhood in our own English Channel, for there we will hold them fast. Fear you not, madam; we will not let so much as one bold don set foot upon your soil, nor countenance one Spanish seaman's anchor in your harbours."

"I do not fear," said Elizabeth truthfully, and she was smiling. "Mayhap I have not the sinews of a man, nor the brute strength to wield a sword to defend my realm, but I am my father's daughter, and from him have I inherited all that is needful to protect my people. My heart is stout, my spirit strong, and my determination, strengthened by the fiery passions of the Tudor Kings, will furnish me with the armour I shall need to withstand my foes and confound my enemies. And what I lack, my lord, you shall provide. You, and those other sons of mine, whose valour and quality rouse in me an everlasting pride and make me give constant thanks to God for my good fortune."

She nodded a little and held out her hand again.

"Go you now, Nick, and give such aid as you can to my Vice-Admiral, for he is hot for war. Go you, and God keep you safe, sire, for whilst I live, I shall have need of men like you."

And Nicholas went, bowing low from the audience chamber, his heart beating a trifle faster than usual, wondering, not for the first time, what magic this Tudor changeling had in her small, thin body and bright, watchful· eyes which made him long to beat the Spaniards single-handed for her sake.

How could this wrinkled, faded woman with the painted, raddled cheeks, rouged lips and outrageous gaudy wig make his pulse race and his blood leap wildly in his veins as he bent his knee before her?

It was a mystery that he could not fathom, and a puzzle to which he had no key, but as he made his way along the corridor towards the chamber where Drake awaited him, it did not seem to be of importance. No matter what sorcery Elizabeth used, she used it with an unerring hand, and with a subtle power which was all her own, and Rokeby was smiling gently as he tapped upon Drake's door and waited for his summons.

During that day, Rokeby spent many hours with Drake and the other English leaders. He talked with Frobisher and Edward Hoby, Lord Burghley's nephew, and exchanged notes with John Hawkins as to the fitting of his ship, and finally rose to bow to England's Lord High Admiral; Charles, Lord Howard of Effingham.

Howard was a tall, gentle man, with kindly eyes and a prim little smile, and his men held him in great affection.

Rokeby had been right when he said he was not a seaman, but this was of no moment, for he had that rare quality of seeing the best in those who served under him, allowing their talents full rein. His birth and heritage was such that none had quibbled at his appointment, all honoured to serve a man of such distinction, and thus, with this one major stumbling block removed, Howard had found it a simple enough task to draw his men round him to face the task before them.

He listened to them complaining about the lack of guns and powder and the poor state of the food, which was already rotting in the ships' holds, and sighed a little when Lord Henry Seymour waxed violent about the stinking water in his drinking barrels.

With his customary tact and wisdom he soothed his men's complaints, and steered them gently towards a different topic, urging Rokeby to tell those assembled what he had learned in Spain. They all listened eagerly, nodding and murmuring amongst themselves, whilst Drake sat rubbing his hands together in ill-concealed pleasure.

" 'Tis almost certain," he said finally, " that the dons are now lying in the waters of the Tagus, and that when they are given the order, they will take sail to Belem. This done, they will turn and make for Finisterre and thus on to the open sea until they sight the Lizard."

" Then will we light the beacons," said Thomas Fenner briskly, " that all England shall know of their coming and thus make such preparations as are needful."

He glanced at Drake. " When will we have word, my lord? What scouts have we at sea to give us first warning?"

" There are two pinnaces in the Bay of Biscay and three more standing out to sea from La Coruña, keeping a watchful eye on the ships that guard the coast there. We should have their signals in good time, but for the moment the winds are rude and boisterous, and there may yet be more delays before we can put our mettle to the test."

The talk became general, and when Nicholas finally made his escape, he faced the unwelcome task of bidding Jane Mordaunt farewell, for enjoyable though he had found the stolen hours he had spent with her, he knew the time had come to make an honest ending.

On his way to Jane's room, he encountered Eleanor Strickland, who kissed him warmly and turned a glowing face to his.

"Dear Nick," she said and hugged him tightly. "How glad I am that you have returned, for now I have discovered that which you wished to know."

For a moment he looked puzzled and she laughed.

"Do you not remember, Nick? You charged me to discover Stephen's dark secret, lest he proved unfit to be my husband." She chuckled. "Oh, Nick! So foolish! 'Twas merely that he had once offered for the hand of a girl whom he had known since his youth, and did not wish me to know of this. How blind he was, for I would not care, now that he is mine."

She implanted another kiss on Rokeby's cheek and danced away leaving Nicholas to smile wryly as he continued on his way.

He found Jane in her chamber, clad in white silk, with her corn-gold hair shining softly in the dimness of the room. When he reached her, he kissed her hand, but made no other move to touch her, and the sudden spark of hope died quietly in her eyes.

"You have come to say good-bye, Nick?" she whispered finally, and touched his hand with light fingers. "To tell me that we shall not meet again; is that it?"

He looked startled, and she laughed softly. "Did you think I would not know, Nick, when the moment came?" She rubbed her cheek against his hand, holding it tightly as if to comfort herself. "I knew, dear love. I knew as you walked towards me. When you kissed my hand as if I were a stranger, and put up a barrier in your eyes so that I could not read your thoughts."

Rokeby frowned. "Sweet Jane. I would not hurt you for all the world. You have been dear to me, and have given generously of your love, and no matter what may come, I shall not forget this. But now I have to leave Whitehall and join my ship, and who knows when I shall return?"

"But that is not why you bid me farewell, Nick." She met his gaze sadly. "You have sailed away many times before, but never like this. There is another reason why you now speak thus. It is a woman, is it not? I have lost you, not to your ship, Nick, but to a woman."

He sighed gently and released her hand, but he did not lie to her, for he cared for her too much for that.

" It is another woman," he agreed finally. " I would not have had it happen, Jane, for I was happy enough as I was, but Fortune spun the coin and broke my precious tranquillity in two."

" Is she beautiful?" Jane's voice was low, but the light was not strong enough for him to see the tears in her eyes. " Is she, Nick?"

He smiled, and when she saw his face her last drop of hope ran down her cheek in despair.

" She is the most beautiful creature I have ever seen," he said, and there was an awe and wonder in his voice that made Jane wince in pain. " She was fashioned by the gods for man's undoing, and for all my life I shall love her with all that is in me, although I know that she can never be mine."

Jane's eyes widened and she brushed her cheek quickly with a shaking hand.

" I do not understand, Nick," she said unsteadily. " If you love her thus, and she is of such beauty, why can she not be yours?"

He sighed again, more deeply now, and she felt the sorrow in him.

" I took from her one whom she held most dear. I had no choice, and would have given all I had to have spared him, but it was not to be. I killed her brother, Jane, and for this she will not forgive me."

" She is angry, Nick? She hates you for what you have done?"

Nick shrugged. " She has shewn no anger, Jane, nor spoken of her hate, yet it must be there, hide it though she may. She is too gentle and good to berate me for what she knew I had to do, but that cannot cure the bitterness in her heart, and I will not force myself upon her and thus add to her burdens.

No, there is no future for us; my Catalina and I. But though I must let her go, I have nothing left now for any other woman, and this I had to tell you with honesty, for I would not cheat you."

Jane felt moisture on her lashes again, and once more she took his hand.

" I will pray for you, Nicholas," she whispered, " and perhaps one day you will find you are wrong, for were I this girl, I would forgive you anything in the world. But should you be right, and if you are left alone, remember this. When you need comfort and love, Nick, come back to me, for I shall not ask you for anything, nor expect ought from you. If you are sad and filled with loneliness, come back to me, sweet, and I will give you what I can for your heart's ease. It will not be much, but it is all I have to offer, and it is yours for the taking."

Nicholas caught her in his arms and for one moment held her tightly to him, then turned quickly from her and was gone, leaving Jane to bury her face in her hands and sob her misery away in helpless tears.

Whilst Nicholas Rokeby was thus engaged in England, Philip of Spain, now back in comfortable seclusion in the Escorial, read with his customary patience the latest protest from the Duque de Medina Sidonia.

He laid the parchment down with a faint sigh and glanced round the bare little room with satisfaction. The peace was like a benison; deep and tranquil and fulfilling, and for a moment he sat in silent contemplation, enjoying the isolation afforded by his barren cell-like chamber.

Philip had built the Escorial to satisfy a dream and to fulfil a vow which he had made when his armies had won a splendid victory at St. Quentin on the 10th August, 1557. In honour of St. Lawrence, whose feast day it was, Philip had planned his palace in the form of the gridiron on which the Martyr had died. It was to be a palace, a monastery and a mausoleum, and to achieve this triple purpose, the King had commissioned Juan Bautista de Toledo to bring his skills to bear.

Philip, with all Spain at his feet, chose for his site the foothills of the barren rocks of the Guadarrama mountains, for there he found the stillness and peace which he sought. It took many years to achieve his dream, but whatever else Philip lacked it was not patience, and he watched contentedly enough as year by year the great edifice rose from the rough grey earth beneath it.

The walls were of *berroquena*, a bluish stone which blended quietly into the landscape, and the roofs were topped with a dozen towers and cupolas to give the palace a regal grandeur as it soared upwards into the clear cloudless sky.

But if the sierra at whose stony feet the palace sat was austere, there was no lack of ornament and rich embellishment within. From Burgo de Osma came jasper, and from the south, the wonderful, delicate marbles from which the pillars and floors were made, whilst from Granada and Seville were transported fabrics of such magnificence that the eye was dazzled by their shimmer and myriad of colours. From his Flemish looms, Philip summoned the exquisite tapestries which hung upon the walls, and from Milan, still part of Philip's mighty empire, came gold, silver and precious stones to make the palace sparkle.

He filled his libraries with the rarest of books and manuscripts, and furnished his music rooms with the finest instruments which man's hand could fashion, scouring Europe for all that was best of sculpture and paintings to enrich his *castillo*.

The great vaults were designed to hold the coffins of Spain's royal family, and here to the Escorial, Philip brought the bones of his father, the Emperor Charles, and here also he laid to final rest, three of his wives, and those of his children who had not lived to see this miracle of which their father had dreamed for so many years.

The *capilla mayor* was the pinnacle of Philip's ambition. It boasted a screen which rose a hundred feet into the air, and its walls were alive with the glow of sacred paintings and precious polished marbles. Flanking the chapel were the open oratories with their figures of bronze and silver, and to guard this sacred heart of the palace, the King brought the Hieronymites to offer perpetual worship to God, and to pray continuously for the souls of men.

And when it was finished, and when the last fishpond had been filled with carp and perch, the last canvas from Venice placed in position, and the final piece of sculpture from Naples set in its niche, Philip had given a deep sigh of satisfaction and made his way back through the great domed corridors to his small bedchamber, where the walls were adorned with strange, unpleasant pictures of horned monsters and gross demons which tortured screaming, writhing voluptuaries in a fiery hell of their own making. None knew whether they were intended as a salutary reminder to the King of the sins of the world around him, or whether he derived some queer, unnatural pleasure from the sufferings of these damned souls, but since none were close enough to the King to enquire his reasons for the nature of his grim frescoes, the mystery remained unsolved.

Philip set his altars ablaze with light, and knelt in rapt adoration before the Blessed Sacrament. He wandered along the silent passages and through the empty music rooms and libraries, hearing nothing but the gentle music of a chiming clock or the faint chanting sound of the monks at their offices. He had created an earthly paradise of stone and marble and gems, but it was completely without life. It had three hundred rooms and nearly three thousand windows, but it had no spirit, and its eyes looked in upon itself in eternal blindness.

Over eighty fountains played gently in the summer sunshine, and it boasted no less than fifteen cloisters and sixteen courtyards, but it seldom heard the sound of a child's laughter, nor the step of a woman upon the satiny marble stairs. It was like a great frozen jewel, set amongst the most formidable mountain range in Spain. A prison of all the talents of the world; a trinket box of the wonders of the earth, but it was as dead and lifeless as the mouldering bodies lying in rigid quietness in the great porphyry mausoleum. Philip had built a spectacular tomb, and now he gathered its icy stillness about him like a cerecloth, waiting patiently for the day to come when he could lie in ultimate silence in his cold, priceless necropolis.

Apparently unaware of its shortcomings, and appreciative only of the pleasure it gave him, Philip was about to dip his quill into the inkwell to begin his reply to his Commander-in-Chief when a secretary crept silently into the room, bowing low and murmuring his apologies. Philip laid down his pen and listened to the man's words, no frown of annoyance or irritation marring his brow as he learned of the presence of Cristóbal Lanuza, who had arrived unannounced and unheralded at the Escorial, and who was now begging the privilege of an audience.

The King nodded and bade the secretary bring the Marqués to him, and carefully set aside his fresh sheet of parchment until the moment came when he could return to it. Time was not important to Philip. He could never be hurried or rushed, and what he could not achieve on one day, he would accomplish on another. " Time and I are as one," he would say to his long-suffering counsellors, and then with the greatest repose, would select yet another out-dated letter from his growing pile of correspondence, and begin his spidery, scrawling answer.

When Cristóbal Lanuza came into the presence of the King, his bow was low and he went humbly on one knee to his sovereign but Philip saw the blazing anger under the Marqués's outward calm.

He sighed gently, for he was not a passionate man himself and found it difficult to deal with the emotions of those who were, but his smile was kindly enough as he bade the Marqués rise and state his business.

Philip listened impassively to the torrent of rage which spilled from Lanuza's mouth, making no attempt to stem the current of vituperation which seared the air and filled the room with the acrid smell of hatred.

Finally, when Cristóbal paused to draw breath, the King raised one hand.

" Compose yourself, my lord," he said quietly. " It is not good to give way to such anger. And I have already been told of the disappearance of Sir Nicholas and his companions."

"And *Señorita* Catalina, sire?" The Marqués's yellow eyes were raging bright. "Hast been told of this also, and of the child, Margarita?"

Again the King motioned the Marqués to silence. "I have been told," he said equably. "It is clear to me now that we have been misled. This man, Rokeby, was sent by Elizabeth and her ministers to pry into our secrets, and to probe our plans. It is to be hoped he found little to help him." Philip's smile was a trifle sour. "But if he took back to England with him Don Fernando's daughters, we must reconcile ourselves to the fact that their brother's life is in jeopardy."

"And Catalina's honour in the dust," snapped the Marqués, "for this English dog would not have taken her if he had not meant to possess her himself."

The King's expression did not change, but his voice was a shade cooler.

"It must not be supposed, my lord," he said calmly, "that all Englishmen are rogues and vandals, nor predators of women, for if we assume this, we should be making a false judgement. I lived in England, long years ago, and there are many men there who hold their honour as highly as do we, Don Cristóbal."

"But, sire, why should he take Catalina if his purpose was not an evil one? Doubtless he has discovered that Don Manuel was sent to England, and probably he has found out the reason for this, but once this intelligence was known to him, why then should he spirit Catalina away?"

Philip shook his head. "That I do not know, Don Cristóbal and thus I cannot answer your question, but of one thing I am sure. This man Rokeby is not what you think. I spoke with him, and had time to take his measure. I have some understanding of men, my lord, for I have had a lifetime to study their ways, and I trust my own judgement in these matters. Whatever motive he had for taking the *Señorita* Catalina from our Court, it was not a base one, nor will he misuse her. I regret your loss, sire, and I am angered that we have been tricked, but I have no fear for my ward, for she will be as safe at the Court of Elizabeth of England as she would be under my own protection."

"I will kill him," said the Marqués, and again the amber eyes burned with an unholy light. "I will destroy him utterly and completely for what he has done. He has grossly insulted me, and made a mock of me, and for this I will tear his heart out of his living body."

Without the faintest flicker of expression, Philip picked up his quill again and considered it thoughtfully.

"You will have every opportunity to do so, Don Cristóbal," he said in his soft, dispassionate voice. "For on the 4th May the Armada will sail. You will join your ship immediately, and prepare to leave with the Duque de Medina Sidonia, and when you have met with the Duke of Parma and set foot upon the shores of England, you may seek out this impudent Englishman, who has made a fool of you, and do with him as you will. *Vaya con Dios.*"

He dipped the quill into the ink and drawing the parchment towards him began to write his letter as if the Marqués did not exist, and with a smothered curse, Don Cristóbal bowed his way out of the room, closing the door none too quietly behind him.

When he had gone, Philip raised his head and looked after him, and although he had long since ceased to interest himself in the quarrels and disputes of men, for one moment he permitted himself the luxury of wondering what would be the outcome of the meeting between this fiery nobleman of his and the man whom he had met at Valladolid, who had unhesitatingly risked his life for the safety of his Queen.

# 12

BUT THE time for the Enterprise had not yet come, and although England was now fully prepared to meet the Spaniards, the hand of God, on which Philip relied so greatly, held back his ships in Lisbon Harbour. The rude winds and gales which tore round the coast, kept the Duque de Medina Sidonia neatly pinned down for a full three weeks, and when at last his spectacular line of greatships and galleasses shook off the restrictions of the harbour, it was only to sail as far as La Coruña, where the Duque, desperately short of both food and water, decreed that the fleet should pause for re-victualling.

Thus they crowded into harbour, not more than half the ships managing to drop anchor before night fell upon them, leaving their less fortunate brethren standing out to sea, praying hard for first light.

Just after midnight, when men groaned in fitful sleep and muttered prayers as their tired bodies crouched on the decks and in the holds of the gently rocking ships, there was a sudden dreadful sound which roused the crews to instant attention. The wind had risen. Not gently, but like a raging torrent as it spat its turbulent rainfall over the churning seas like a thick wet pall. It roared and screamed and cursed as it buffeted the ships first this way, then that, nor did it seem inclined to hurry in its work of destruction.

232

For thirty-six hours the storm blew with unrelenting harshness whilst Philip's commanders tried every trick and device they knew to save their ships and their lives, but when at last the exhausted hurricane swirled itself off to seek fresh pastures for its fury, no less than seventy greatships had been driven from the safety of the harbour and waters close to La Coruña and were now drifting far out in the unwelcoming arms of the Atlantic.

It took four days for Medina Sidonia and the pinnaces he sent out to find the missing vessels, to calculate the damage done, and to recognise that for the time being, the Invincible Enterprise could not set sail for England.

The Duque, his distaste for the undertaking greatly enhanced by this calamitous beginning, continued to bombard the King with pleas to call off the expedition, and patiently Philip answered each and every one of Medina Sidonia's urgent requests to him with the same unfailing courtesy and flat, unequivocal refusals, signing the gentle rebuffs with the familiar scrawl, 'Yo el Rey'.

Medina Sidonia turned pathetic eyes to the Council of War to support his petition to the King, but by now it was as full of determination as Philip and would not heed him.

Philip had learned of the first disastrous ordeal of the Enterprise without moving a muscle, and when he had finished giving orders for a *novena* to the success of his fleet, he sat down and wrote to the Pope, assuring him that this small setback had in no way dampened his purpose.

Sixtus V, whilst eager to see England brought back to obedience to the Church of Rome, was less eager to see Philip's power increased, and whilst he had reluctantly promised the King a million ducats, to be paid on the day the Duke of Parma set foot on the soil of England, he was not prepared to countenance Philip's claim to the English crown. Finally, as a compromise, it had been agreed that Philip's son should have Papal recognition as the claimant to the throne of England, and since Philip did not want to discourage the Pope in his somewhat dubious acquiescence, his letter to the Holy Father was longer and even more indecipherable than usual.

Whilst the Duque de Medina Sidonia shook his head sadly and set about the re-ordering of his ships and the search for more men to replace those lost in the storm, Philip plunged whole-heartedly into further plans for his Enterprise. He did not concern himself with the shortage of gunpowder, nor the fact that the food was both sparse and rancid and that the water was unfit for hogs to drink. Instead, he wrote a painstaking edict forbidding the men to swear or blaspheme during the course of their voyage, laying down meticulously the punishments to be meted out to them should his orders be disobeyed. The normal custom of allowing prostitutes to accompany the men was also forbidden, and to ensure that his crews were faithful in their prayers, and that their confessions were made regularly, he sent monks and priests to swell the numbers on board, charged with the task of keeping pure and unsullied the sacred purpose of the Enterprise.

He chose with care the banner which the Armada was to bear with it; Christ upon the Cross, flanked by the Blessed Virgin and St. Mary Magdalene, the words: *Exurge, domine, et vindica causam tuam* embroidered in scarlet beneath the stiff, inhuman forms.

He arranged an elaborate procedure whereby on each day there should be a new password to be used by his fleet; Most Holy Trinity, All Saints, and Our Lady being the first of the sacred names he chose for this purpose.

By the middle of July, the Duque de Medina Sidonia was aboard his flagship, the *San Martin*, and the other Spanish leaders were engaged in last-minute adjustments in their own vessels. Aboard the San Pedro, Cristóbal Lanuza strode the decks, barking out sharp orders and supervising the loading of last-minute supplies of arms and ammunition. He had not lost one iota of the destructive rage which had beset him when he had learned of Rokeby's flight with Catalina de la Vega, and whilst he bowed humbly enough before the severe looking prior who had boarded his ship with two cheerless, grey-clad Brothers in attendance, it was not in the name of God that he sailed to meet Parma, but for the purpose of seeking out and destroying the man who had flicked his pride raw with his calm insolence.

But at last all was ready, and Philip's Armada set sail from La Coruña, and by the 15th July, was within sight of the English Channel. Here, the Spanish fleet encountered once again the rough tongue of the wind as a *tormenta* screamed through their sails and shot walls of spray over their bows, but finally, from the masthead of the *San Martin* a man cried out the news for which all had been waiting. Land was in sight. Hard ahead was the first glimpse of the Lizard, and with a deep, foreboding sigh, the Duque de Medina Sidonia raised the sacred banner, blessed by the Holy Father himself, and King Philip's long-awaited crusade against the English heretics had begun.

On that same fateful day, Drake, Frobisher, Hoby and Fenner, together with others of their companions, were engaged upon a quiet game of bowls on Plymouth Hoe. Lord Howard of Effingham was also present, but he had no time for games, for the weight of responsibility on him was great, and he had none of Drake's light-hearted enthusiasm for what lay ahead. Rokeby, Grey and West had joined Drake at his request, and their ship, the *Bullen Lass*, was anchored far below them in the Sound.

Peregrine had lost some of the corpse-like pallor which had caused his companions such concern, but the gaiety and life which had once burned so strongly in him seemed to have gone, as if washed away by that one terrible hour he had spent in the *plaza* at Valladolid. He had a certain tenseness and watchfulness about him, as if he were waiting for something to happen, and only when mention was made of the forthcoming struggle with the dons, did some flicker of emotion stir behind the hazel eyes.

Drake, looking remarkably pleased with himself, was enjoying his game. It was true that he had not been able to wrest from the Queen quite so many men as he felt he needed, and

235

certainly she had been blindly parsimonious with money for ammunition. whilst the quantity and quality of the food left much to be desired, yet to Drake, smoothing the wood between his sinewy fingers, these were mere details. He had waited a long time for this affray; half a lifetime, but the waiting had been worthwhile. Now, at last, he could be done with the petty harrying of Philip's vessels in the far-off oceans of the New World, and the stripping of his treasure ships as they dipped their graceful bows through white feathers of foam on their way home to Spain.

The dons were almost upon them, and he could be done with filching a few chests of gold coins, or a handful of smooth white tusks of ivory stowed carefully in the dark hold. Now he could turn his guns upon the warships of Spain and spill the blood of his foes over the rain-washed decks of their galleasses.

Nicholas, watching him, smiled a little. There was so little they had in common; this stocky, merry man, born of Puritan stock, with the sharp, intelligent eyes and jaunty little beard, and the thin, Catholic patricians who worshipped at the shrine of their own honour and pride in Philip's stilted Hispanic Court. They were a hundred worlds apart, with no common language or mutual beliefs to link them, and their only possible meeting ground would be the rolling decks of the great-ships, or the pebble-strewn beaches which Drake proposed to defend with his life.

Drake was drawing back his arm, squinting as he attuned his eye to the shot he was about to make, when a sudden cry made him pause and straighten up. A man was running over the long green verge on which the men were assembled; a man who waved his arms as he ran, and shouted in words which were carried away by the capricious mischief of the wind.

When the man drew nearer they saw it was the captain of one of Drake's pinnaces which had been sent to watch for the coming of the dons, and Drake smiled broadly, raising his hand in welcome.

"Well, sire, and what news do you bring? Have they been sighted yet?"

The man nodded, gasping for breath and holding his sides in pain.

"Sire, yes, yes! They are off the Lizard. A great host of ships, my lord, stretching as far as the eye can see. Sire, we must hurry; there is no time to lose."

Drake cocked one eyebrow, and weighed the wood carefully upon his right hand.

The others watched him closely, drawing nearer as they heard the news for which all England had been waiting, holding their breath a little as Sir Francis considered his captain's words.

"God bless me, sire," he said finally and laughed a little. "There is time enough." He turned to Hoby. "Sir Edward, see that the bonfires are set ablaze, so that the dons' path is well lit for them. Let England know of their coming and thus rejoice with us, for now comes the time of reckoning. They have ventured into our waters, and there, my lords, will we meet them with joyous hearts and ready guns. We will shew them that victory is not born of the weight of ships nor in the length of a gun barrel, but in the steadfastness of men's hearts. Go you, my lord; put your torch to yon beacon, and then send word to her Majesty at Tilbury that our hour is come."

"And you, sire?" Nicholas was smiling faintly. "What are you going to do?"

Drake grinned cheerfully and tossed his wood lightly in the air.

"I, good Nick? I am going to finish my game; what else?"

Whilst England's beacons burned like a thousand winking stars, the Armada sailed slowly and with immeasurable dignity past the Lizard on its way to Plymouth.

It was, perhaps, the greatest irony of all that Philip, that most implacable enemy of the Infidel, should have been master of a fleet which chose to sail in the form of the Turkish Crescent, but it was nevertheless a brilliant conception.

In the central position were the galleons of Castile and Portugal, with the *San Martin* at their head. Behind them, tucked safely away from the enemies' guns, were the urcas and store ships, and sweeping back like two graceful wings were the horns of the crescent under the command of Juan Martinez de Recalde, Pedro de Valdez, Martin de Bertendona and the handsome young Don Alonso de Leyva.

The vessels stayed in perfect formation, not moving so much as one sail out of their chosen pattern. It was an inspired design for defence, for the fiery little English ships could not mount a full-scale attack against such a close-knit, impenetrable mass. To challenge the tips of the cresent was to encounter Medina Sidonia's strongest vessels of war; to bite into the weak ships in the centre was to invite the powerful galleons on the wings to close in upon them and crush them in a vice.

As night fell, the Spanish fleet dropped anchor outside Plymouth Harbour, but when the clear pale moon rose in the early hours of the morning, it had its first taste of Drake's seamanship. Under the cover of darkness, the swift, manoeuvrable English ships had slipped out of port, and now lay behind the Spaniards, seizing that most vital and necessary of advantages, the wind-gauge. The first move on the chessboard of war had been made.

The passage of the Armada along the English Channel was one of the strangest battles ever fought, for the opposing sides each sought to use their own methods of warfare, without success. The Spaniards had little taste for blowing the enemy out of the water with long-range guns. The *grandeza* regarded this method of destruction as crude and dishonourable. They preferred the tried and tested method of grappling and boarding, but it was impossible to put their age-old procedure into operation, because the low, fast English ships danced away from them like silver fish, not coming sufficiently close, nor pausing long enough for a single tackle to be thrown over the side of a solitary vessel.

Nor were the English able to press the advantage of their superior guns, on which Hawkins had lavished so much care, for the superb control of the Spanish formation made this impossible.

True there were incidents. Howard's flagship was rammed, and hemmed about by enemy galleons, but before the Spaniards could make capital of their small gain, the *Ark Royal*'s boats had towed her round and she sped away at a pace which left her adversaries gasping.

Then one of Miguel de Oquendo's greatships exploded, and whilst Medina Sidonia was rescuing the screaming survivors and taking the ship in tow, Howard attacked again. His challenge was answered by Recalde and by Pedro de Valdez, whose ship, the *Nuestra Señora del Rosario*, accidentally rammed hard into another vessel and broke its bowsprit.

This time the Spanish commander's efforts to rescue his crippled ship failed, and the *Rosario* was left to its doom, as the Armada sailed on, its rigid structure unbroken and barely dented by its clash with the English.

When Howard's captains met on the *Ark Royal* on the night of July 21st by the Julian Calendar, or the 31st, if calculated by the Gregorian Calendar, they all agreed that Medina Sidonia was likely to seek some anchorage near to the English coast until he had received a message from Alexander Farnese, the Duke of Parma, that his men were ready. Thus, the decision was taken to remain behind the enemy, using the advantage of their windward position to keep Medina Sidonia on the move, and frustrated in his attempts to pause for respite.

The action wore on with grinding slowness and with little to shew for the endeavours on both sides. Drake captured the sinking *Rosario*, and Pedro de Valdes, finding it was the *Revenge* which challenged him, made no attempt to fight, but surrendered into Sir Francis's possession a rich prize, for very little effort, and much later, the *San Salvador* was also taken, loaded with much needed powder and guns.

On the 23rd July there was a fierce engagement, and on the following day another, and it was then that the *Bullen Lass*, cutting her way dangerously close to the left tip of Medina Sidonia's quarter-moon, found herself cornered by a huge galleasse, her great square rig and bold prow a formidable challenge as she bore down on the smaller English ship.

Rokeby on the bridge, cursed under his breath, but shouted quickly to his master-gunner and the ship's master to prepare to turn about and meet her. The *Bullen Lass*, a galleon of nine-hundred tons with a hundred foot keel, had thirty heavy guns aboard and twelve light guns. Her culverins could fire shots of eighteen pounds and her cannons were capable of hurling a sixty pound shot seventeen hundred yards into the sides of an enemy ship, whilst her falconets, minions, sakers and robinets could spit short sharp venom against her foes at close quarters.

In the waist of the ship, where lay the upper deck, netting had been fastened to ward off boarders seeking this vulnerable spot, whilst the other decks were covered to conceal the heavy guns whose vicious mouths breathed fire and smoke through the gaping portholes.

She had three masts; the great mainmast, the foremast and the mizzen, and her long bowsprit jutted out defiantly like a swordthrust from the hull.

The two ships grew closer, and now Peregrine and Nicholas could see clearly the name of the ship, painted boldly upon her, and could see the eager faces of the men who clustered threateningly along her sides.

" The *San Pedro*," said Nicholas reflectively as he drew his sword. " I have heard tell of her. I recall that her name was mentioned whilst we were at Valladolid, but I cannot think whose vessel she is."

" It is Lanuza's," said Peregrine softly, and his hand was clasped lovingly round the hilt of his blade. " Cristóbal Lanuza's, for I heard him boast of this on more than one occasion." He was very still and quiet amongst the noise and turmoil about them. " God is good, Nick," he said, and now he was smiling a little. " I have prayed for this, as I have never prayed for anything before, and now, when there are so many ships which might have come upon us, it is this, the *San Pedro*, which seeks to ram and board us. God be praised."

Rokeby had no time to share his bitter-sweet enthusiasm, for now the battle was enjoined. They were too close to use the heavy guns, and the smaller guns could do little harm against such hordes of men, and for once the Spaniards had the opportunity of fighting as they liked.

They swarmed like angry bees over the sides, hurling the heavy grappling irons and hooks on to the *Bullen Lass* with cries of triumph. Rokeby glanced back behind him, but the other English vessels were too far away to give him aid, and with a grim face he turned to the task of repelling the screaming boarders.

The minor guns did what they could; the curriers, the slings, the fowlers and the rabinets. They spoke tersely and lethally as they cut down the first of Don Cristóbal's invaders, but in the end, it was the personal encounters which mattered. Men hacked and struck at one another with cold steel; caught choking throats between powder-blackened hands; struck fists into mouths which poured with blood, and jammed knees hard into groins and stomach. They flung themselves upon one another like two packs of wolves, with as little care for the refinements and niceties of chivalrous warfare as the animals they resembled would have exhibited. It was a blood-bath; a welter of bright red death which trickled unceasingly on to the heaving deck.

When the Marqués de Avila y Manrique swung himself lightly on to the deck, from which the netting had now been slashed away, he raised his head and saw Rokeby rip his sword out of the writhing body of one of his compatriots. The Marqués's eyes brightened. Completely without fear, and wholly insensible to the pain and slaughter about him, he had felt the quick, rewarding exhilaration of success as he boarded the English ship, but his pleasure was increased a thousand-fold when he saw Rokeby pause in his task and look down upon him with hard, unflinching eyes.

"*Buenos dias*, Sir Nicholas," shouted the Marqués, and made a mock bow. "This is a pleasure I had not expected. I had not thought that Fate would so quickly bring us together again, but I thank the gods of chance which have brought about our meeting."

Rokeby dropped easily down to the deck and the two men

stood some eight feet apart, slightly away from the worst of the fighting. They eyed one another like wary dogs, each measuring the other with icy calculation and nerveless precision. Don Cristóbal wore his uniform with the same elegant nonchalance that he had worn his silks and velvets. His breastplate, gorget and morion shone brightly against the darkness of his tunic, and it was typical of him that the long, supple boots on his strong, shapely legs were untouched by so much as a speck of the dirt and filth which now washed the decks.

"It is a mutual pleasure," said Rokeby finally, and his fingers tightened slightly on his sword. "I had not hoped either for a second opportunity to match my steel against yours, sire." He smiled, and his smile was as terrible as the carnage about him. "This time there will be no quarter given, my lord; no mercy asked, and none given, for I have several debts to pay. Moreover, I would have this rabble swept from the decks of my ship that it may be clean again. I would have the stench of your Spanish *campesinos* driven from my vessel, that it may have to bear the odium of your presence no longer than is necessary."

Cristóbal Lanuza drew his sword in a lightning movement and now the light eyes were fierce and stormy.

"Then, sire," he said softly. "Let us waste no further time, for when I take this ship in tow, I will have its Captain strapped to the mast for the crows to feed upon as we sail into your English harbours and make them our own."

Nicholas raised his sword, but before he could make a move, Peregrine Grey slid down the rigging and came quickly to his side. He had a naked sword in his hand, and something in his face which was scarcely human.

He raised his blade and held it traverse across Rokeby's breast, forcing him gently backwards.

"No, Nicholas," he said, and in the clamour his voice could barely be heard. "Not this time. This time it is for me to give the Marqués a lesson; not in swordsmanship but in retribution." He turned and looked at Lanuza, who was regarding him with faint, mocking disdain. "He is mine, Nick;

mine. Do not seek to take him from me, for I would kill you should you try."

Nicholas hesitated, but the Marqués waved his blade airily and laughed.

"Let him come on, *señor*. When I have disposed of him, I will deal with you. Do not stop the *cachorro*, I pray you. Let him come on."

Rokeby fell back as Peregrine pushed him aside and made for Lanuza and he held his breath as their blades engaged. Peregrine was an able swordsman, but no match for the polished perfection of Lanuza, and Rokeby grimaced as the Marqués flashed two brilliant strokes which almost ripped the sword from Peregrine's hand.

It seemed there could be only one end to this; a brave and gallant death for Peregrine, who no longer had the will to live, and a quick victory for the arrogant Marqués, but Rokeby had underestimated the quality of the corrosive hatred in his companion.

All the experience and adroitness of the Marqués, allied to the venom which supported his skilful knowledge was not enough to withstand the spark which he had lit in Grey's heart when he had had Antonia Ruiz dragged through the streets of Valladolid and burned to death before Peregrine's eyes.

Grey was like a man possessed by demons. It did not matter that he knew less than half the strokes and passes of the sword which were the Marqués's strength; it was not important that Cristóbal was quicker and lighter on his feet, and moved like a graceful dancer as he wove a dangerous pattern of death about his opponent. In the end it did not signify, and what burned like a sacred flame in Peregrine's mind was all that really counted.

He could not give the Marqués any pointers in the art of the *duelo*, but on the foam-washed decks of Rokeby's vessel of war, he taught him a lesson in the power of love, and the destructive force of hatred, as he drove into Lanuza, using his weapon like a bludgeon.

For all his speed, and for all his practised grace, Lanuza had not been prepared for a passage of arms with a madman, and for those short eight minutes, Peregrine Grey went quietly but unmistakably berserk.

Rokeby stared with widened eyes. He had never seen the like of it before. He had not thought it possible that Grey could stand up to Lanuza for more than two minutes, but as the time ground slowly on, he felt his hand slacken on his sword as a strange numbness overcame him.

All around them the noise of battle went on, but oddly enough none had found their way to the place where Peregrine Grey and Cristóbal Lanuza stripped all pretence away and bared their souls to one another. They turned and twisted, jumped and leaped, and spun aside like tops. Their blades screamed at one another and hissed through the air like singing whips, and their breath was harsh and painful in their throats.

And gradually and inexorably, Peregrine began to force the Marqués on to the defensive. Don Cristóbal Luis Lanuza, who had only once before had to defend himself, being normally the aggressor, now found himself fighting for his life. But he had already lost his claim to living. He had surrendered this privilege on the day that he took from a drawer the evidence which was to condemn Antonia Ruiz to the stake, and since then, he had lived on borrowed time, blithely unaware that the passing of each hour was draining away his very existence.

When the end came, it came quickly, for Peregrine had no time to spare. Lanuza made one unexpectedly awkward feint with his blade, and it was all over. Grey's steel cut across his face like a scythe, slashing the flesh of his cheek to the bone and severing the nose. In a flash Peregrine threw his sword aside and leapt on the Marqués, catching his falling body and jerking his head back in a sickening thrust which broke his neck instantly. The blade fell harmlessly from Lanuza's hand and his blood-stained head lolled helplessly against his steel neck-piece which had become unfastened in the struggle.

Without a word, Peregrine lifted Lanuza's body in his arms and staggered over to where the fighting was at its thickest. With a superhuman effort he started to climb the rigging, the corpse slung over one shoulder, its life-blood still pouring from it. When he had reached a sufficient height for his purpose, he steadied himself and holding on tightly with one hand, let his right arm take the full weight of the Marqués's body. Watching him, Rokeby was amazed at the fantastic physical strength Peregrine displayed. He knew him to be at the peak of condition, and to have the sturdy fortitude of his forefathers, but to see him clamber up unsteady rigging after such a fight, bearing the dead weight of Lanuza's body, was a breathtaking spectacle.

Suddenly Peregrine cried out. His voice was loud, and something in it seemed to penetrate the deafening chaos of sound below, for as he repeated his cry, the struggling masses at his feet slowly began to fall apart and turn their faces up to him, their weapons slackening a little as they stared at the sight above them.

" The Marqués would join you, gentlemen," called Peregrine harshly, and hitched the body a little nearer to him, apparently unaware of the colossal strain on his arm. " Take him, and make what use you can of him, for I am done with him."

And with that he hurled the body down into the midst of the crowd, which threw itself away just in time to dodge the useless mass of flesh and bone which hit the deck with a shattering thud.

Rokeby, pulling himself together with an effort, took a flying leap towards the mêlée and shouted to his men.

" Come, gentlemen," he called, and now he was violent in his resolve. " We are at least one Spaniard less; now, what of the rest?"

And from that moment the fight was really finished, for the sight of the Marqués's distorted body had unnerved the Spaniards, and as they turned to meet their foes again, the fire and spirit had gone out of them. They died on the decks, were transfixed on the riggings, thrown over the sides of the ship into the churning sea, or trampled underfoot as their companions tried to get back to the *San Pedro*.

In a matter of half an hour the struggle was over and Rokeby, drawing the *Bullen Lass* back to suitable gun-range, turned his heavy cannons on the galleasse and gave his order to the gunners to light the tapers.

The *San Pedro* died hard, for she was a strong ship and a well-built one, but she was helpless against the spite of the the murderous English bombardment, and there were none aboard her capable of answering with like shots. She reeled and jumped under the continuous onslaught of the heavy cannons and finally a well-placed ball hit her magazines and she burst into flames.

Rokeby watched the ship die with no regret. It was a prize ship, and worth a fortune, but he wanted no part of her and no reminders of her existence. He watched with a glad and thankful heart as the water began to lap over her decks, and then turned to clear up the turmoil in his own ship.

It was an hour later that he encountered Peregrine. Grey had a head wound, and an ugly cut on the leg, but when Nicholas looked into his hazel eyes, he found they were calm and tranquil and devoid of hate, and with a quick sigh of relief, he went back to the bridge and turned the *Bullen Lass* back to the safety of the English fleet.

Faithful to his master's orders, Medina Sidonia sailed on, retaining his tightly packed design, and eschewing any forays along the English coast as he made his way to his rendezvous with the Duke of Parma.

He had engaged the English, and they had shewn their teeth, but he had not allowed them to halt his passage and by the end of July he had reached the waters off Calais where he dropped anchor and prepared to wait for word from Alexander Farnese. It was perhaps as well for his peace of mind that the Duque was unaware of Parma's inability to keep his rendezvous. Farnese could not find the flat-bottomed craft he needed to get his troops through the shallows off the Lowlands. He had the army, but no way of getting it to Medina Sidonia's greatships, and he raised his fists to heaven and heartily cursed the Enterprise, for which he had never had much time, and in which he had practically no faith.

Whilst Medina Sidonia waited in uneasy obedience for Parma's message to come, the English captains once more met aboard the *Ark Royal* and put their heads together. The English fleet was at anchor behind the Spanish ships and it was now clear that the long guns which they had hoped would give them victory, would not suffice, not least because they were now almost out of shot and powder.

There was only one way to break the perfection of Sidonia's mighty crescent, and Drake and his companions knew what it was.

They filled eight ships, some as large as two hundred tons, with all the explosives and powder they could muster. They stuffed the vessels with all they could find which would burn, and left their rigging and sails flaunting boldly above the choked decks and holds.

Medina Sidonia, not unmindful of the danger of such a move, for, above all, fire was a ship's greatest enemy, was watching carefully for such a visitation and had sent his pinnaces out with orders to grapple any fireships which came their way, and to tow them off from the fleet.

Amongst themselves the Spaniards whispered nervously of a new and devilish plan which the English had. A weapon more deadly than a mere fireship; a secret instrument of war which embraced a novel form of explosive a hundred times more terrible than mere flames and smoke.

But Howard had no such secret. He simply sent his eight ships forth, all their guns fully loaded, their hulls blazing in the darkness with such a force that it seemed as though the midday sun was shining. They sailed on with calm determination, like floating beacons as bright as those which had warned England of the coming of the dons.

Medina Sidonia had ordered his ships to slip anchor, should they be in danger from the fireships, and to stand out to sea, leaving a buoy to mark the place their anchors fell, but all his instructions and planning were to no avail.

When the Spanish pinnaces came upon the fireships they moved in to tow them to the shore as ordered, but just as they drew close enough to throw their grapples over them, the white-hot guns on the ghost ships started to explode. The pinnaces scattered in confusion, and the fireships sailed serenely onwards toward the fleet. Hearing the noise of guns, and seeing the red glow in the sky, and believing the English had unleashed their new device upon them, the Spanish fleet began to disperse. No Spanish vessel was touched by the flames, for they moved too quickly for that, but their impregnable crescent was at last broken, and at first light Lord Howard of Effingham split his ships into squadrons and began to chase the Spaniards.

Drake took the *Revenge* in gleeful pursuit of the *San Martin*, followed closely by Frobisher in the *Triumph*, Hawkins in the *Victory* and Rokeby in the *Bullen Lass*. Medina Sidonia answered them with all he had left, but though he was joined by his comrades, sailing hastily to his defence, he had in fact precious little remaining to hurl in the teeth of his tenacious enemies.

Despite the shattering blow the fireships had dealt the Spanish fleet, it still managed to re-assemble and began to limp away in its former half-moon design, but now its powder was spent and its guns were silent, and at last the English were able to use their guns as they had first intended.

The Spanish fleet suffered much in that encounter, and the decks of its ships ran red with blood, but in the end it was not the English gunpowder and deadly cannons which brought Philip's dream to an end, but the savage winds which changed direction and blew hard to the north-west. The Armada found itself slowly but surely drifting on to the Zeeland Sands, and such priests as were left aboard, offered earnest prayers for the souls of the doomed men. Then, when death seemed almost upon them the wind changed its direction yet again, and the trap of the Zeeland Sands was exchanged for the menace of the open ocean which roared its displeasure as they sailed into its teeth.

And so it ended; the greatest naval action ever undertaken by man had failed. Through a tangle of bad judgement, fatal mis-timing, and a complete lack of understanding of the nature of the task which faced it, the Spanish fleet was left to sail, hopelessly battered, up the east coast of England, round the shores of Scotland and on to Ireland, in a desperate effort to regain a Spanish port, there to lick its wounds and reflect bitterly on the Invincible Armada which had met the even more invincible winds of God and the bold, unyielding hearts of the sea-dogs of England.

It took some time for the news of Spain's defeat to penetrate to the whole nation, but when the tiding were fully known, the country rejoiced with heartfelt thanks to God for its deliverance, ringing its church bells in a paean of gratitude, and Nicholas Rokeby went back to Devon with Peregrine Grey and Greville West, to face an undertaking more difficult than the subjection of the dons.

The Lady Caroline met him as he came through the door, exclaiming at his pallor and the wound upon his arm, but he smiled her concern away, making light of what had come to pass. When his aunt had satisfied her curiosity, and got from Rokeby such details as she was able to drag from him, she opened her fan and swept it calmly to and fro.

"Well, Nick, now that you are back, should you not see how your guest is?"

Nicholas looked up quickly and found his aunt looking remarkably innocent.

"I doubt that she will wish to see me," he said finally, and made no move to rise, but the Lady Caroline snapped her fan shut and tapped him sharply on his sound arm.

"That is for her to say," she said shortly. "It is neither seemly nor courteous that you should ignore her. She is in the summer-room, Nicholas. At least go and greet her civilly, if you can find nothing else to say to her."

Reluctantly Nicholas got to his feet, and eyeing his aunt with some disfavour, made his way slowly to the summer-room and pushed open the door with a doubtful hand.

Then he saw Catalina. She sat on a satin-covered settle by the open window, her face turned towards the gardens where the hum of the bees was soothing on the ear, and where the perfume of the flowers made a rare sweetness in the lazy, sun-lit afternoon.

He watched the perfection of her profile against the light, and the way the sun shone on the dark, silky hair piled high on her small, proud head, and he felt his heart begin to pound in a way that no Spanish warship had been able to make it beat.

He tried to summon enough courage to speak to her, but whilst he sought feverishly for words, she turned her head and looked at him, and he saw her lips part in a smile which made his heart turn to water.

She rose from her seat and came towards him, and as he bowed, he was conscious of the delicate scent she used and felt his senses swim helplessly under its spell.

For a moment he held her hand in his, then he led her back to the settle, and enquired as to her health and the welfare of her sister.

He could see no sign of hatred in her, nor even dislike, for her eyes were shining with something he dared not let himself believe, and for a while he contented himself with pointless small talk, until finally Catalina laughed a little and laid a hand on his arm.

" Sir Nicholas," she said, and her gaze was warm. " I am grateful to you for your concern as to my welfare, and thankful for the sanctuary you have given me in your home. My debts I can never repay, but . . ."

" You owe me nothing," he said almost curtly. " It is I whose debts cannot be repaid, nor wiped out by mere words of contrition."

She sighed a little, but she did not withdraw her hand.

" You speak of Manuel," she said sadly, " and I understand

your feeling, but you must not blame yourself for that. It was not your fault, and I understood why you would not let them take him to London. For this, as for so much else, I am grateful to you."

He raised her hand to his lips for a second and then let it go.

"My thanks, *señorita*, that you found the understanding in your heart for which I asked."

She blushed a little, and he tried to think of something else to say to prevent the sudden wild desire to catch her in his arms from overwhelming him, but before he could embark upon some safe and harmless topic, her smile had faded, and she said slowly:

"*Señor*; I must find a way of getting a message to Don Cristóbal. Although he may no longer wish to marry me, nor, indeed, to acknowledge me should we meet, yet I must tell him that I am safe and well, and assure him that he need no longer concern himself for my sake."

Rokeby gave a short laugh. "I doubt that he ever concerned himself about you, madam, and a message would be difficult to deliver where Don Cristóbal has gone, for I know none who would venture into the depths of hell to carry your letter to him."

Her eyes widened and her lips parted slowly, and for a frozen moment Nicholas fought to control himself, thrusting down the craving to cover her entrancing mouth with his own.

"He is dead, my lord? Is that what you say? The Marqués is dead?"

"Very," said Nicholas bleakly. "An odd quirk of Fate, madam. His ship, the *San Pedro*, tried to ram mine, and Don Cristóbal and his men boarded the *Bullen Lass*. A thousand to one chance, but that was how Fortune threw the dice."

"And you killed him?" There was a faint, lovely colour in her cheeks, and again he ached to take her face between his hands and to stop her questions with a kiss which would last for ever.

"Not I," he said, and kept his longing hands rigidly still. "It was Peregrine who killed him, but the end was the same,

251

Lady Catalina; he is dead, and you need fear him no more."

She gave a sigh of pure relief, and her lips curved into a smile.

"Then I have no ties left in Spain, Don Nicholas, and am free to make a home for Margarita here, for you must see the manner of my flight from Valladolid makes it difficult for me to return to Spain again."

"That I see." He paused, then said hesitantly: "I will find you a house, *señorita*, wherever you wish to live."

"But I have no money," she whispered. "All my possessions are in Spain."

"I have money," he said briefly. "Enough to buy you a hundred houses, if you will."

"One would do," she murmured, her mouth twitching a fraction. "But may I not stay here, my lord, at Monks' Walk, for I have grown to love it since you brought me here?"

He looked a trifle startled, but seeing her gaze travel affectionately round the summer-room, he nodded.

"If that is your wish, madam. I will make arrangements to leave here as soon as I can."

She turned dark, beautiful eyes back to his face and he caught his breath.

"I would not have you go, *señor*," she said gently. "For this is your home, and I will not drive you from it."

"But . . . but . . . I can hardly stay if you . . ." He broke off and bit his lip. "If you wish to live here, Catalina, I cannot myself remain, for it would not be . . . be . . ."

"Fitting, sire?" She was laughing at him, and he longed to slap her for her mischief, for he felt it was entirely the wrong moment for such levity when he was searching desperately for the right words to bid her farewell.

She veiled her eyes with the dark extravagant lashes and put her head slightly on one side.

"Of course, my lord, it would be difficult for us both to live here, unless . . . unless . . ."

Then her courage failed her as a sudden realisation of her

temerity and brazen immodesty overcame her, but at last Nicholas had understood, and slowly and unbelievingly he reached out and caught her shoulders.

"You would marry me?" he asked, half-fearfully, half-incredulously. "Despite what I have done; you would still consent to be my wife?"

"If you were to ask me, Don Nicholas," she said demurely, and closed her eyes in blissful happiness as he pulled her fiercely into his arms and bent his head to steal a kiss with true piratical ruthlessness.

In his small, quiet room, deep in the heart of the Escorial, Philip of Spain read the last of the despatches which little by little had told him of the failure of the Enterprise.

The secretary who had brought the latest missive of bad tidings, waited apprehensively for some sign of the fury which he thought to find in his royal master, but the King's face was as impassive as if he were reading a routine report on the anticipated fruit harvest in Seville.

Finally Philip laid aside the document and picked up his well-used quill, drawing a sheet of parchment towards him.

The secretary hesitated, but then, taking his courage in both hands, ventured a comment.

"It was a disaster, your Majesty," he whispered, and his eyes were fearful. "Our losses were great, for many ships were destroyed and the full reckoning of lives is not yet known."

Philip paused in his task of dipping the pen into the ink and said coolly:

"It is as well, therefore, is it not, that God has favoured me with the means to raise another fleet of equal strength, for what I did not achieve on this occasion, I will attain at another time."

"But . . . but . . . sire!" The secretary's face was anguished, for his quick Spanish pride was deeply wounded, and he could not understand the apparent indifference of the King to the total failure of the mission. "We were defeated."

"But not by the English," said Philip softly. "I sent my

ships against men, not against the winds of God. Close the door quietly as you leave, Lopez."

And with that he dipped his quill into the inkwell once more and began to write a tactful and diplomatic letter to the Pope.